Quartet Qrime

FAMILIAR SPIRITS

LEONARD TOURNEY

Familiar Spirits

QUARTET QRIME

First published in Great Britain by
Quartet Books Limited 1985
A member of the Namara Group
27/29 Goodge Street, London W1P 1FD

First published in the United States of America by
St. Martin's Press, 175 Fifth Avenue, New York, N.Y. 10010, 1984

British Library Cataloguing in Publication Data

Tourney, Leonard
Familiar spirits.
I. Title
813'.54[F]   PS3570.0784

ISBN 0-7043-2547-0

Printed and bound in Great Britain
by Nene Litho and Woolnough Bookbinding
both of Irthlingborough, Northants

For Martha, Anne, and Megan

AUTHOR'S NOTE

THIS is a novel of detection and of the supernatural. The persons, events, and more specifically the phenomenon described in the book as the Chelmsford Horror are figments of the imagination. The place, time, and psychological atmosphere, however, are real. Chelmsford was—and remains—a town in Essex, England; and during the reign of Elizabeth I over two hundred men and women were hanged for witchcraft there, an act of carnage that dwarfs the better-known episode of a century later that made immortal the name of the little town of Salem, Massachusetts.

It is small consolation in this more rational age to think that the great majority of those accused, tried, and hanged in Chelmsford were innocent—or, at worst, guilty only of being old, in most cases female, and, in the eyes of their neighbors, strange. Hardly more consolation to consider that a minority of the alleged witches may have been witches in fact! Innocent or guilty, either would have cause, were it possible, to rise from their graves to avenge themselves on their accusers. One must keep an open mind in such matters.

CHELMSFORD, ESSEX, ENGLAND

September, 1602

PROLOGUE

IN the dark, gloomy house on High Street, things were going from bad to worse. Susan's master, a glover by trade, was afflicted by a mysterious ailment that his physician was unable to diagnose, much less cure. The glover's wife, a terrible termagant in the best of times, had become more shrewish and willful than ever, and poor Susan herself, one of the two remaining servants in the house, had fallen afoul of a strange melancholy humor that made her continually nervous and morose. For weeks she had been moving about in a fog, starting at every knock, creak, rattle, or slam, shunning certain rooms in the house as though they were under heavy curse, and performing strange rituals, many of her own devise, that gave her small comfort in her condition of helpless and seemingly inexplicable dread. Before she made a bed, scoured a pot, swept the rushes, or fetched water from the well, she blessed herself. Not once but thrice! When passing an old woman in the street, she would quickly avert her eyes. She avoided strange dogs, especially black ones, and around her neck she wore an amulet, a small leather pouch filled with sweet scented herbs. Ursula had given the amulet to her. Ursula was her friend. Susan believed the amulet would protect her, and although she suspected it was the cause of the skin rash on her breast, she was afraid to take the amulet off.

Her melancholy had developed to such a state that Susan regularly forgot to perform the most ordinary and essential chores, which is how it was that on a certain evening in mid-September, darkness having already enveloped the street like a cheveril glove, she had quite forgotten to empty the upstairs chamber pots. Her master's young nephew and houseguest, alerted to her negligence by the reek, gave her a terrible scolding. He called her a dumpish whey-faced slut and lazybones. He said she wasn't worth the food she ate.

Blubbering and disconsolate, she threw a wrap around her shoulders and carried the offending pots out-of-doors, casting a nervous eye at the big back yard with its cluster of shadowy outbuildings. She made her way down the long garden path without a moon to guide her steps, listening to the crickets' chorus and the flutter of her heart. She hated the dark more than anything, and the darkest of places was the privy.

The wooden shed, decked with a lush growth of vines and scarlet runners, loomed before her. She took a deep breath of the warm night air and kicked open the door. The stench assaulted her nostrils. She bent down for the low lintel and entered. The door creaked shut behind her.

Worse than a hundred rotting corpses in the charnel house, she thought, braving the stench to empty the pots. She groped in the darkness until her hand found the lime bucket, and with the little handspade kept therein she scattered a fine layer of the stuff over the ordure, like the priest swinging his censer. Then she pushed the door open and went out into the lesser darkness of the night.

"Susan."

She froze at the sound, then spun around in the direction it came. Next to the privy was a ragged gorse bush, and just beyond its shadow she perceived a shape that she knew was no part of the bush. The shape was motionless but in dim outline female, as the voice whispering her name had been.

"Who's there?" she asked, her voice quavering. "Who is it that calls my name? Brigit, is that you?"

The shadow stirred and slowly moved toward her. Her heart leaped into her throat, and in her fright she let the pots slip from her grasp and they went clattering onto the cobbled path. "Oh, Christ my Saviour! It's you, Ursula. Oh, Jesus

God, Ursula. You gave me such a fright! You make no more noise than a cat."

Her friend laughed, advanced until Susan could see the girl's features quite clearly, even in the dark.

"I thought you were a ghost," Susan said.

Ursula laughed again. "We're meeting tonight," she said. "In the loft."

The invitation was softly uttered. Susan hesitated. A little voice inside her head seemed to say: *Go back to the house straightway*, but something else, something as strong and dark as the night around her, urged her to follow. She clutched the amulet at her breast, her heart racing. Walking softly as in a dream, she followed Ursula.

Susan retrieved the pots the next morning. Her mistress, who had wanted to ease herself during the night and had found no receptacle for that purpose, threatened to beat her black and blue if she did not fetch them.

OCTOBER OF
THE SAME YEAR

O N E

CONSTABLE Matthew Stock looked out his shop door and had one foot on the cobblestoned street when he saw the hangman bearing down on him like a galleon under full sail making for port.

"Good morning, Constable Stock!" the hangman cried in very good humor.

Matthew returned the greeting, closed the shop door behind him, and shook the hangman's hand. The hangman screwed up his eyes to peer at the sun. "We're well met," he said in the same jovial tone of his greeting. "Since our destination is the same. Both late too, if heaven's clock tells truly."

The two men threaded their way down the busy street, Matthew lengthening his stride to keep pace with his companion. As they went, Matthew glimpsed in the little square panes of shopwindow glass the many reflections of himself.

They made an odd pair for a morning's walk, the hangman and the constable. Matthew was somewhat below the mean in height, stoutish—of unprepossessing figure if the truth be told. He wore a heavy fur-faced gown of the sort successful merchants wear, and a flat velvet cap pulled down to a point just above the brow and covering almost completely his thick black hair. Beneath the cap was his earnest, well-meaning face, forty years in the making, dark like a gypsy's, smooth-shaven and intelligently affable. Little lines around his eyes and a determined set to his small mouth gave his countenance additional character.

The hangman, on the other hand, was a veritable giant—a good six feet or more if he was an inch. Sims by name, he had broad, muscular shoulders, a tree trunk of a chest, and sturdy thighs and calves taut with energy. He wore a leather jerkin without sleeves and russet hose, and he had a wide freckled face and huge hands downed with curly hair of the same burnished gold hue as that which crowned his head in rich profusion. Astride, bent on his mission and happy for it, he was an intimidating presence who looked more like a forester or a blacksmith than a barber, which is what he was when he wasn't making a few shillings extra by lopping off the bodily parts of malefactors or stringing them up on the gallows tree for their own good and the entertainment of the town. Tucked beneath his brawny arm was the black hood he wore when he engaged in official duties. A grin of cheerful anticipation lighted his freckled face.

"Marvelous fair morning for a hanging, eh, Constable?" remarked Sims as the two men maneuvered around a farmer's wagon lumbering up the street and then stopped suddenly to avoid collision with a pedlar carrying a long staff and his gear piled high upon his back.

When they continued on their way, Matthew agreed with Sims's comment. It was market day in Chelmsford. High Street was full to overflowing with citizens and countrymen come to buy, sell, or just gawk at those who did, and it was fine weather too—a late-October morn with a sky as bright and blue as a robin's egg, not a wisp of a cloud, and the pleasant smoky wood-fire scent of autumn in the air. It was a marvelous fair day indeed. For some.

Sims began talking about the condemned, ticking off their names with the nonchalance of a storekeeper inventorying his goods—as though Matthew didn't know who they were, the three malefactors Sims humorously referred to as a "pair and one." Sims did not break his stride as he talked, looked aside only to wave at a friend leaning from a doorway or to acknowledge the greeting of another poking his head from a window. The crowd in the street was thinning out. Sims picked up speed.

Matthew knew them all, the condemned, and marveled at Sims's cold-bloodedness. Here was a rare gift—either of God or the Devil, who could tell?—Matthew thought as the two men crossed the bridge into the neighboring hamlet of Moulsham. Within the hour, Sims would string up three souls and take their bodies down again and all his contemplation was a casual remark about the weather! A fine day for a hanging indeed!

Well, it was a wondrous fair day and Matthew thanked God for it, but he himself had no love of hangings. He thought them cruel, gruesome affairs, and only his civic duty, such as beckoned him now, prodded him into attendance. How awful it all was. That terrible moment when the slender coil of hemp fell heir to the body's weight and, like an obdurate landlord, evicted the soul from its temporal lodgings. If the neck did not snap with the force of the fall, the condemned man—or woman—would wriggle in helpless torment. The eyes would start from the skull and the black swollen tongue protrude obscenely. The pendent body—hardly human now—would become a mockery of its former self. Would dangle like a thing to scare crows. The head would loll foolishly, as though to declare: "See now, gentles, how easily the trick is done. A moment before you saw me quick who now am dead. Avoid my fate—if you can."

We live in hope to 'scape the rope, the constable quoted to himself when, the houses falling away on either side, he could see in the distance the place of execution. Sims pled the need to hurry, leaving Matthew to a more leisurely approach to the scene.

In a broad meadow, the scaffold had been erected, raw and grim in the still morning air. The constable mingled with the large and varied crowd. It was, indeed, a veritable anatomy of society—a great press of all ages and conditions such as a clever artist might depict on a broad canvas, from the gentleman in courtier's hose, doublet, and cap to the poor scraggily bumpkin with his undernourished flea-bitten dog at his feet and hardly a breechclout to his name. Matthew saw women with young children in tow, sad-faced merchants and clerks, a rout of apprentices, and an equally large number of schoolboys released from their Latin exercises of the morning for the greater edification of a public execution. There were balladmongers and vendors of sweets and fruits, laborers and mechanics, alehouse wenches, the poor of the town mingling with the gentry of the county, learned divines, and at least one prominent knight, decked gloriously in a scarlet cape, his manhood celebrated by the monstrous codpiece he wore.

The constable greeted those he knew and pushed his way toward the scaffold where the hangman had now taken his place and was testing his equipment. Hooded and anonymous, Sims seemed even larger and more threatening a personage. Sensing himself the center of attention already, although the prisoners were yet to arrive, Sims was making a great show of these tests, yanking back the lever that operated the trapdoor and then jamming it forward again. The trapdoor fell open with a clatter, banged shut, clattered open again. He seemed to take pleasure in the simple mechanical operation.

He began testing the rope. He put his whole weight on it, then lifted himself up, his brawny arms bulging.

The crowd, increasing in number by the minute, watched it all with interest. They pressed in around the scaffold, talking excitedly. A few applauded when Sims, apparently satisfied with the good working order of his tools, stood back and took a braced stance at the rear of the platform.

While this was going on, Matthew had worked himself into a good position in front of the crowd. He could see the scaffold clearly, and the slight elevation on which the structure had been erected afforded a sweeping view of the spectators as well. He thought about the deaths he would presently witness.

A pair and one, Sims had said. That meant two men of no unusual demerit, and a single woman whose offense was as pernicious as it was damnable. William Hunt had stolen five swine—and poor underfed creatures at that!—from Jacob

Stone, a neighbor and kinsman. Matthew knew Hunt well. The other man was Diggon Ruttledge. Ruttledge was charged with having declared the Queen's teeth and hair were none of her own, which everyone knew to be the truth but had the wisdom not to publish out-of-doors.

Last would come Ursula Tusser. Ursula was a pale, thin girl of about fifteen, a servant of Thomas Crispin, the tanner. It was her death the crowd had come to see on this fair morning. Not only come to see, but to relish.

A bell tolled in the distance, sweet and clear in the thin air. The crowd quieted. Matthew heard the clomping of horses and the creaking of wheels.

It was the prison cart, preceded by about a dozen men on horseback, some officers, others town officials. One of the dignitaries was the high sheriff of Essex, resplendent in his chain of office. The procession moved slowly toward the scaffold, the crowd drawing back to let them pass.

The three prisoners in the back of the cart were very miserable in countenance. They were dressed in prison garments—garments that would also serve as their winding sheets. Matthew watched as they were taken out, their manacles and leg-irons struck. The parson led the first of the condemned up the steps to the platform, followed by three of the sheriff's men with halberds, the sheriff's clerk, and the sheriff himself. When everyone was in his place, the parson stepped to the front of the platform and addressed the crowd.

He was a young man with fresh ruddy cheeks, fair hair, and a serious expression. Dressed in his cassock and surplice and with a copy of the Geneva Bible in his hands, he presented a satisfactory image of ecclesiastical authority. He spoke slowly and confidently, addressing the crowd as though they were his own parishioners, which in fact most of them were. In solemn tones he admonished them to take good heed to what they would presently see and reminded them that while all must die, to some it was reserved to die by the law's hand for numerous crimes he proceeded to summarize. He said he hoped there were none present so frivolous of mind to find more pleasure than instruction in the death of their fellow beings—miscreants as they might be—and then he bowed his head and recited a long prayer.

When this was done, the parson indicated to the sheriff in charge that the secular powers might proceed with the business at hand. The sheriff directed one of the clerks to step forward and read the charges against the prisoners. The charges were lengthy, couched in legal language, and it was doubtful that many hearing them could make sense of it all, although their sum was clear enough: death. Then, without further ado, William Hunt was brought forward beneath the rope.

Hunt was a ne'er-do-well farmer, a big, swarthy fellow. He would leave six children behind him and a sickly wife but few others who would mourn his passing. Belligerent and quick-tempered before his arrest and conviction, he was a changed man now that death was his adversary and not some meek-mannered shopkeeper or hapless farmboy. Facing the eager crowd, Hunt stood pale and quaking, and the final words he was allowed and that indeed were expected of him were few and punctuated by loud sobs. He said he was sorry for his sinful life, asked the prayers of his neighbors, and warned the youth of the town to avoid his example.

When he was done, the hangman went quickly to work. The noose was placed around Hunt's neck, tightened, and the trap sprung. After a minute of futile struggle Hunt was dead. The crowd cheered.

Matthew had averted his eyes during the agony. Now he looked up at the scaffold again where two of the officers were getting Hunt's body down. One had him around the middle and was hoisting him up while the other worked to untie the noose. Then they dragged him by the arms across the platform and handed him down, headfirst, to their fellows on the ground, who without ceremony heaved his body into the cart. It was all quickly and efficiently done.

Now Diggon was made to climb the ladder. A simpleminded lad of about twenty-five, he had the crowd's sympathy, since it was generally felt his fate was undeserved. Some treasonmonger from a nearby town had fingered him, and the authorities had been obliged to investigate. They had taken him to an alehouse, filled him full of cheap wine, then invited him to express his views. What did he really think of the Queen? Well, she was a very old woman for all her majesty and dominion. Diggon spilled all.

Now he stood on the platform obviously confused about what was to happen to him and why. He looked out at the crowd and met the eye of many a friend, then at Sims, who cut his hair once a quarter, then at the parson, whose sermons he enjoyed without understanding half of them—the utmost of his religious knowledge was the Paternoster and six of the Ten Commandments. On his face was his usual expression of good-natured guilelessness. His pale, wide-set eyes seemed mildly amused, as though the throng before him had come seeking some other form of entertainment than his own demise and he would presently enjoy the spectacle with them.

Diggon was not given the privilege of final words, although his neighbors would have gladly heard them. It was feared he would repeat his calumnies. Thus the ceremony of his death was brief. The parson prayed on his behalf, a simple plea for mercy and the promise of a glorious resurrection. When he was done, Diggon thanked him for his pains, gave Sims a penny—for someone had schooled him, at least, on that piece of etiquette—and grinned self-consciously while the noose was placed around his neck.

Sims went to work. It was all over quickly for Diggon— without fuss or struggle and with only a scattering of cheers afterward, and those by the handful of strangers who knew neither the man nor his crimes.

Matthew turned his back on the scene, his gorge rising. His gaze swept over the crowd, but he found no relief there either, for the death was now imprinted in his memory and the horror he felt he saw mirrored in many a face before him. He would have pushed his way through them, left them to their grisly spectacle, had duty not stayed him. Gladly would he have found solace in a pretty prospect of countryside, or in a book, or in a snatch of melody. But the crowd remained, and so must he. Behind him the sheriff's men were disposing of Diggon as they had Hunt. Matthew could hear the scraping of Diggon's heels on the planking as his body was dragged toward the ladder. The trapdoor slammed shut.

Suddenly from the back of the crowd a strident female voice shouted, "Ursula! Give us Ursula!"

The demand was picked up by other voices, became a chant. He turned back to the scaffold. Ursula Tusser was now standing beneath the noose. He thought: She's a child, a boy. A mistake surely. They've got the wrong one, those imbeciles. But it was no mistake. Ursula's hair had been brutally cropped in prison. The coarse-spun garment she wore hung on her thin shoulders like a sack and extended to her ankles, hiding her sex. Next to the towering hangman she seemed diminutive, pathetic. Her small heart-shaped face and large eyes, green and subtle like a cat's, stared at the spectators accusingly.

The parson approached her to ask if there was anything she had to say to those whom she had abused so vilely. She shook her head. She didn't look at the parson, but kept her fixed stare on the crowd.

"What, woman? Not even a word of repentance?" the parson said.

"What sins I have, I have confessed to God in my cell," she said in a soft but audible voice. "It will avail me nothing to repeat them here. I am come to die, not to preach. I'll leave that to you, Parson."

"It is fit you confess your sins before God and before this company, if only that those here may not follow your lewd example," the parson remonstrated, his young man's face furrowed with vexation.

"Yes, confess, confess!" screamed a voice in the crowd.

The demand was taken up as a chant: "Confess, confess!" It thundered in the constable's ears. He watched Ursula. She seemed unmoved by this display of public hostility. The parson was angry; he was keeping his irritation in bounds only with the greatest difficulty. Finally he turned to the crowd and raised his hands to signal that the chanting must stop. It died away. The parson turned to Ursula. He said she was a wretched girl whom the wicked one had possessed entirely. He said her soul was utterly damned.

The girl cast an indifferent eye on the parson, muttered something inaudible, and then fixed her gaze on the crowd. A smile slowly formed on her lips. It was a humorless smile, cruel and vengeful, and it did not go unnoticed by the crowd. Many taunted and cursed, but others blessed themselves or hid their children in their skirts or turned aside themselves so as to avoid the accused girl's stare.

There was nothing more to be done but hang her. The crowd demanded it, and Sims moved forward to perform his office. He placed the noose around Ursula's neck, tightened it, stepped back, and, without further ado, pulled the lever releasing the trapdoor. The door clattered, the body fell. The constable watched in horror.

Ursula was dead. Her body swung lifeless in the still morning air. A thing to scare crows.

There was no cheering—not at first. First there was a silence, deep and inexplicable. The crowd gaped at the body, which the officers made no move to take down. Then someone shouted, "Good riddance to her and her kind!"

Suddenly the spell was broken. The crowd roared as if on signal. Caps and hats flew into the air. A group of schoolboys standing near Matthew howled with delight, and the faces of many otherwise grave matrons beamed with pleasure. Children gathered about their parents' knees were now hoisted to their shoulders to see the sight on the scaffold.

Finally the officers took the body down and Matthew had his last view of Ursula's death grimace, which had somehow managed to preserve her vengeful smile. He pushed his way through the cheering crowd but quickly found himself immobilized by the press of bodies. It was a public celebration, the jubilation of a people freed from a curse. Some strange fascination was holding them there. He wanted to shout, "Go home! It's all over. Go home!" But it would have done no good. He would not have been heard, and if heard, not obeyed. Even after Ursula's body had been thrown into the cart with the others, even after the cart had been driven off, the spectators stayed to talk, to congratulate one another. It was like a marriage or a baptism.

He got himself free at last and made for the road. He passed the parson, who was talking to another clergyman. He heard the parson say it had been a good day's work, especially the execution of Ursula Tusser. The parson quoted the Scriptures, thumping his Bible for emphasis. "Thou shalt not suffer a witch to live," he quoted sonorously.

The other clergyman agreed.

Matthew saw that carrion birds had gathered in a nearby tree and were staring toward the now empty gallows. He heard a balladmonger singing a song about Ursula Tusser, the infamous witch of Chelmsford, and he thought about what he had to do the rest of the day—visit the scrivener, see a carpenter about the repair of one of his looms, meet with the town bailiff and aldermen about a new ordinance regarding the use of the town muckhill. Depressed as he was by the hangings, he almost welcomed this round of mind-dulling chores, even the last, which, given its controversial nature and the personalities involved, would probably consume the entire afternoon.

T W O

As the church clock struck six, Matthew Stock came home, weary in his bones. By trade he was a clothier—a pillar of the Worshipful Company of Linen Drapers—and he lived with his wife and their servants and apprentices in a handsome house on High Street, the front ground floor of which was his shop. His constableship was a civic duty. For four years, his fellow townsman had conferred it upon him, despite his protestations of ineptitude. What did he know of crime? How could such a one as he, mild of manner, affectionate by nature, disinclined to any variation from the most direct road, which was to say he was as honest and straight as a carpenter's rule—how could he play Argus with his hundred eyes to all the mischief, malfeasance, and devilry of which the human heart was capable?

Yet year after year they elected him, and the truth was the honor pleased him, pleased him more than his profits as a shopkeeper. He did his job not only conscientiously but, incredible to him, with great success. He had built a reputation as a clever man, although he read little, spoke without eloquence, and wrote no learned or witty books or poems. His London connections, some of whom were men of renown, were at a loss to explain it. His virtues were simple: dogged determination, an eye for detail, and a clever wife.

Ah, his wife. Joan. Standing on the threshold of his shop, he felt dumpish still from the hangings, despite the intervening busywork that should have provided the solace of distraction. What he needed at the moment was a good talk with Joan.

He opened the door and entered as the shop bell tinkled pleasantly. His assistant Peter Bench, a young man of about twenty, looked up from behind the counter.

"Good evening, sir," Peter said, his long pale face cheerful and ingratiating.

Matthew returned the greeting and asked Peter about business.

"Tolerable," Peter replied, tallying up the day's receipts. Sales had been better than expected, but then, Peter noted, it tended to be so in the fall when thought naturally was drawn to the colder weather in the offing. Peter grinned and waited for his employer's expression of satisfaction at his report.

But it was slow in coming. Matthew's mind was far from cloth. He glanced distractedly over the trencher tables heavy laden with bolts of linen, russet, white frieze, lockram, woolen cloth, and kersey—ells and ells of it. His stock in trade, but far now from his mind.

"Oh, very fine, Peter," Matthew finally returned absently. "Very fine indeed. You can close up now. There'll be no more business today."

"Yes, sir, Mr. Stock. Good night, sir."

"Good night, Peter."

Matthew went through the narrow passage that connected the shop with the kitchen of the house. It was a big, cheerful kitchen with a great stone hearth, and he paused on the threshold to watch his wife at work. She was standing with her back to him, decked winsomely in her white cap and apron. Her pretty oval face, when she turned at his greeting, was flushed with the warmth of the fire and her forearms were bare and plum-colored in the firelight. But even before she returned his greeting and, following it, his embrace, he sensed something was wrong.

"Is the witch dead, then?" she asked, turning back to the hearth.

"She is," he said, placing his cap on the rack behind the long, well-scrubbed trestle table that was the kitchen's chief item of furniture and the center of household activity as well. He sat down and regarded his wife cautiously. Joan dipped the ladle into the pot and withdrew it, then blew upon the savory contents and tasted.

"That will do," she said to Betty, the cook, who had just come in.

Betty greeted her master and began setting the table. Joan sat down opposite Matthew. Betty began to serve. The cook was a woman of about fifty, rotund and slow, with a plain, cheerful face. The stew steamed; the salad of mixed greens harvested that very day from what remained of Joan's fall garden pleased the eye. They drank strong dark beer of Joan's own brewing and supped upon pewter plates.

"It's a crying shame, if you ask me," Joan said between mouthfuls, ignoring the fact that she had not been asked.

"The girl? Yes, I suppose it is. Her death was awful."

"Justice, you men call it," she said with sarcasm.

"A jury of women found the mark." He thought of the ghastly smile, the body swinging in the still air. A witch.

"Oh, the mark. Well might they find a mark. What body is perfect, then? Who without some superfluity of nature between the top of the head and the sole of the foot? What was hers?"

"A nodule, an ulcer—beneath the left breast," he answered, trying to remember. His memory of the trial was vague. He had not attended. It was the week he'd been down with the ague.

"Oh, indeed, beneath the left breast, was it?" She grinned derisively. "And that mark the learned jury determined was the infamous witch's teat. Where the Devil sucked upon her. Why, had they stripped me naked and searched me through they might have found more than that to feed their credulous eyes upon! What of that small ruddy birthmark upon my upper thigh? Or the mole upon my left knee? And might one of our daughter Elizabeth's poppets, much tattered now but dear to us still as keepsakes of her childhood, not be found at the bottom of the chest to lay the groundwork for my conviction and damnation as a notorious witch and malefactor?"

"Come now, Joan," he said in a feeble effort to temper her growing heat. "No one would think *that* of you."

"Marry, sir, there's a man of overweening faith, I warrant," she replied shortly.

"I believe in witches," he responded firmly, draining his cup.

"Nor do I deny them," Joan said. "And yet I believe too in obnoxious old women their neighbors would gladly rid themselves of, and foolish maids with idle hands and minds who make much of necromancy and fortune-telling to call attention to themselves. In truth, such have no more power than a dog has to bring down from the tree the squirrel beyond his paw's reach."

"They say the evidence against her was strong. At her hanging she smiled—"

"Strong! Smiles! Evidence like a reed in the wind. Come, husband, your brief against the girl. Tell me your strong reasons. Her smile offended, you say?"

"It was no brief of mine, wife," Matthew declared, growing heated himself now, for he had not looked to find Joan's disapproval of the jury's verdict to be heaped upon himself. "I levied no charge against her, but merely executed the magistrate's writ."

"That's true," she conceded.

"I was no juryman. I was home abed the morning of the trial."

"I remember it."

"The facts are well known," he continued. "The evidence seemed more than enough. Two of her friends testified that she bewitched them. She cast fortunes and claimed to raise spirits from the dead. She frequented with familiars, which thing the Scriptures expressly condemn. Mrs. Byrd testified she had seen Ursula in the company of a cat of most foul visage and strange behavior. Indeed, she had many cats about her."

"Ha! Sound evidence *that*," Joan responded. "Who in Chelmsford has not come upon that same congregation of cats, forced to make a home for themselves in the fields and woods. I have heard it said Ursula was a great lover of animals. She would often take in strays, or at least feed them kitchen scraps. Simple charity to God's creatures, if you ask me."

"Yes, but what about her necromancy? What, will you dispute the reality of spirits? Have you fallen into that awful atheism of which the parson has spoken more than once lately?"

"I am no atheist!" she protested. "Were there no spirits, nor indeed conjurers to bring them alive again through Satan's power, sacred writ would never speak of the Witch of Endor, who raised the prophet Samuel's shade. But for that it does not follow that every simple girl wanting the judgment to mind her business and avoid the appearance of evil must be confederate with the powers of darkness. Why, what necromancy did she perform that she should be brought to trial for it?"

Matthew conceded that no witness to such performance had appeared.

"Well may you grant that none appeared. For the truth of the Scriptures I will attest and grant Samuel's spirit was raised as an article of faith, but do not try to persuade me that Ursula conjured up some familiar spirit to reveal to Brigit Able or that other girl—Susan Goodyear—that her future husband should be tall or short, ride a brown horse or a gray. Stuff and nonsense, the whole of it. I swear this town has lost its senses in the matter of witches, ever since Elizabeth Francis and old Mother Waterhouse and that vindictive daughter of hers met their ends upon the gallows in our parents' time."

They finished their stew. It had been a long day for Matthew and he took no pleasure in these wrangles. What had he wanted upon returning home but a quiet meal, his wife's companionship, and then to bed? He dared not tell her about his horror at Ursula's death now, about that vengeful smile that had made his blood run cold. Joan was in no mood to be sympathetic. The best he could hope for was a change of subject. If he dropped the subject of witches, would she? He regarded her face as she finished her meal and wiped her mouth on her napkin in the delicate way she always had, as though she must not press the lips too hard. From long experience he knew the ways her thoughts ran, like an oft-trod road where every rock, bramble, and tree is known and bears a familiar name. Her jaw was still set in her humor, her eyes brooding dangerously. No, there would be no dropping this subject.

Dropping. The word caught in his throat, lodged there as though he had spoken it aloud. The scaffold again. Ursula Tusser limp and smiling. Should he concede, then? Admit the girl had been falsely accused, her condemnation an outrage against reason, morals, true religion? And what if Ursula had been innocent for a fact, the victim of malicious gossip? Yet the jury had returned a speedy verdict. All those testimonies. The bewitched girls. He had heard it all—by hearsay, of course, since he was ill at the time. Could the whole town have been wrong?

"I heard she would not repent on the scaffold," Joan said, bringing him back to her, the table, their kitchen.

"No, she did not. The parson could not prevail upon her, nor the crowd. You would not believe the uproar. She died keeping her counsel."

"Then she had much integrity for one so young," Joan said sadly. "Why should she answer to such ridiculous charges?"

"Why, to save her own neck," he said. "It was a poor pitiful defense of her life that was made. Why, look you now, even her brother could hardly do more in her behalf than swear no ghost came from the grave at her bidding. It was never in dispute that she was the leader of the group of idle young persons who met in Malcolm Waite's barn loft to practice curious arts. Even Ursula admitted *that*."

"Be that as it may," Joan said, "there was no small envy in the accusations. Consider her accusers—Brigit Able and Susan Goodyear—green girls and lazybones, the both of them. The Devil will find work for idle hands to do. What is upon their minds at that age but young men and mischief?"

"They claimed Ursula had bewitched them, cast a spell upon them—"

"Ha!"

Betty cleared the table, brought more beer. Joan continued: "I suppose her brother has taken his sister's death very ill. She was his only kin, you know. Both were orphans. Thomas Crispin showed much kindness in taking them in when their father died."

"And no little risk, since he got the brother in the bargain," Matthew said. "There's a strange young fellow, Andrew Tusser. He's much in demand when Chelmsford plays Moulsham in football, but otherwise he isn't worth a farthing. Thomas Crispin complains of his idleness. I suppose the tanner will be rid of Andrew now."

"I don't think the boy would want to stay in Chelmsford, not after this," Joan said. "It's a wonder Andrew wasn't cried out against as well."

"Oh, he's a kind of simpleton, harmless."

"Well, surely he'll leave the town now."

With that Joan did drop the subject of the Tussers, to Matthew's great relief. The remainder of the evening was pleasantly spent. Joan stitched while Matthew, who had a fine tenor voice, sang.

In the weeks following, the weather turned wet and gloomy, and talk of the Chelmsford witch subsided, as such talk will, replaced by fresher news of town, county, and court. It was said the Queen was sick abed and near to death, that the little Scots King, James, was to be named her successor. There was a nervousness, it seemed, throughout the land, fear of treasons and sedition, an alertness for signs and portents of things to come. Meanwhile, to Joan's surprise, Andrew Tusser did not leave Chelmsford. He was seemingly unaffected by his sister's death and disgrace. Idle and shiftless as ever, he apparently enjoyed the attention he was now receiving, and if there was revenge or resentment on his mind, his countenance did not reveal it. Thomas Crispin, the tanner, kept him around for odd jobs—perhaps, the Stocks conjectured, out of simple charity. He was, after all, an orphan.

Then, one Sunday while Matthew was at table relishing a succulent pork pie, a knocking came at the door. It was Jeremiah Carter, a near neighbor, complaining that while out for an afternoon stroll he observed a group of men and boys playing at football in the widow Singleberry's meadow.

"On the Sabbath!" exclaimed Matthew, wiping his mouth with a napkin.

Jeremiah Carter nodded grimly.

Casting a regretful eye at the pork pie, Matthew did his duty. The playing of football was expressly forbidden by law, save on Christmastide at home. Such a bloody and murderous game was particularly obnoxious on the Sabbath.

He told Joan where he was off to and went at once to the meadow, which was no more than a half mile from his shop door. Even before arriving he could hear the shrill excited cries of the players. There were several dozen men and boys, most from the neighborhood, scrapping around after a brown leather ball and kicking up clouds of dust. Conspicuous among them for his speed and agility was Andrew Tusser.

Matthew had thought to break up the game and send the players home with a stern warning, but fate decreed otherwise. Matthew witnessed the strange accident and later described it to Joan.

Andrew had the ball, having emerged from a boisterous and violent melee of bodies with a shout of triumph, and was racing toward the opponent's goal line. The ball skipped along ahead of him. Andrew ran fast. The other players were hard put to keep up with him. The hapless defender of the goal, seeing Andrew's advance, came running out to stop it and the two young men collided.

Matthew called out to the players but none paid attention to his call. They were all gathered about the fallen bodies. Both players lay prone in the dirt. Matthew hastened forward, was seen by one of the players, who gave the alarm, and then they all scattered. The goal defender into whom

Andrew had smashed was helped to his feet and hurried off with the rest. Only Andrew remained. Motionless.

Matthew knelt down beside the fallen youth and spoke his name. There was no response. Not a tremble in the limbs or a flicker in the eyelids. The boy's face was streaked with dirt and sweat, but the flush of his recent exertion was fast fading into a morbid colorlessness. Alarmed, Matthew listened for a heartbeat, felt for pulse of life.

There was nothing. By all the signs he knew, Andrew Tusser was dead. The only mark on him was a slight discoloration on the forehead.

Behind him now, Matthew heard a voice. Turning to look over his shoulder, he saw approaching a handsome man of about thirty-five, with broad chest, ruddy cheeks, thick, curly black hair, and neatly trimmed beard.

"How now, Mr. Stock? An injury, is it?"

"Good morning, Mr. Crispin," said Matthew. "More than an injury, I fear."

The tanner came over and recognized his servant. "It's my bird, is it? I wondered where he'd flown. What ails him?"

"I think he's dead."

"Great God in heaven!" Crispin exclaimed incredulously, kneeling down beside the body and beginning to shake it as though Andrew's unconsciousness were feigned and a little roughness would bring him to his senses again. But it was no use. The shaking did nothing, and shortly the tanner gave it up. He groaned and stood, staring with unbelief at the body. "Dead," he said somberly. "Of football! Would to God he had worked for me with half the effort. This is sad news, Mr. Stock. First his sister, now him."

Matthew agreed. The death was as sad as it was strange. It was only a tiny bruise and swelling, no more than a man got for not watching for a low-hanging tree limb.

Evidently the news of the accident had spread. Across the meadow several persons were coming from the town to see for themselves. One of these offered to help Thomas Crispin carry his former servant home.

THREE

FOR the next several days, Matthew kept himself very busy in his shop. When he wasn't behind the counter, he spent long hours inventorying his goods, making lists and revising them, haggling with suppliers, or poring over his accounts with such fastidious zeal that one would have supposed the Judgment Day at hand and the clothier's trade goods the very substance of the great summing-up. All the while, Ursula Tusser remained in the back of his mind like the twinge of a disquieted conscience.

For a while he had put her out of his mind. Now she was back with a vengeance. It was her brother's death that re-opened the wound and left it raw and bleeding. The whole town talked of it, marveling that the young man should have been struck down so mysteriously, wondering that death should have taken both brother and sister in so short a span. Fate seemed bent on wiping out the Tusser race. In anxious whispers the town speculated on the meaning of it all. Was it a mere coincidence, or divine retribution upon the ungodly?

Matthew thought it pure coincidence but avoided debate. Still he was haunted by the thought that Joan might have been right. What if Ursula had been innocent, after all? That vengeful smile of hers had made his flesh crawl, but there was no sin in smiling. Doubt robbed him of his peace of mind. He became moody about the house, hectored his apprentices, lost interest in singing. Joan watched his change and said nothing. Then a disturbing incident occurred that brought the whole issue to a head.

It was about a week later. The Stocks had retired early after a long day in which Matthew and Joan had worked side by side to prepare a large shipment of broadcloth for London. They had been asleep at least an hour when they were awakened by a desperate rapping at the door. Half awake but knowing from experience what such a nocturnal summons portended, Matthew crawled drowsily from bed, put on his dressing gown, and stumbled downstairs, taper in hand.

He opened the door and saw standing in the street a girl of about fifteen with sharp, anxious features and a petulant mouth. He recognized her before she identified herself. She was Brigit Able, the serving girl who had testified against Ursula Tusser at her trial. Her cap was askew and her plain russet smock looked as though it had been put on in great haste and disregard for appearance.

"Oh, Mr. Stock!" she cried, gasping for breath. "Come see what has befallen my master."

"Malcolm Waite?" said Matthew. "What, does he need a physician, then?"

"He's beyond that, sir," said Brigit, her eyes wide with horror, her lower lip trembling.

"Dead, is he?"

"Yes, sir, he's dead."

Matthew felt his heart sink. He counted the glover a friend. In his mind's eye he saw the cold white body, already laid out.

"How did it happen? His long illness, was it?"

She shook her head, terror still shining in her eyes. She began a confused account of the death, punctuated by frequent sobs and prayerful utterances. From what Matthew could understand, she had been working in the kitchen when she heard her mistress scream. She had grasped the import of the cry and run to the parlor where Mr. Waite—by whom she meant not the dead man but a nephew residing in the house—interposed himself between her and the threshold.

Beyond him, she had glimpsed her mistress, pale as death herself, all tearful and gasping and carrying on about a window and a face.

"Whose face?"

But she didn't know. She said she had seen the master too. The sight was awful, she said. The nephew told her her master was dead. She was to fetch the constable straightway.

Matthew told the girl to come inside and wait while he dressed, then went back upstairs where—without waking Joan, who had fallen back asleep—he groped around for his clothes, got them on, and went downstairs again. Brigit was waiting. Her lantern guided them down the street to where the glover lived.

Matthew had known Malcolm Waite all his life. About ten or twelve years Matthew's senior, the glover had been moderately successful until recent years, when failing health and foolish investments had allowed his competitors the advantage and his trade had diminished to practically nothing. As his debts mounted, his friends began to avoid him. His wife was a proud, domineering woman named Margaret, given to dressing beyond her means and wearing thick layers of powder and rouge to hide a distressed complexion. They had two grown sons—glovers like their father—established in other towns.

Shortly the glover's house came into view. It was a two-storied house of timber and plaster behind which was a spacious, if unkempt garden, a meadow, and several outbuildings, one of which, the dilapidated barn, had been the scene of Ursula Tusser's nocturnal gatherings. The upper part of the house was dark, but through the bay windows of the shop Matthew could discern a glow of light coming from somewhere in the back of the house.

Brigit led the way through the shop. It was small and untidy. They passed through an adjoining room and were on the threshold of a third when they were met by the dead man's nephew.

John Waite was a young man of about twenty, thin and neat. Smelling of tobacco and pomander, he was dressed in a loose-fitting dressing gown of good cloth, decked with stars and crescent moons, and he had a nightcap on his head. His hair was lank and oily and came down below his ears, and on his upper lip there were the beginnings of a mustache. His expression was intelligent but not altogether pleasant. His mouth, left to its own devices, tended to sneer, even when its owner had no occasion for it. He spoke in the clipped speech of London, from whence he came, and although he had been living under his uncle's roof not more than a month or two, his citified manners and contempt for Chelmsford had already aroused local resentment.

At the moment, he seemed more irritated at the fuss his uncle's death had caused than grieved. He spoke sharply to Brigit, telling her to go to bed. Then he beckoned Matthew to follow him into the next room.

It was this room—a kind of parlor with a hearth and old faded furnishings—the lights of which Matthew had observed from the street. The fire in the hearth had died down to practically nothing, but there was a lamp on a long table in the center of the room and it illuminated the corpse. The glover was sprawled in a high-backed chair facing a window with its curtains pulled back. His long arms hung loose to the floor, the wrists as angular as though they had been broken. A table napkin or similar piece of cloth had been placed discreetly over the glover's face, but Matthew recognized at once the massive head of white hair that had been Malcolm Waite's most distinctive feature.

"We thought it best not to move my uncle. He died in his chair, as you can plainly see."

Matthew nodded to John Waite and, without saying anything, went over to examine the body, removing with appropriate reverence the napkin and placing it on the dead man's chest. Under the great mane of hair, Malcolm Waite's face seemed shriveled, wasted by his recent illness. The pores of his large, hooked nose seemed unnaturally conspicuous and a week's growth of grizzled beard bestubbled the cheeks and was oddly dark contrasted with the pallor of the flesh. The dead man's jaw was slack, exposing pink swollen gums and two missing teeth. The tongue reclined upon the lower lip. Most strange and terrible was the expression of the eyes. They were glazed and stark. It was the expression of one whose last mortal view is too terrible for utterance.

Avoiding the dead man's stare, Matthew hastily examined the body for signs of violence while the nephew looked on without comment.

"Why was I summoned?" Matthew asked when his examination was done. "By all appearances your uncle died a natural death."

John Waite explained that he had been out for the evening with some friends and upon his return had been alarmed by his aunt's screams. He had rushed into the house to find the aunt hysterical and his uncle in the state in which the constable now found him. When he had succeeded in calming her, she told him what happened. He reiterated the fact that nothing had been touched. Summoning the constable had been his aunt's idea, he remarked in a tone implying he would not have done so without her pleadings and was therefore blameless for disturbing the constable's sleep. It was because of what she said was the peculiar manner of the glover's death.

"Your uncle had been long ill—"

"Yes, very long. The physicians despaired of a cure. The death was not unexpected and yet . . ."

"And yet?"

"My aunt told a most incredible tale."

"What sort of tale?"

John Waite sighed and frowned. With a motion of his hand he suggested the two men move away from the body, the presence of which was making Matthew uncomfortable too. Matthew replaced the napkin over Malcolm Waite's face and followed the young man to two chairs that were placed directly in front of the hearth. John Waite picked up some faggots and got the fire stirring again, and then he asked Matthew if he would have some wine.

There was a flagon on the table and some cups. The nephew filled two and brought them to where Matthew was sitting in one of the chairs. Matthew watched the flames in the hearth while he waited patiently for the aunt's story.

"Ursula Tusser's trial and execution was most upsetting to my aunt and uncle, as you can imagine. The cursed girl had practiced upon our servants, you know, filling their heads with all sorts of nonsense. Even my uncle was taken in by her devilry—for a time, at least. My aunt was the worst. It was all rot to me, this business of witchcraft. Like alchemy or a similar fraud. I tried to reason with them, my uncle and aunt. Of course when Ursula was accused, they changed their tune. Claimed to have nothing to do with her then."

John Waite paused to refill his cup. Matthew listened carefully. He had not realized the depth of the Waites' involvement, but of course it stood to reason. It was, after all, *their* barn and *their* servants who had been allegedly bewitched. The wonder was that the couple had escaped being accused themselves.

"They thought they would be implicated," the nephew said, picking up on the constable's own thoughts as though he were a mind reader. "Their solid reputations saved them—that and testifying against Ursula themselves."

"You said your aunt and uncle were . . . patrons . . . of Ursula's. What would they have had from her—some charm or familiar to advance their fortunes?"

John Waite smiled and shook his head. "My uncle could well have used spiritual advice on his investments, but it wasn't that. My aunt had a brother once, much beloved of her, who was murdered ten or twelve years ago. You may remember him. Philip Goodin was his name."

"I think I do," said Matthew. "A tavern brawl, was it not?"

"A robbery, according to the evidence. His body was found a week after. It had been deliberately covered with leaves so as not to be found until the spring following. Now, as I said, my aunt loved this brother and ever after mourned his death. She wanted nothing more than to know whether he was in heaven or hell. Ursula promised to conjure his spirit and put her doubts about his redemption to rest."

"And did she?"

"According to my aunt, she did, but not at once. Ursula said conjuring was not easy work. She said that if it was an ordinary familiar my aunt wanted, then she could provide that easily enough, but a member of the family was a different matter. That took time, she said, and the performance of good works."

"Good works?" exclaimed Matthew. "That's curious terms from a necromancer. What good works were these?"

John Waite took another long drink and then smiled grimly. "Ursula called them evidences of good faith. She meant money, of course. My aunt was to give her money and other valuables. A silver bowl and a set of spoons and a lace handkerchief she had of my aunt, as though my uncle's business losses were not a sufficient misfortune. Oh, it was all a gross imposture, the lot of it, but my aunt is very credulous, you see. The town sent the wench to the gallows for witchcraft, but in my book she was a common mountebank who, had she lived, would have been able to set herself up nicely in London on the ill-gotten gains of superstitious women."

The nephew laughed bitterly, and asked the constable if he would have more wine. Matthew declined politely and reminded John Waite that all of what he had said was prologue to the tale his aunt had told, which Matthew was waiting eagerly to hear.

"Oh, yes. Forgive me. But the background is important. You see, according to my aunt, my uncle was frightened to death."

"Frightened to death. By what?"

"It seems a ghost, sir."

A wry smile played about the nephew's mouth. Matthew was astonished. "Whose?"

"The girl's. Ursula Tusser's."

"Ursula's!"

John Waite nodded, wiped his mouth on his sleeve. He was about to speak again when they were interrupted by footsteps in the passage. Both men turned.

"How do you do, Aunt Margaret?" John Waite said.

Margaret Waite was dressed in a loose shift that revealed white shoulders and thin forearms. Her long, sensitive face was haggard and drawn and bore no paint or other attempt to hide her blemished cheeks and her present distraction. Her nether lip was swollen and trembling, and the dark shadows beneath her eyes were accentuated by the lamplight into whose circumference she now glided like a spirit herself.

"I do as well as any wife so newly come to her widowhood," she said. She nodded a greeting to Matthew and then cast a fleeting glance at her husband's body. Her brow knitted in pain.

Both men had stood at her entrance. Matthew remained standing while John Waite walked over and leaned against the mantel as though to warm his backsides by the fire. Margaret Waite sat down and invited Matthew to do likewise.

"I prayed for sleep, but my prayers went unanswered," she said after an awkward silence. Matthew leaned forward and regarded the widow intently. She had begun to cry softly and plucked at the loose hairs about her ears and neck.

"I am most sorry for your husband's death," Matthew said in an effort to console the woman. "Malcolm was a good man, a just man. He will be much missed."

"Missed?" she replied, laughing bitterly through her tears. "Missed by his wife, his sons. None other. He was ruined, Mr. Stock. You know that. By the way, did John tell you how my husband died, the horrible manner of it?"

"He said there was a . . . manifestation of some sort."

"Manifestation indeed," she asserted, snorting, then glancing reproachfully at her nephew as though she expected him to confute her claim. Not responding, he turned his back to her and began to warm his hands at the fire as if the apparition and the terror it had caused were the farthest things from his mind. "It was *she*," Margaret reiterated to Matthew in a hoarse whisper.

"She?"

"The witch."

"Ursula Tusser? So your nephew told me."

"*He* doesn't believe me," Margaret said.

Matthew heard the nephew heave a cynical sigh. So John Waite was paying attention, after all.

"I saw, myself," Margaret said.

"You saw the ghost?"

"I did."

"Where?" Matthew looked around the room.

Margaret twisted in her chair and pointed a shaking finger toward the window. She spoke slowly and with a tremor: "Malcolm and I were sitting here conversing and reading, our custom of an evening. Suddenly there came a little incessant rap at the window, like someone begging to come in. We both heard it—I first, but he, laying his book aside, rose, went to the window, and drew the curtain to see who or what thing it was there. The next moment, I heard him gasp, as though seized with a sudden pain, then cry out a most strange and ungodly scream. It was as though the air had been half sucked from him, and with what little remained he blurted out an appeal to heaven. I remember his exact words. I never shall forget them. 'Oh, Jesus God,' he said. 'It's *she*. Forgive my treachery.'

"I jumped up and ran to my husband, who had fallen back in his chair. He was muttering incomprehensibly. His eyes were rolling in his head. He didn't seem to recognize me. I went to the window. Without a thought of danger to myself, I pulled the curtain back to see what he had seen. Oh, horrible! It was the face—the girl to the life. Her visage, pressed to the pane, was pale and ghastly. The lips were curled in a vengeful smile. Too terrified to scream, I turned again to my husband and saw now that the vision had been the death of him."

Margaret broke off her narrative and hid her face in her hands, while her nephew, who was now pacing the room, stopped long enough to pour her a drink and encourage her to regain control of herself. Matthew walked over to the window to peer out into the darkness. He started at his own reflection, a wide, fleshy face with deep-set eyes. He shaded the light and could see dimly. The Waites' barn loomed beyond the garden.

"Her face appeared at this window?" Matthew asked.

Margaret nodded. "I *saw*," she repeated.

"Aunt Margaret, Ursula Tusser has been dead a month, six weeks," said John Waite in an impatient tone of voice.

"Had she been dead a year or twain, a century or more, yet she was at the window this night," Margaret pronounced solemnly. "My husband saw her and the sight killed him. His last words seared my soul. Her face was as it was while she lived, her hair long and lank about her shoulders, like flax on a distaff. And her eyes, so accusing."

"By now her body is food for worms," John Waite said matter-of-factly. "How could she then appear as she was? What—did she appear decayed?"

"She appeared as I have said," his aunt replied firmly. "As I and my husband saw at the window. Oh, poor dear husband. What shall become of me now?"

The nephew made a gesture of exasperation and resumed pacing. Matthew asked some more questions about what the couple had been doing when the ghost had appeared.

"Strange it was," said Margaret, drying her eyes with a handkerchief her nephew had provided her with, "but we were speaking of Ursula about that time. We testified against her at her trial, you know. My husband and I. My husband encouraged me. He said if we did not, the town would believe we were witches too. I complied with his wishes. But he too regretted it afterward. When this last week her brother died, we thought the guilt of them both confirmed. My husband was happier. Then the ghost." She shuddered and ceased to speak.

"Isn't it possible, Aunt Margaret," suggested the nephew, pausing again in his course, "that your very converse on this topic invited the apparition? Often the thought provokes the vision itself. So say scholars."

"Scholars may say what they will. I know what I saw," Margaret said, casting a reproachful glance at her nephew. "Had you seen her, Mr. Stock, you would know that no idle fancy or trick of thought could project upon that glass a visage such as I and my husband saw there. What, will the fancy kill as her horrid shape did? Never believe it. The specter was real, as real as my own flesh. Had I then the courage to open the window, I could have reached out and touched her face."

"Spirits have no flesh, so says the Church," corrected the nephew in his caustic vein. "After the resurrection, yes—before, the body grows to dust where it was planted. If you did see something at the window, I am of the mind it was a trick of your own overheated imagination and your vain regret for having testified against the girl. Consider now what you yourself have admitted. You were discoursing upon her. Suddenly she appears. Reason tells us the ghost was in your brain."

"In my husband's brain too—in both brains at once? Nephew, *your* reason is addled," Margaret said shortly. "My husband, if you must know, was reading the Scriptures. See, there on the floor they lay still, where he dropped them in his fright. Some passage he came upon awakened a thought. A passage concerning bearing of false witness. It was that which brought Ursula to mind. As I have said, after the trial we had second thoughts as to what we had testified to at the trial, thinking that we might have kept silent or, like my sister and her husband, spoken in the girl's behalf to mitigate her crime. But Andrew Tusser's wondrous death laid all our fears to rest. So we thought."

Margaret had spoken of her sister and her husband, and the Crispins, as if by summons, now appeared. Their expressions of sadness made it evident that someone had apprised them of Malcolm Waite's death.

"Oh, sister, thank God you've come!" Margaret said.

Without a word, Jane Crispin, a tall, attractive woman in her mid-thirties with smooth, pale complexion and striking blue eyes, moved forward to embrace her sister. For a few moments condolences were offered, then Margaret repeated her story of her husband's death. She omitted no detail from her earlier version; the Crispins listened intently but noncommittally. When Margaret had finished, Jane said, "You poor dear," and then, casting a glance at the dead man, suggested that it was high time the body was removed from the parlor and that the men might perform this duty while she ushered Margaret upstairs. "My sister is exhausted," she said. "She must rest."

When the women were gone, the three men moved the body to an adjacent room, a small office that during the days of Malcolm Waite's prosperity, he had used daily. There was a table there, cluttered with papers, which, when cleared, provided a place for the body. Waite was very tall. His legs hung over the table end. John Waite found a coverlet; a candle was placed at the dead man's head. Then the three men went out, shutting the door behind them.

John Waite now begged to be excused to go to bed, leaving Matthew and Thomas Crispin to wait the return of the tanner's wife.

When they were alone, Matthew asked Crispin his opinion of Margaret's story. The tanner stroked his beard thoughtfully. "It's a very strange story, I'll say that for it. That something was observed at yonder window I make no doubt— Margaret Waite is an honest woman, for all her faults. But that it was Ursula Tusser come for revenge I wonder at, allowing of course that ghosts *are* and have as much ground in true religion as do angels and other heavenly spirits. Sometimes, however, the conscience works upon the imagination in curious ways and—"

Matthew interrupted to ask whether the tanner's wonder was at the reality of the apparition or its motive for appearing in the window. Crispin pondered this, rubbing his hands together as though in a moment he would separate the palms and from between them the answer to the constable's question would appear. "If Ursula's spirit has risen from the grave, I suppose it could be with cause. Malcolm and Margaret testified against her at the trial, but then so did others in the town."

"I understand from what I have heard that you spoke well of her at her trial."

"Spoke justly of her, you mean," replied Crispin somewhat uneasily. "I extenuated in no way her mischief, nor did I magnify it by falsehood or exaggeration. Do not misunderstand, sir, I imply no criticism of Malcolm or Margaret. Their testimony was theirs. I said what I knew. Ursula was a good servant but given to silly fancies as young girls often are. I don't believe there was any malice in her. Stories about her consorting with demons in the shape of cats and toads were just that—stories. We never saw her with any creature more terrible than a homeless cat or stray dog she would feed kitchen scraps to. I tell you, Mr. Stock, she was unjustly hanged, and if her spirit has visited this house it will not be the last house in Chelmsford she visits."

This ominous prediction caused Matthew a certain uneasiness. He looked toward the window where the ghost's form had been seen. For a moment he thought something moved there, but to his relief he saw no pale, vengeful face, only his own reflection.

Jane Crispin now returned from upstairs. The signs of strain were beginning to show in her smooth features. "She's asleep, poor dear," Jane said, speaking of her sister. She cast an eye on the empty chair at the window and seemed relieved to find the body gone. Then she went over to stand by her husband, who was staring moodily into the fire.

"How will my brother-in-law's death be interpreted—officially, I mean?" she asked, regarding Matthew intently.

"I found no marks upon him to indicate the death was anything other than a natural one. For death by specter the law makes no provision, nor could it do much to bring such ghostly forms to justice if it did."

"I have advised my sister to say nothing more of the apparition—at least outside the house," Jane said. "It will only cause more alarm in the town and a deal of new gossip as well. Cousin John believes the ghost is a figment of my sister's imagination. I am inclined to agree. The less she says about it, the better."

Crispin nodded his head in agreement. Matthew considered Jane's advice and then said, "As far as I am concerned, the death, though strange, was God's will. I don't know what Malcolm Waite saw in the window—flesh, spirit, or image of the mind—but his heart must have been over-taxed by his long illness. The power of suggestion is strong. Hearing her husband's cry, the wife may have *thought*—"

"Yes, that's very likely it," interrupted Crispin impatiently, as though he had something else on his mind now and needed desperately to get to it.

"My sister's sons must be notified of this," said Jane.

"I'll send someone at first light," said Crispin.

"Once again, my condolences to the family," said Matthew, preparing to leave.

"I have a lantern. If you do not, Mr. Stock, I'll see you home," said the tanner. "You will keep Margaret's story to yourself, won't you? We would consider it a point of friendship."

Matthew promised he would. He agreed it would only cause alarm if Margaret's tale were noised around. Surely it would mean more suffering for the widow.

He went home, Thomas Crispin guiding his way. Later, cracking his shin on the bedpost in an effort to undress himself in the dark, he uttered a mild oath and woke Joan. She wanted to hear the news, she said, every bit of it, and would not be content to wait the light of day.

FOUR

MATTHEW kept his promise to the Crispins and—except for Joan, from whom he could keep very little—told no one about the strange circumstances of Malcolm Waite's death. But his discretion was to no avail. Someone else told and must have told again. By eight o'clock he noticed a crowd gathered outside the Waite house. It was a small crowd and orderly—he thought little of it. Deaths always attracted some attention, questions, sympathy. When at midmorning he took the time to look down the street again, he saw the crowd had become a great one and he went to investigate. It was then he discovered that the appearance of Ursula's ghost was common knowledge. Most of the crowd were neighbors of the dead man, drawn by curiosity and not a little fear of this new supernatural manifestation. Others were strangers, who, informed of the reason for the gathering, acted as concerned as the neighbors. The crowd remained orderly; they stood in the street in little clusters whispering, watching, and pointing. But the sentiments Matthew overheard as he moved among them were not kindly disposed toward the house or its occupants. The consensus was that if Ursula Tusser had chosen the Waite house to haunt, then that was hardly an endorsement of the godliness of the Waites.

"Good day, Mr. Parker," Matthew said to the prosperous corn-chandler, who stood with the others gazing at the house. "Your business has moved into the street, I see."

The corn-chandler scowled in response to Matthew's attempt at wit. He was a thickset, burly man of about fifty with a broad, flat face, a liverish complexion, and very thick brows. He had been one of the jurymen at Ursula Tusser's trial and was obviously unsettled by this strange news of her reappearance.

"I would fain know what you intend to do about this, Mr. Stock," Parker grumbled, knitting his thick brows threateningly.

"Is it some disorder you fear?" Matthew asked, looking up at the house, which seemed unusually quiet and deserted for this time of the day. Of course the glover's shop was closed. A long piece of black crepe had been hung upon the doorframe as a sign of mourning. The upper windows of the house were shuttered, and no smoke curled from the chimney.

"No," said Parker. "No riot in the streets, but disorder within the house. We thought we had cleansed the town with the death of the witch. Now it appears she has left behind a nest in which to breed more of the Devil's vermin. You've heard the news?"

"I have heard that Malcolm Waite is dead," Matthew replied, pretending ignorance of more in order to determine just what version of the incident had spread abroad.

"Why, that she-devil herself, Ursula Tusser or her shape, appeared yesternight. With her was a legion of spirits in monstrous shapes that entered at every window and door, came down the chimney, and hovered above the house an hour or more, screeching and threatening as if all hell broke loose."

"A mighty tumult," said Matthew dryly. "I wonder it did not raise the town."

"It was observed by many," Parker said.

"Who, pray?"

"A great multitude," said Parker.

"You saw it yourself, then? At what hour did it happen?"

The corn-chandler scowled at the question and made a gesture of impatience. "No, not I. Samuel Jenkins and Jeremy

Barnes saw it. Two or three other townsmen as well. It was about midnight."

"I wonder they were abroad at so late an hour."

"Well, sir, they had been at a tavern and were on their way home."

"I see," said Matthew. "And these men brought the news to you?"

"No, I had it of my wife, who got it from her neighbor Mrs. Miller."

"I see," said Matthew again, well aware of this particular chain of communication.

"Now it is clear Ursula was not the only witch in Chelmsford," Parker said, stroking the loose flesh of his neck thoughtfully.

"How's that, sir?"

"Why, it must take a witch to raise one from the dead, for surely the spirit of Ursula Tusser would not have returned save she were beckoned by some secret incantation. Thus do witches work in summoning spirits to have intelligence of them regarding the future and to work their curses upon their enemies. You must find Ursula's confederate, Mr. Stock, and soon, or else we are undone."

At that moment the corn-chandler was drawn away and the necessity of Matthew's responding to his charge went with him. Matthew continued to circulate among the watchers. He entered into casual conversation with others of his acquaintance, especially those who lived nearby and might have seen the new manifestation of which the corn-chandler had spoken. By several of the wives he was informed that Ursula Tusser's spirit had visited elsewhere. She had been seen just before dawn in the form of a large blinking owl atop the church tower calling out strange words in Hebrew.

"Hebrew!" exclaimed Matthew to the wide-eyed matron who had conveyed this news to him. Knowing the woman to be no scholar, he asked, "How were you able to discern it was Hebrew and not some other tongue—say, Latin or Greek or Dutch?"

The woman pondered this. "Hebrew is the Devil's

tongue," she asserted vigorously. "What else therefore could it have been she spoke but that?"

The woman made a face to suggest her logic was irrefutable, and Matthew walked on. Her eyes had been full of fear and conviction, and he realized it would be futile to argue with her.

He was about to go up to the house to see how the family had spent the night when he, and everyone else in the street, was startled by a sudden cry of alarm.

"There she is, there she is! It is the witch's shape, her very shape!"

A few feet away from him, a gaunt woman with a pack on her back was pointing up at the house and trembling. All eyes turned in the direction she was pointing. A tiny window under the eaves had opened and the face of a young woman could be seen peering down to the street. Though the face was visible for only a moment, Matthew recognized it as that of Brigit Able.

But by now, the damage had been done. The gaunt woman's alarm had triggered a general panic. Others were pointing at the now closed window and screaming. A woman next to Matthew fell to the ground in a faint, and there was a rush away from the house and a great commotion. People tripped over each other as they fled. In vain, Matthew called out after them that it was no ghost they had seen but only one of the Waites' servants. His explanation did little good. Soon he found himself before the house with only a handful of companions, mostly close neighbors who had seen Brigit's face and knew it was Brigit and not Ursula. The neighbors were not easy in their knowledge and they immediately began to complain.

"It must be burned. It must be sanctified of the evil within," cried a small fellow, an unemployed carpenter named Hodge, who spent much of his time in the alehouses of the town and had been suspected more than once of setting fires to hayricks and barns.

Another suggested the widow be arrested for witchcraft

without further ado, for she had given the evil eye to her neighbors and thereby caused the aborting of many a calf.

"Yes, Constable Stock, arrest her," demanded a third, a grocer who usually was mild-mannered and had a good word for everyone he met. "And that knavish nephew as well," added the grocer, making an obscene gesture with his fist.

Matthew was unsure how to respond to this animosity toward the Waites, but he told them he would look into the matter, mumbling something about writs and warrants. These words, charged with the authority of the law, seemed to pacify them. They wandered off, not without a final glance of scorn and fear at the offending house.

But the rest of the crowd, those who had scrambled for fear, were now venturing forth from their hiding places. Slowly they moved toward the house, whispering ad pointing, their faces fixed with concern. Some looked only curious, and among these Matthew spotted two men who had on earlier occasions served him well as deputies. He beckoned to one of these, a young man named Arthur Wilts, and charged him to stand guard outside the house while he went inside to speak to Mrs. Waite and her nephew. He then repeated in a loud voice that it was Brigit Able's face that had been seen at the window and no spirit's. But his announcement did little good. The crowd, grown considerably larger and more hostile now, continued to murmur and cast dark looks at him as though he and his deputy were confederates of the Waites and his explanation of the facts a strategy to subvert their quite reasonable terror. Arthur Wilts eyed the crowd nervously.

"I don't like this, Mr. Stock," he whispered. "There's only the two of us and a great many more of *them*."

"I'll send for the magistrate," Matthew replied. "He'll bring help."

"He'd better bring a company, for time will not improve the disposition of this rout," Arthur said. "We have no weapons but our fists, and precious good they'll do outnumbered as we are."

Eyeing the hostile faces before him, Matthew shared

Arthur's concern. Many of these faces were unfamiliar to him. Now that a riot threatened, his timid neighbors had taken refuge indoors, were shuttering their windows, bolting their doors. At the forefront of the crowd were shabbily dressed laborers and ruffians from the alehouses, opportunists of sorts, spoiling for some ground to legitimize their bilious tempers. Those among them who had not heard of the specter were now being informed of it with many embellishments, and the story grew more complicated and horrific as it passed from mouth to mouth. Matthew spotted the grocer's apprentice standing out of the way of the main throng and beckoned to him. Fearfully the lad responded to the summons. Matthew gave him a penny to go fetch the magistrate.

Then Matthew went up to the Waites' door and knocked. It was some time before he had any response, and when it came it was only a voice from within—small and fearful but recognizable as John Waite's. Fear had taken the edge from the normal curtness of his speech. Matthew identified himself, assured the young man that the door could be safely opened, and presently heard the sound of heavy objects being moved. The door opened slowly to expose a part of John Waite's anxious face.

He motioned to Matthew to enter quickly, and then shut the door and barricaded it with one of the glover's counters, explaining as he struggled with this task that the family had been aware of the uproar outside for some time and had barricaded the house for fear of their lives. The nephew had an old sword that he had searched out in a desperate moment, believing, as he explained again, that an invasion of the house was imminent.

"You had good reason to be fearful," said Matthew, "but I believe you are in no immediate danger. The crowd is hostile enough, but they want a leader and as long as they lack one they're not likely to do more than stand in the street and shake their fists. They'll grow weary of that too, come dinnertime," he concluded, hoping it was all true.

The nephew received these assurances with a skeptical expression but didn't stay to argue. He led the way into the back of the house where Margaret and the two servant girls had taken refuge.

Matthew greeted the women, and then Brigit Able confirmed what he had suspected. She had overslept and, opening her little window for the morning air, she had been startled to see the street so full of people. When the woman screamed, she shut the window at once and ran to wake her mistress, who had also lain abed late. Then Margaret apologized for the untidy state of things and seemed more embarrassed for the disarray and her own unsightliness than for the danger presented by the crowd at her door. About that she was much confused. Why had the crowd gathered in the first place, she wanted to know.

"Someone has told them of the apparition," Matthew said, casting a sidelong glance at Brigit. But the girl showed no sign of guilt. She seemed as surprised as anyone else in the house that the story had got out. "When the woman saw Brigit at the window, she thought it was the ghost again. The idea caught on, and in an instant the crowd was beyond being persuaded otherwise."

The nephew laughed bitterly, his wonted sneer returning full force. "What did I tell you? Is this not too perfect for words? Why, had a dog made water before the house they would have thought it the Devil in disguise marking his territory."

Margaret now seemed genuinely alarmed. She was even more so when Matthew informed them that the entire household was under suspicion of witchcraft. She turned deadly pale and was forced to sit down. She was not a well woman, she declared in a weak, pathetic voice. First her husband's death, now this. She complained of a headache, of palpitations.

Brigit went into the kitchen for a cordial. The other servant, Susan Goodyear, went upstairs to fetch a coverlet for her mistress. John Waite began to ridicule the allegations against his family. He waved his arms threateningly and challenged Matthew to identify the persons who had so slandered him, for he intended, he said, to take legal action against them. "Fools and liars all," he declared.

"The accusation is common, on everyone's tongue," Matthew said. "You would have to sue half the town. It would be futile."

The conversation was interrupted by a round of loud knocks on the door. Matthew went with the nephew to see who it was. Thomas Crispin and his wife, two other women, and the parson stood waiting. The women had come to help wash and enshroud the body of the dead man, the parson to console the widow. Crispin had been out of town all morning and had only just heard of the uproar, which had subsided considerably. There was still a gawking crowd, but it seemed quieter, less hostile. The ruffians had gone off somewhere for a drink. However, the neighbors were back, watching, and the little party had had to endure their insults.

"They showed small respect for the Church," the parson said, smoothing his cassock and staring in bewilderment at the improvised barricade and at John Waite's drawn sword. "Constable Stock, can nothing be done to quell this riot?"

"A greater, more ear-piercing broil has never been seen or heard in Chelmsford," remarked one of the women, who also objected that her mission of Christian mercy should be so ill-regarded. She was an ironmonger's wife, a woman of some substance and reputation in the community. She had come at the parson's behest and had never been so vilified in her life, she complained, regarding Matthew with great severity as though he were responsible for the indecencies visited upon her.

Everyone went into the parlor, where Brigit was administering the cordial to her mistress and Susan was tucking the coverlet underneath her chin. Margaret looked up, relieved to see her sister. She smiled wanly. After preliminary conversation and condolences Matthew took a chair with the others. The rude crowd was now forgotten.

Brigit built up the fire while Susan offered a semblance of hospitality. The two servants disappeared, and the parson commenced a sermon on excessive grief that lasted nearly half an hour by Matthew's reckoning. This was followed by much talk about the deceased, and since everyone present, except for the parson, had known Malcolm Waite all of their lives, there was a generous supply of anecdote to dwell on. At length the widow made a sign to indicate that the time had come for the body to be laid out. She rose and led the other women into the adjoining chamber.

At once John Waite resumed his complaints about the town as though he were talking with one of his London friends and not Chelmsford residents, characterizing the citizenry as a rude, credulous lot of busybodies, drunken louts, and villains, predisposed to riotous assemblies and ignorant of logic and reason. He spoke of the last two abstractions as though they were special intimates of his.

Matthew and the other men endured this diatribe impatiently; however, since no one seemed willing to defend the town at the moment, the nephew was allowed to rave on. When he finished, the men began to speculate about how the word of Ursula's apparition had spread. Matthew confessed he suspected Brigit or Susan.

"Most likely," said John Waite with a supercilious sneer. "Both are saucy wenches whom my aunt would do well to put out-of-doors now that her husband is dead. It was he who favored them, not out of any unwholesome lust, but rather a simpleminded charitableness and a weakness of will when it came to disciplining servants."

The parson looked to be on the verge of defending charity when the women came filing back into the room. At the same instant, Susan entered to say the undertaker's men were at the door. Margaret told her to show them in. Presently heavy footfalls could be heard on the wooden planking of the shop floor and the two men entered. They were shabbily dressed and dour; they eyed the room curiously, walking heavily with their load, the empty coffin. Margaret showed them to the room where her husband's body lay, and wept into her handkerchief when, moments later, they returned with the body inside. It was clear from the expressions of the men that their task, unpleasant in the best of circumstances, was the worse for the present case. They had heard the commotion in the street, the whispers. They regarded the widow with obvious caution and seemed eager to be gone.

Outside, the appearance of the undertaker's men and their burden caused another stir among those who had lingered during the noon hour. Neighbors explained to newcomers in hushed tones whose body it was that was being carted away and how the man had died. Matthew had accompanied the men outdoors, watchful of further trouble. Since things seemed calm enough now, he sent Arthur Wilts home to his dinner, asking him to return afterward to resume his watch. Then Matthew went into the parlor, where a discussion of funeral arrangements was in progress. The parson was expressing concern about the possibility of further demonstrations. He said he hoped no unruly gathering would desecrate the holy precincts of the church. The remark set poorly with both Thomas Crispin and John Waite, and a heated exchange followed, the conclusion of which was the parson's stalking out with the ironmonger's wife and her friend, all in very ill humor and mumbling about the ingratitude of those whose deserts were in grave doubt, given the circumstances. After this, attention was paid the widow, who had been made very upset by this dispute. Matthew took the opportunity to inquire of the nephew if he might speak to the two servants.

"Upstairs they went," said the nephew moodily. "Speak to them as you will, Constable."

FIVE

THE upper story of the house consisted of a dark, narrow landing opening into three rooms—the great bedchamber, in which the glover and his wife had slept, and two smaller rooms, one of which was being occupied by the nephew during his stay. The floors were strewn with fresh rushes, but the rooms themselves were meanly furnished. The walls were bare and cracked. There was also a tiny closet that contained a steep flight of stairs leading to the attic. Even as Matthew ascended, he could hear the two girls whispering.

The whispering stopped before his head emerged into the open space. The attic, which sloped with the pitch of the roof, was lighted by small square windows on either side, tucked under the eaves as an afterthought. Against a wall stood a trundle bed, hardly more than a cot, and on this single piece of furniture the two servants were sitting.

He greeted them pleasantly, but they did not return his greeting. They both seemed nervous, and it was obvious that the younger of the two, Susan Goodyear, had been weeping. He told them he had come to speak to them about their master's death—with Susan first.

At this, Brigit rose, cast an uncertain glance at her companion, and said she would go downstairs to see if her mistress wanted anything.

When Brigit's descending steps had faded away, Matthew walked to the tiny window where earlier he had observed the startled face of Brigit from the street below. It was a simple casement without glass, a commodity too expensive to be wasted in an attic window. He opened the casement and peered down at the street. Traffic moved as normal for the time of the day. Arthur Wilts stood talking with a man Matthew didn't recognize. He closed the casement and turned to the girl on the bed.

Like her fellow servant, Susan Goodyear was a plain girl of undernourished figure. She wore a little cloth cap that tipped slightly to the left ear, and beneath this her small face with its long jaw and discolored teeth reflected the meanness of her existence. She had testified at the trial of Ursula Tusser, and this earlier experience of interrogation seemed to Matthew the cause of her anxiety in his presence. She fidgeted nervously and stared at him with wide, fearful eyes.

Matthew felt a surge of pity for her plainness. "I mean you no harm," he said kindly.

"I've done nothing wrong, sir," Susan said in a tearful voice.

"That's good—I did not think you had. I want to ask some questions of you."

"Of me?"

He explained he had not been at Ursula's trial, had not heard her account. Would she tell him what had transpired between them, how Ursula had bewitched her?

She made no objection to telling her story. In a thin, uncertain voice she explained how she had become one of Ursula's circle. She had come to work for the Waites a little over a year earlier—about Michaelmas or so, she said, computing the date in her mind with great earnestness and difficulty, as though the moment of her first employment was not only germane but crucial. The association and, ultimately, friendship of the two girls seemed inevitable. They were of the same age, both servants. They dwelt in adjacent houses of kinsmen. Comings and goings between the two families were constant. In her first month of service, Susan had been homesick beyond endurance. Her mother—a poor widow with a large brood to care for—lived in Colchester. Susan had thought of running away. Then Ursula, a quiet girl like herself, had made signs of friendship, bringing her nosegays, which Ursula had found in the meadow, and once a funny black kitten, who had unfortunately died the same day. As Susan continued to describe her relationship with Ursula, it was clear the Crispins' servant had taken the place of an older sister for Susan.

"What of Brigit?" Matthew asked.

"Oh, she was not yet come. Then I was the only servant. Philipa Carey had died of the fever a week before I came."

"So you became friends—you and Ursula Tusser."

"Oh, we were *that!*" Susan exclaimed in a little transport of happiness at the recollection. "Of nights we would walk together in the pasture behind the houses. Ursula had most wondrous ways with animals. She knew the names of herbs and plants, their powers to cure and hurt. All she had from her own mother, she said, who was a cunning woman in her town. The birds would fly to her outstretched hand. Foxes came at her beckoning. Once I saw her charm a little snake so that it coiled and uncoiled its silver sheen, coiled and uncoiled again. Oh, sir, she did indeed play most wondrously with the snake, and she showed no fear of it at all, nor it of her."

"Yet she bewitched *you* at last," Matthew reminded her.

The thin smile of happiness faded. Susan's face turned gray at the memory. She was vague about just *how* Ursula had bewitched her and *why*. The bewitchment itself was murkily described. She had not been lamed or made sick; she had not been driven to do something against her will or to feel passionate longings for forbidden things; she had not been inflicted with ghastly visions or threatened by demons or specters—until now, at least. But she reaffirmed her charge, nervously yet with conviction. Bewitched she had been. Brigit Able too.

Matthew listened, asked questions, allowed the girl to take her story where she would. At the same time, he sensed the lie. Sensed it the way a spectator at a play, viewing the imitation of life, is caught up by the tale but at the same time recognizes it as the concoction of the poet's fancy. Susan

Goodyear's bewitchment was fanciful. She had lied at the trial and was lying still to protect the first lie.

Matthew imagined the jury—their sense of Ursula's guilt a foregone conclusion, heady with their power of life and death, and eager to get to their verdict—greedily gobbling up the lie and savoring it. *Bewitchment.* Why, the very word caused a tingle in the spine, a reverberation in the brain. It was all clear to Matthew now what had happened and why. Neither Susan nor Brigit was clever, but they knew well enough how to get themselves out of trouble. Representing themselves as Ursula's victims, they had in truth been her accomplices, to what degree Matthew could not determine. The wonder was that Ursula, seeing herself betrayed by her friends, had not in turn denounced them.

He would have liked to tell Susan that he knew she had lied and was lying still. But he knew his accusation would serve no useful purpose. A confession would do Ursula no good now. She was dead. If the truth were known, the circle of guilt would only be enlarged, increasing the gallows fodder and enriching the hangman. What concerned Matthew now was the apparition. He asked Susan why she thought the specter had appeared to her master. To revenge itself on the house? He asked her if she feared the specter would appear to her.

The girl shuddered at the very suggestion and turned pale. It was obvious her conscience was uneasy, her fear well motivated. She had betrayed a friend, lied under oath before God. About the apparition she would say nothing. She had seen nothing, heard nothing. With her lips she denied the existence of what her expression affirmed. Matthew glimpsed the depth of her terror.

Feeling her resistance strong now, Matthew decided to change the subject back to Susan's relationship with Ursula.

"You met with her in the barn loft?"

"I did—along with others."

"I don't care about them. I care about *you*. I want to know what it was you saw."

"I told at the trial." She began to whimper.

"I know you did, but I wasn't there—remember?"

"We were mostly Ursula's audience. She spoke, we listened."

"Spoke what?" he asked, more insistently.

"What would befall each of us," she said.

"What did she say would befall you?"

"She said I would marry."

"Well and good. Who, did she say?"

"She named no names."

"I should think not."

"She said I would marry a man not of this town. She said he would be mounted on a fine bay horse, have a full purse and a merry wit. She said I would be happy and bear many children. She said my mother and brother and sisters were well at home and that William, my youngest brother, would suffer a fall but not be hurt by it, which thing turned out to be the truth indeed, for the week after she told it me my mother came from Colchester to see me and said that William had fallen from the haycock and had lain without his wits for an hour's time, then woke refreshed as though he had been asleep. By this I knew Ursula spoke the truth."

"How was she able to know these things?" Matthew asked.

"She had a familiar."

"Ah, it was witchcraft, then?"

Susan nodded. "Her familiar, she said, was an old Greek who had died long before. She said he came to her in the form of a cat and whispered things."

"Things about anyone?"

"No, just about her circle—about us."

"What other powers did she claim by this cat, this familiar?"

"She said that if anyone threatened us, she could protect us and cause them harm who threatened. By the cat she knew these things. She would also make images of wax or clay, sometimes of swollen radishes that, lain overlong in the ground, would grow into human shapes with bellies and limbs. These she would set over the fire until the man or woman so depicted would waste away with continual sickness. She also claimed knowledge of uncouth poisons, which she would use to cure or cast on disease, and she knew of certain roots which, concealed beneath the bolster, could make the barren wife fertile or the husband impotent."

"This is all truly witchcraft," Matthew said sternly. "Why didn't you shun her, knowing as you did what evil she designed?"

"Why, sir," returned Susan with an expression of injured innocence, "she told us it was not of the Devil at all, what she did. Christ, by clay and spittle wrought together, opened the eyes of a blind man, showing that there is indeed virtue in such combinations of elements."

"A foolish argument, and you the more foolish for believing it," said Matthew. "Satan is a subtle creature. That miracle of which you speak our Lord did of his own virtue, not that of the clay or spit, else that would be the common method of healing the blind and no miracle at all."

Susan made no answer to this; her head hung dejectedly.

"How long did you practice these things with her?"

"About three months."

"Did she ever raise spirits of the dead—either for herself or for others' use?"

"No, I don't think so."

"But she did claim to have the power to do so?" said the constable, remembering what John Waite had said about his aunt's participation in these mysteries.

Susan admitted that Ursula claimed to have such power, but she insisted she had never seen her use it.

"Were there others in this circle who claimed to have like power?"

"To raise spirits?"

"Yes."

"Only Ursula. None other."

Only Ursula. From his memory he retrieved the image of the hanged girl, the child-woman. Harmless and pitiful she had seemed to him in her predicament, diminished by the towering hangman, the hostility of the crowd, the furor of the law. And yet in her vengeful smile Matthew had sensed the evil of which she was possessed. He had not fully recognized the cause of his unease then, thinking it merely his doubts about the justice of her execution. But it had been more than that. Surely Susan was telling the truth about *this*—the images and concoctions, the familiars and the demonic prophecies. If these things were not the substance of witchcraft, what was?

He told Susan to find Brigit and send her up to him. While he waited for the older girl, he went to the window on the opposite side of the attic and looked out on the back parts of the house. He knelt down on the splintery floorboards, and the barn appeared within his view. He thought of the witch's circle. Of Susan and Brigit. Of Malcolm Waite and Margaret. Of Mrs. Byrd, who had been the first to denounce Ursula. And he thought of Ursula—pale, thin Ursula—with new respect. What power she must have possessed that such a self-willed woman as Margaret Waite would seek her counsel. It was all passing strange.

When he heard Brigit mounting the stairs, he rose and faced the stairhead. Her head emerged. She stared at him with an expression suggesting that she knew what questions he would put to her and that her resolve was firm to answer only the questions that pleased her.

The brief interview that followed plowed much the same furrow, only deeper and more irregularly. Like Susan, Brigit had first been drawn to Ursula's company by the other girl's proffers of friendship. Once the friendship had been established, Ursula had introduced Brigit to her various arts, beginning with the relatively innocent fortune-telling and then moving to the more arcane and forbidden areas of necromancy and magic. Brigit denied that she herself conjured, denied seeking familiar spirits or the employment of images on her own behalf. She claimed that it was not until she felt herself bewitched that she became aware of the satanic origin of Ursula's powers. Like Susan, she was unable to specify just what manner of bewitchment had been visited on her. Matthew was able to determine, however, that the alleged bewitchment happened after Mrs. Byrd had complained of Ursula's conjuring to the authorities. This made him even more certain that Brigit's bewitchment, like Susan's, was a desperate effort to divert attention from her own participation in Ursula's craft. It was equally clear to Matthew that Brigit was as terrified of Ursula's apparition as was Susan, and yet Brigit made no denial that the apparition was real.

"Do you believe it was Ursula's shape your master saw in his window?" he asked.

"I believe it was, sir," said Brigit with quiet conviction and a noticeable shudder.

"What do you suppose she wanted?"

"In coming to the window?"

"Yes."

"Why, to show the mistress she could not be got rid of so easily. She'll be coming to me and Susan soon, I fear. There'll be no stopping her. Not my mistress—not you, sir, not even the magistrate. Not the Queen herself. There's no shackles upon the dead," she pronounced gloomily.

The light in the attic was bad; it came only from the tiny windows, and Brigit's narrow, pinched face, pale with fright at her own words, seemed corpse-like. The attic was cold too, cold as though Ursula Tusser were already making her presence felt, not as a visible shape but as a draft of chilling air. Suddenly, Matthew had a great desire to get out of the attic and of the house. Had her terror infected him?

As he descended the stairs, he took a last look at the girl. She sat transfixed in a thought. There was no need for her to tell him what the thought was. If she had lied about being Ursula's victim at the trial, her testimony had ironically become true. She was Ursula's victim now. Brigit had seen the specter herself. Matthew was as certain of that as if he had been a party at their meeting.

Matthew returned to the parlor, where he found the members of the family conferring quietly. "In the resurrection," Jane Crispin was saying to her sister, "we shall see him as he was—in a body made perfect of its deformities."

"Yes, made perfect," said Margaret absently. Her gray eyes were cavernous with fatigue and grief.

Jane rose and with a glance at her husband indicated it was time for them to go. There was a short exchange of farewells, and then Matthew followed the Crispins to the door. Before he could leave, however, John Waite took him aside and whispered confidentially, "I gather you found the servants sufficiently communicative?" The nephew's expression suggested he would have been interested in just what the two girls had told Matthew, but Matthew felt no obligation to gratify the young man's curiosity. He confirmed only that he had spoken with both and that they had answered his questions to his satisfaction. John Waite seemed disappointed but said nothing further.

When Matthew went into the street, he saw that Arthur had returned from his dinner and had resumed his station. He waved to him and then said good-bye to the Crispins, whose own departure from the house had been delayed by Jane Crispin's having to run back inside. Some last word about funeral arrangements, she had said upon rejoining Matthew and her husband.

"You were best to look out for your sister-in-law," Matthew advised Crispin. "It's quiet enough now, but I can't promise it will remain so."

"Never fear, Mr. Stock. My wife and I will keep a faithful watch on Margaret and her house. We can depend on your help too, can't we?"

Matthew assured both of them he would do what he could. "Over there stands Arthur Wilts," Matthew said, pointing to his deputy watching them from the opposite side of the street. Now that things were quiet again, Arthur was obviously suffering from the tedium of his assignment. "If there's trouble, he'll come to fetch me. I'll be at my shop."

No sooner had Matthew said this than he saw two of the town's aldermen approaching. They cast unpleasant looks at the Crispins and then informed Matthew that the magistrate, who had been away from home when the morning's trouble started, had now returned and been apprised of it. Matthew was to come with them to the manor house at once to make a full report.

S I X

JOAN'S husband had been gone nearly an hour when the women descended upon her in a flutter of excited talk. They were her friends—her gossips, as Matthew was fond of terming them in his droll humor: Alisoun Monks, the scrivener's wife; Elizabeth James, a plump loquacious person who had persisted in her widowed state for such a long time that hardly anyone in town could now remember her husband; and tall, stately Mary Carew, who put on airs and whose husband, like Matthew, was a clothier.

The women brought the news. They had been hurrying on their way to visit Joan when they were attracted by the crowd outside the Waite house. Curious, the women had mingled long enough to be witnesses to the extraordinary manifestation of satanic power that was now the talk of Chelmsford. In fact, as their subsequent accounts to Joan revealed, none of the women had *seen* the apparition that was said to have shown itself in the upstairs window. What Mrs. Carew had seen was the terrified expression of a poor woman's face who had seen it, and *that* was sufficient testimony for her.

The other two women fell into agreement, the way in a team of three horses running abreast all stumble if one does.

"Oh, it was a dreadful sight," exclaimed the widow James, pressing a plump white hand to her ample bosom. "A most awful and portentous visage."

She made a face to emphasize her horror and the other women looked on sympathetically. "Just imagine it," she said, "in broad daylight with a hundred or more Christian souls looking on."

"One poor wretch fainted dead away," added Mrs. Carew, and made a clucking noise of disapproval. "The grocer's wife and her child were nearly trampled by the crowd."

The women had seated themselves at the long trestle table in the kitchen and were being served hot caudle to take the chill from their bones, but by the flush on their faces it was evident that their excitement had warmed them enough. When had such a sight been seen in the town?

While her friends gave their reports, adding or correcting as they saw fit, each vying with the others for the most horrendous version of the scene, Joan listened, applying her hands to her stitchery, pausing only long enough to sip her drink. The spicy caudle was pleasant on her tongue, but she thought the women's news very bad indeed. Of this strange supernatural occurrence she trusted Matthew would tell her upon his return, but she did not like the sound of riotous trampling of women and children, and she was concerned for her friend Margaret Waite. What a state the poor widow must be in with a husband to bury, a riot at her door, and a ghost in her attic!

"Did any of you see my husband?" she thought to ask.

"Marry, he was there in the flesh," said Mrs. Carew, who had always been a little jealous that it was Joan's husband and not her own who had been repeatedly elected by the freemen of the town to the important office of constable. "But he could do little good, given the size of the press and him but one man."

"Strangers have flocked to the town to see the wonder," remarked Mrs. Monks with a satisfied expression on her face. "On High Street it is like market day for the throng. The alehouses and taverns will do a great business."

"Yes, but the honest merchants of the neighborhood must close up shop for fear of invasion of these riotous wondermongers," said Mrs. Carew disapprovingly. "Let us pray the authorities can keep order and protect the decent and God-fearing from these enormities."

Joan winced under the implied criticism of her husband and looked up sharply at Mrs. Carew. "I'm sure the town will suffer no great damage from this," she said coolly.

The tone of Joan's response caused a shift of topic and the women began to speak of Margaret Waite. They had all known her for years, but it was evident that none except Joan had liked her very much. She had been distant and haughty, even after her husband's business failure. A woman with a successful husband was supposed to carry herself proudly, but one in other circumstances should at least affect humility. At any rate, that was the women's opinion.

During this time, Betty brought a plate of cates and marchpane and distributed the sweets among the women, who continued to talk while they ate. The conversation narrowed in focus—Margaret Waite's relationship with Ursula Tusser.

"I say Mrs. Waite was as thick as her serving girls with the witch," affirmed the widow James, looking around the table for support for this proposition.

Mrs. Carew agreed. "Were Margaret's body to be scrutinized, I warrant we'd find the mark," she said with scarcely concealed relish. "Why, I tell you she was one of the circle. Twice weekly they met. In the Waite barn, that horrible rat-ridden place. It ought to be torn down."

"Burned," said the widow, munching.

"Destroyed completely, even to the foundation," added Mrs. Monks.

Mrs. Carew made a disdainful face, and the image of the offending structure floated into Joan's mind. Mrs. Carew said, "What more proof of complicity would a reasonable woman want than that? Pray, would a Christian family abide such practices under its own roof?"

The question hung in the air, and since its answer seemed obvious none of the women responded. Joan held her peace. She had her own ideas, as her husband had discovered, but she was not prepared to advance them at the moment. She felt decidedly at a disadvantage. She had not been in the street, not seen the new apparition of Ursula Tusser. Ursula's activities she knew by hearsay alone. Her sense of fairness precluded any snap judgments.

Mrs. Monks now stated that her scrivener husband had done some small services for the Waites. "I learned a thing or two," she said, nodding her head judiciously.

"What did you learn?" asked Joan, looking up from her stitchery.

"Marry, that Margaret was all agog over Ursula's arts, despite what she said at the trial. My husband said that Malcolm Waite told him he was grieved over his wife's curiosity about these matters. He urged her to give over these preoccupations and trust in God, but she would not be schooled so."

"Why, could the good man not impose his will, control his wife?" asked Mrs. Carew, who always made much of masculine authority in her talk with friends but ruled the roost at home.

"Not Malcolm Waite," observed Mrs. Monks with a brittle scornful laugh. "He was a milksop, always allowing his wife her will."

"A husband who will do that may find she's allowed him his horns," cackled the widow James, whereupon they all laughed.

The women went on to the subject of Ursula Tusser. Joan's friends did not share her doubts about the young woman's guilt. Outnumbered and disinclined at the moment to debate, Joan continued to listen as Ursula's enormities were recounted and, she suspected, embellished. Mrs. Carew claimed Ursula had conjured regularly and kept open company with familiars and imps. Then Mrs. Monks said the girl had given her soul to the Devil, and reminded them all of the Devil's mark that had been found beneath her right breast.

"It was the left," said Mrs. Carew, smiling tolerantly. She had been on the jury of women examiners and had seen the mark herself. Examined it with finger and eye, she stated.

Mrs. James, not willing to be outdone by her friends, then told how the girl had caused a great swelling in her nephew's groin, so that the surgeon had to lance it, whereupon black pus oozed forth to the amazement of the surgeon, who declared he had never seen the like. And Mrs. Monks related a new story of how Ursula bewitched a pail and made it run downhill after her, and the widow James confessed that she had once in her girlhood been tempted to conjure that her sow might breed the more but resisted the temptation. She also admitted buying a charm of a traveling tinker, which, he assured her as he pocketed her tuppence, would enable her to find hidden treasure. The charm had not worked and she cast it away, she admitted sadly.

Mary Carew wanted to know then what manner of charm she spoke of, and the widow said it was a smooth white stone about the girth of a peach pit, and Mrs. Carew declared she had a stone exactly like it and, by flinging it into the air behind her and then walking to where it lay, she had once recovered a silver spoon one of her babes had lost in the grass. She said the widow was very foolish for casting off the stone so readily, but the widow, although her face was sad enough, declared she thought the stone was a hoax.

After some additional talk about the properties of stones and charms, the women speculated that Ursula's circle might well have encompassed more persons than those identified at the trial, and proceeded to name several elderly women of the community and at least one man who, Mrs. Carew was sure, kept female imps in his closet to satisfy his lustful pleasures.

Joan felt very uncomfortable and worried with this line of talk, realizing that once such suspicions began and were voiced, there would be no end to them. Every person with a grievance against his neighbor would find cause to accuse him of the black arts, and the same charge would be returned until no one in the town could trust another. It was a great relief to her when about noon her friends excused themselves and left her to mull over a tangle of truth and fantasy that seemed more hopelessly confused than ever. It was her feeling now that the charges against Ursula had doubtless had some foundation in fact, although whether or not the girl deserved hanging she continued to question. But what was she to make of this most recent apparition?

When the dinner hour passed and Matthew had not returned, Joan began to worry more than ever. During the long afternoon, she busied herself but could concentrate on nothing. Restless beyond endurance, she told Betty she was going out, collected her cloak and cap, and went into the street. Within minutes she was standing before the Waite house.

The crowd of gawkers was gone now and no signs of a riot remained. Shops nearby were open but doing little business. The afternoon sky was solemn and threatening, the air chill and damp. The handful of persons passing the house seemed at pains to avoid it, and those she knew made no effort to greet her or stop to talk. The only friendly face she saw was that of Arthur Wilts. He was leaning against the doorpost of the glover's shop as though he himself were the proprietor. He wished her good day.

"Good day to you, Arthur."

"The constable told me to question any who came," explained Arthur when Joan inquired what business of his it was what she wanted with the occupants of the house.

"Arthur Wilts, you know me well enough," Joan said crossly. "Make way. I want to see my friend Mrs. Waite, if you must know, and comfort her on the death of her husband. Is that so strange?"

Arthur smiled sheepishly and stepped aside.

She knocked at the door, and presently it was answered by Susan Goodyear. The girl explained that her mistress was abed and in her chamber, but invited Joan to come in and wait. Joan was shown into the parlor.

While Susan revived the fire with a few faggots, Joan took in every detail of the room with her careful housekeeper's eye. Its furnishings told the story of prosperity fallen into adversity. The wall hangings were faded and dusty; the great sideboard was bare of pewter, doubtless sold off to pay the family's debts. Above the hearth there had once hung the sword and breastplate of a martial ancestor. She remembered them well, but the mementos were gone now. It was all very sad, and she wondered in which of the straight-backed chairs Malcolm Waite was sitting when he died.

She waited alone in the room for what seemed an hour, pretending to read a collection of dry sermons she had found on the mantelpiece but hardly progressing beyond the first page. Why should she read sermons when the chamber spoke one so eloquently? *Sic transit gloria mundi.* Her only Latin. She contemplated the thought and grew more melancholy than ever. The dark house reeked with the odor of disappointment, failure, death. She found it overpowering.

Then Susan returned to say her mistress would be down shortly. Joan thanked the girl, and, finding the chamber no longer to be endured, she told Susan she would walk in the garden in the meantime.

Joan passed through the empty kitchen and out the back door. Emerging into the bracing air, she gave a sigh of relief. Before her lay the rectangular patch of herbs and greens that was Margaret's garden. The patch was overgrown, and the outlines of an earlier regimen of squares and circles—an artful geometry—was now barely discernible. Beyond the garden was the ivy-enshrouded privy with its door ajar, beyond still a low stone wall and the meadow sloping to the river. To the right of the garden stood the barn.

This now infamous structure caught her attention and for a few moments she stood regarding it. The rough-timbered barn was much weathered and tottering, with a high-pitched roof of rotting thatch and with gaping front doors loose on their hinges. At one side of the building was an empty swine pen in which weeds and thistles grew wantonly; at the other an enclosure for ducks, geese, and hens. The fowls cackled and honked, but the familiar notes of their discourse soon passed from her awareness. The sight of such disrepair and neglect renewed her melancholy, but the infamous barn aroused her curiosity as well. She did not mean to snoop, and yet, with no one around to tell her stay, she felt the urge to explore.

She followed the path that led around the garden and then fanned out before the barn doors. She was halfway to her destination when she paused. Suddenly she felt she was being watched. She surveyed the garden, then turned to look back at the house, half expecting to see Margaret or one of her servants or perhaps the nephew observing her progress, critical of its intent, preparing to call her back. But she saw no one, either at the door or at the windows. The house might have been deserted for all the signs of life she could see. A dead house. She cast a quick nervous glance beyond the garden to the meadow, then looked toward the neighboring houses and their similar complement of gardens and outbuildings. There was nothing. Under the glowering sky a vast stillness had fallen, and she felt unaccountably afraid.

But she was not inclined to go back. The barn beckoned to her. She continued along the path and was nearly to the doors of the barn when she saw the cat.

Lithely it came from out of the dark interior, as though to meet her, and took up a position of watchfulness, mewing plaintively. It was a large brindled cat with a flat face, bristling fur, and eye slits that opened to reveal hard gemlike eyes. Since she was fond of cats, she greeted it pleasantly, but as she did the cat arched its back and hissed.

"Now there's a good gentle cat," she said, extending a hand to stroke it, bending over. The creature struck at her with its paw and made a hostile snarling noise.

She recoiled, her heart thumping. "Inhospitable devil to use me so ill," she said in a quaking voice.

The cat ignored the rebuke and continued to glare menacingly. She told herself the cat was but an ordinary cat, probably a capable mouser and—if a male, as its size seemed to suggest—a patriarch of some eminence in the neighborhood. And yet it blocked her way and threatened with an uncanny purposefulness.

Then it occurred to her that the cat may have been Ursula Tusser's familiar, and the thought triggered another spasm of apprehension. It was almost as strong as a premonition. For what seemed a long time, she stood in a quandary, uncertain whether to proceed or to return to the house. She had almost decided to return when the cat unaccountably forsook its position and bounded off into the weeds.

Now that her way was open again, she began to breathe

more easily. Slowly her courage returned. With an effort of will she reasoned that the gaping doors of the barn presented an opportunity. The Waite house returned to normal might not permit such unsupervised investigation as she intended. Having convinced herself, she resolved to go on, if only to spite the impudent cat, who, she concluded in her more confident frame of mind, was a mere cat, after all.

She stepped across the threshold into the barn, bending her head for the low lintel and leaving the doors ajar. The chamber was without windows, and it took a moment for her eyes to adjust to the dimness. The air was moist and rank with the odor of horse dung, and presently she could see the originator of this stench: the Waites' mare, standing in the first of a line of stalls. The horse shook its head and whinnied, and at this friendly greeting Joan's apprehension began to fade. She approached and stroked the mare's nose and withers. The mare nudged at her ear affectionately. "Poor creature," she said softly, in a deliberate undertone as though she expected her conversation with the animal to be overheard. "To endure such filth. Do those lazy louts never clean your stall or let you graze in the meadow?"

The horse wheezed and stamped to share Joan's complaint. Her desire to explore revived. At the end of the stalls she could see a ladder she knew would lead to the loft. She walked toward it, glancing as she did at the dark empty stalls, filled with trash. She came to the ladder and looked upward at the rectangular opening in the ceiling, dimly perceiving, beyond the underside of the roof, the gaps of light in the rotting thatch. Testing the rungs of the ladder and finding them sturdy, she began to climb.

The great door of the loft was closed but light came in through the chinks in the wallboards. On a summer day the loft would have been an oven, unbearable. Now the layer of matted hay, turned into compost by moisture from the leaking roof, exuded a warm, earthy smell. It was not unpleasant, and while she remained on her guard, her heart beating like a drum, she admitted to herself the loft was not the chamber of horrors she had expected. There was little to be seen—certainly little evidence of secret ceremonies or incantations that had given it its local reputation. A mouse watched her with its beady little eyes, then scampered off. In dark corners she could make out the skulls and bones of birds who had found their way into the loft but not out again. Spiders and their webby habitations. A few rusting tools. The pendent shapes of bats in their black cloaks waiting for the true dark. Now that she was here, what was she to do? There remained an edge to her curiosity as though she had not seen all there was to see.

She noticed a pitchfork standing against the wall, and without a definite sense of what she was looking for she began to poke around in the matted hay. It came up in clumps, sticking to the prongs, revealing dark moldering underlayers. At length her explorations were rewarded. She found a piece of red ribbon, the nub of candle (what mischief had it illuminated?), a fragment of yellowing paper upon which she could just make out the word "whereas" written in a fine, secretary's hand. Heartened by these small discoveries, she persisted in her labors and was ready to give over her task when her tool struck a hard object. Kneeling down, she extracted the thing with her hands, then took it to the wall and a ray of light the better to inspect it. She saw, cleaning it off with her hands, that it was a carved figure of human shape, with eyes, nose, and mouth carefully etched in soft wood. The figure was armless, but two legs had been crudely represented. In the groin was an obscene parody of a male member, raised and bloated.

She cried out in disgust and cast the image into the corner. She knew what it was, the image. She knew its purpose—the laming of an enemy or his cow or his horse, the spoiling of crops. At its most innocent, causing love, or lust, to flourish in an obdurate heart. But even that was witchcraft, were it possible. And even if it was not possible, was not the intent equally malign?

Through the long cracks in the walls she could see outside, down into the garden, if she pressed her face against the wood. She did, and saw Susan Goodyear walking down the path in the direction of the privy. Joan watched the girl. Susan was carrying a chamber pot and walking listlessly, in no hurry. As she passed the barn, she looked up and Joan drew back, fearful of being seen. But she was not seen. The girl walked on, went inside the privy, came out a few minutes later, walked back to the house. Joan watched, waiting. She was ready to leave now, more than ready. She had found what she had come for. She realized there had been something more than gossip behind the charges against Ursula Tusser. She was not convinced yet it was *all* true, but now she believed it was partly so. She shuddered, imagining the scene. The conjurers with their images, their incantations and spells. The awful consequences—loss of valuables, sickness of man and beast, impotency, death. Poor Malcolm Waite. She moved toward the ladder and had her foot on the top rung when she froze.

Whispers. She could hear them, coming from below, male or female she could not tell. She hardly dared to breathe, wondering at the same time why she should be so terrified of discovery. It wasn't as though she were a thief or ordinary intruder. She was a friend of the family. All she had to do was to call out, Hello, is anyone there? But she dared not speak. The whispering stopped. She heard footsteps, the creak of a hinge, a dull thud. Then nothing.

She continued to listen. From time to time she could hear the stirring of the mare. She focused her mind, realizing that she could not remain where she was indefinitely. She peered into the murky darkness below her and saw nothing but an empty stall. Slowly she descended.

All the way down she held her breath, almost afraid to look about her for fear of seeing someone waiting. Worse was the thought of someone grabbing her by the ankle or calf. She could almost feel the iron grip. She stood on the barn floor and stared into the dimness. Nothing but what was there before. She moved quickly toward the doors, noticing that they were closed now although she had deliberately left them open. More evidence that she had not been alone in the barn. She paused to look at the mare. The sad equine face regarded her with its great round glistening eyes. "Who was here?" she whispered, as though the dumb beast would tell.

She pushed open the shaky doors of the barn, emerged from the gloom, and ran toward the house.

SEVEN

JOAN burst into the kitchen to find Susan Goodyear sitting on a stool in front of the fire. The girl hummed tunelessly and did not look up. Her small hands lay idle on her coarse apron and her head hung listlessly as though her physical energy had been sapped.

"I was walking—in the meadow," Joan blurted out in a voice she felt must surely betray how distraught she was. She was still clammy with fear and her heartbeat roared in her ears.

But Susan showed no interest in where Joan had been or why. She ceased humming and looked up slowly, reluctantly drawn away from whatever had held her attention. She nodded her head and said that her mistress had come down, pointing in the direction of the parlor. Joan went through the narrow passage that connected the kitchen with the parlor, pausing only long enough to catch her breath and brush the telltale hay from her skirts. She could feel the heat in her face, the flushed cheeks, and thought how absurd she must have looked rushing like a madwoman from the barn, terrified of a whisper and a piece of wood. But the evil had been palpable. She could not deny it, although she could not make sense of it rationally. Dread still clutched at her heart, and it was only the shock of seeing Margaret Waite that dislodged the thought of the barn from her mind.

At her friend's entrance Margaret Waite rose from a chair near the fireplace and smiled thinly. She was dressed in widow's weeds, but carelessly, as though she had been forced to wear the sable garments. Her face was gray, the features sharpened by grief. Her pockmarked cheeks were hollow, and it seemed to Joan that death, which had so recently seized upon her husband, had somehow already marked her as well. Joan tried to hide her dismay as she took the chair offered to her and sat facing the widow. "God bless you in your bereavement, Margaret," she said. "How is it with you?"

"Oh, Joan, my dear good friend," the widow said in a tired voice, "would that a happier occasion had brought us together after so long an absence."

Joan scorned the consolatory platitudes by which clergy and laity were wont to stifle the natural outpourings of grief, and therefore refrained from talking of heavenly mansions. She knew Margaret wanted more at the moment an ear for her anguish than a tedious lecture. After expressing her sympathy as briefly and simply as she could, she sat back and listened while Margaret vented her grief, mindful at the same time that but for the grace of God this wretched state might be hers too. Margaret spoke fondly of her dead husband, enumerating his virtues as though she had forgotten how long the two families had known one another. Nothing she said would have suggested to a stranger how hard she had borne down on her husband throughout their married life. Now it was all roses, roses without thorns. But Joan did not feel it was her place to dispute this picture of marital bliss, and she noticed too that Margaret scrupulously avoided saying anything about the manner of her husband's death. She wondered if the widow had determined to put the awful business from her mind, or was merely being cautious. Joan listened with a sympathetic countenance, and when the opportunity presented itself, she brought up Margaret's long-dead brother, remembering that it was his strange death that had given rise to Margaret's participation in Ursula's conjurings. "It's a great shame," she remarked, "that you have not your only brother alive to comfort you."

Margaret replied, "Yes, Philip would have been a great comfort, and had he lived I would heartily wish him at my side now, but since he is dead, I would not wish him other than where he is."

Joan concluded from this circuitous response that Margaret was satisfied her brother's soul was in heaven. Joan decided to pursue the topic further. "I quite forget how it was your brother Philip died."

Margaret paused and her brow furrowed as though the recollection caused considerable pain. "He was murdered," she said. "It has been almost twelve years now since his death."

Margaret's eyes glazed with emotion as she recalled the gruesome details. The disappearance, the discovery of the naked decaying corpse, the futile inquiries.

"I do not remember him well," Joan confessed, although in fact she remembered him quite well. He was an ill-tempered youth, prone to quarrel.

"He was a well-proportioned young man," said Margaret, "handsome one might say, with raven hair. He was most beloved of our family, the favorite of our mother, and he had many friends, each of whom would have trusted him with his life if need be."

"Blessed is he who has so few vices," said Joan.

"He had not a one," Margaret asserted. "Or if he did, they were such vices as make men admired by other men. He had a strong will—a hot temper, some would say who knew him least. But I thought it no vice, and he kept clear of violent quarrels such as bring to ruin some young men's lives."

"It is for that reason, then, that your faith is so strong that he is in heaven?"

Margaret looked surprised at the question but answered promptly. "Wherefore should his soul not be in heaven, being the virtuous man he was? Besides," she said, "I have more recent confirmation that sets my old fears and uncertainties at rest." She folded her hands complacently in her lap and smiled at the crackling fire. For a few moments she was lost in her own thoughts, and Joan was certain they had to do with her brother. She sat there motionless, like a figure in a painting, seemingly oblivious to Joan's presence. She started from her trance only when Joan asked in the most casual voice possible just what sort of confirmation Margaret might mean.

There was something about the widow's expression that suggested to Joan that she wanted very much to say, but was afraid. For a moment Margaret's large gray eyes took on a strangely distant look. Joan restated her question. "This confirmation you speak of—the certainty you possess of your brother's state—"

"Ah, yes," said Margaret. "I am certain indeed."

"But how?"

Margaret leaned back in her chair while a thin smile of satisfaction played at the corners of her mouth. Joan felt her friend would presently tell—tell all. She could feel the revelation coming, like the distant rumble that plays herald to a summer storm. "I have had confirmation," Margaret repeated.

"I don't understand," Joan prompted, affecting confusion.

"It passes understanding," Margaret replied mysteriously. The satisfied smile returned.

"Oh, won't you tell me?" Joan pled.

The older woman continued to smile mysteriously.

Frustrated but not willing to give over her effort, Joan decided to resort to an invention, praying the innocent falsehood would be redeemed by whatever truth it uncovered. "I too had a brother," she said sadly. "He died very young."

"Did you?" Margaret responded with what seemed genuine interest. "I never knew. Strange, in all these years I never knew."

"He was only a child when he died."

With her sad expressive eyes, Margaret communicated her regret and sat upright in her chair, as though to welcome Joan's further confidence.

"I would I knew *his* immortal state," Joan said, trying to make the wish sound casual.

"There is prayer, the consolation of the Church," Margaret said hopefully.

"Yes, there is that," Joan agreed. "And yet the confirmation of which you speak—"

"Oh, yes, it was a confirmation indeed," said Margaret.

"If one were only to have a more direct knowledge, to speak with the souls of those we loved. Lift the veil, so to speak."

"Lift the veil," Margaret echoed thoughtfully. "Yes." Suddenly her reserve vanished, or seemed to. She leaned forward so that her face was very close to Joan's and said, "Oh, dear friend Joan, I must tell you. I cannot keep from it for my very life. It is hard to lose a brother and then live in doubt as to the fate of his soul. We trust in Christ and the sacraments, and yet what secret sins may bar the most seeming-virtuous from the heavenly mansions must remain in doubt unless some surer witness be sought—and found, as I have."

"As you have?"

Margaret nodded and looked beyond Joan to the kitchen passage, as though to insure that the message she was about to communicate would be heard by Joan alone. "My fears were assuaged by my brother Philip's own lips."

"But how could that be?" Joan exclaimed.

"I swear it is true." Margaret then began a disjointed account of her dealings with Ursula, which started with her discovery that the Crispins' servants and her own were meeting at night in the barn. She had investigated, determined at first to put an end to such mischief, but when she discovered the nature of the meetings her curiosity had got the best of her. By some strange instinctive sympathy, Ursula had known of her long-standing concern for her murdered brother, and one day when Margaret was chastizing the girl for luring her own servants into idle pastimes, Ursula had told her everything that was in her heart.

"Everything! Certainly she was a witch, then," Joan said, shuddering at the memory of the barn loft.

"She knew of my concern for my brother," Margaret replied defensively, a hurt expression in her gray eyes. "How could she have known *that* unless she had had some communication herself with the other side?"

"With the Devil?" Joan suggested.

"With the other side," Margaret insisted. "I do not think

it is of the Devil. If it were so, why would I have been assured my brother was in heaven? It is not the Devil's labor to console the bereaved with hopes of heaven, where I must go if I am to see my dear Philip again," the widow reasoned earnestly.

"By what means did your brother converse with you?"

"With his very lips, as I said before."

"But how could that be?" Joan asked impatiently.

"It was his spirit that came."

"You saw it with your own eyes."

"No—yes, yes, I did *see*."

Joan looked at the older woman. Her eyes were luminous now with the recollection of the miracle. She stared into the space between them as though the vision were recurring even as she spoke.

"You said both yes and no, as though you were confused," Joan persisted. "Tell me, what was the circumstance of this most remarkable apparition?"

"More than once Ursula had spoken of my dead brother," Margaret said quietly, "how it might be possible to have intelligence of his soul, where it was now, in what abode and what happiness he enjoyed or was deprived of. I begged her to tell me how this might be done, and for a long time she refused to say, explaining that she feared offending the spirit."

"But what of her familiar?"

"Oh, he. She said he came to her of his own will—originally, that is. Afterwards he was at her beck and call. But only after. To summon a spirit from his place of rest was not easily done, she said."

"What caused her finally to agree to summon your brother?" Joan asked.

"I had to make certain offerings."

"Offerings?"

"Yes."

"To whom?"

"Why, to God. It was all of God—not of the Devil, as they claimed at the trial."

"What sort of gifts?"

"The offerings? Money, jewels, trinkets. To me it was all worth it."

"This money went to Ursula, then?"

"No, it went to the poor. She told me so."

"I see," said Joan, trying to hide the skepticism she felt. "And after you gave Ursula money—for the poor—she agreed to conjure up the spirit of your brother to satisfy your doubts as to his condition."

"That is what I did."

"Where was this thing done—in the barn loft?"

"No, although it was there Ursula first spoke of it, taking me aside from the others. They were not to be permitted the vision, you see. Not even my husband."

"Why not?"

"It was my brother's will. Ursula said he wished to see only me, and no other soul. That was one of the conditions."

"And the other?"

"That the thing would be done in her mistress's house."

"At the Crispins'. That seems to me a strange condition."

"About that I do not know, but that was the condition. Oh, yes, I remember now what it was Ursula said. She said the disbelief of my husband's nephew had so offended my brother's spirit that he would not visit the house."

"So you went to the Crispins'."

"I did."

"And they—your sister and her husband—were also witnesses?"

"No, only I."

"I wonder that your sister Jane did not have as great a longing to visit with her brother's spirit."

"I think she did, for she loved him as much as ever I did. Yet her husband had little patience for such business and she feared to offend him."

"How were you able to have the house for yourself?" Joan asked.

"Oh, that wasn't difficult," replied Margaret, smiling her thin smile again. "Ursula knew well my sister and her husband's comings and goings. It happened one night when they were at a friend's house for supper, having taken their two little ones with them. The servants had the house to themselves. On this night she beckoned me to follow her, and we went into the great bedchamber of the house. There I saw my brother's shape as I remembered it, and heard his voice tell me that all was well with him. I asked him what heaven was like, and then he described such a place of wonder and beauty that I almost wished myself dead to enjoy it with him. I asked him if the streets were indeed paved with gold, and he said they were but for such toys the blessed have only contempt, loving gold for its color and brilliance alone and not as a purchase of wickedness. Then I asked him how it was he died and he said he was murdered for his purse. Had I been less amazed at speaking to him, I would have asked the name of his murderers but I forgot myself."

"And his spirit stood before you?" Joan asked, quite caught up in her friend's account.

"In a manner of speaking," Margaret answered after a moment's hesitation. Her brow furrowed and she looked as though she were trying hard to remember exactly how it was. "The chamber was dark and very cold, for no fire had been laid. I remember asking Ursula if we might have a taper the better to see by, but no, she insisted that the darkness would help her put her mind to the conjuring. We sat at two sides of a little table my sister uses to write upon. Ursula held her face in her hands and mumbled beneath her breath."

"Did you hear any of these words?"

"Some I heard but did not understand them. It was a foreign language I think she spoke—or a language of spirits."

"And after she conjured?"

"The conjuring went on for some time. Ursula's voice grew louder, more insistent. I began to doubt, but it was about then that—that—"

Joan urged Margaret to continue.

"I heard a voice behind me. It was my brother's voice."

"How were you sure it was your brother's voice and not some other's?"

"I was not sure, at first, but he called me Meg, by which name I had not been called since a child. I said, 'Who calls me Meg so familiarly?' And he answered, 'What, Meg, do you not know your own dear Philip's voice?' Then I remembered that thus he used to call me. Meg. He used the name when we conversed familiarly. I knew then that it was my brother indeed. The voice sounded distant, as though strained. It came from behind me in the chamber, and when I turned around to see for myself Ursula shouted at me, 'Nay, Mrs. Waite,' she said, 'do not do so, for the spirit expressly forbade it!' 'What?' cried I, 'my own brother forbidding his sister to look upon him?' 'It is for your own good,' she said, 'for spirits, even those of the blessed, are horrible to look upon.'"

"So you believe then it was Philip Goodin himself that you heard behind you?"

"And *saw*, Joan, for before she could warn me of the danger of looking I had turned and glimpsed my brother's form. The spirit was of middle height and dressed as my brother used to dress. The face was in shadows, but oh, I tell you, Joan, I know it was my brother indeed. Never had I felt such joy as then. My gratitude knew no bounds. The agonizing doubt that for years I suffered was suddenly lifted from me."

Joan grasped her friend's hands, which were trembling with excitement generated by the recollection, but Joan could not help asking, "Could it not have been some other standing there, someone who slipped in the door of the chamber and out again without your knowing it?"

The widow gave Joan a sudden sharp look of reproof and said, "The table where I was stood between him and the only door to the chamber. No mortal thing could have slipped by me, for my eyes were never closed and I would have heard him tread upon the floor. No, what you suggest, Joan, is not possible. It *was* my brother's spirit I saw and heard. His words proved it, as did his strange appearance and disappearance. It was the last time I saw the spirit. I did not seek a second interview, nor did Ursula offer to provide one. Within a week she was arrested."

"At her trial you testified against her," Joan said.

Margaret sighed deeply. "That's true," she said. She did not elaborate. Her face was full of guilt.

Joan would have liked to ask more about the apparition, for in her own mind she was less than convinced. The existence of spirits and their ability to communicate with the living she did not dispute, but she reserved the right to doubt whether any single manifestation was a spirit in truth, a figment of the imagination, or a fraud. She was not sure how to interpret Margaret Waite's experience, but somehow she felt it was no true ghost the widow had seen. She was considering this when voices were heard coming from the shop. It was the nephew. With him was Brigit Able. The girl was carrying a heavy parcel, which turned out to be funeral garments. She said she had spent a good hour or two at the tailor's shop waiting for Mr. Osgood to complete them and she was now distraught for all her chores left undone. Margaret told the girl not to trouble herself about the chores but to lay the garments on her great bed upstairs. As Brigit left to do this, John Waite commenced a discussion with his aunt regarding funeral arrangements. Joan rose to go. Margaret rose too and embraced Joan. "Thank you," Margaret said, looking at Joan in such a way as to plead with her not to tell anyone of what she had said. Joan received the message and nodded. Then Margaret showed Joan to the door.

In the street, Joan thought back to the unnerving experience in the barn, and her disquiet returned to do battle with the skepticism aroused by Margaret's account of ghostly happenings. She thought Margaret's encounter with her dead brother had all the earmarks of a fraud—perpetrated doubtless by the clever girl for whom Joan had come to feel less sympathy than before. Ursula's brother Andrew, she suspected, was also involved, and probably played the part of Philip, disguising his voice and using the childish name he and his sister might have discovered from any of a number of persons who had known Margaret as a child. Given Margaret's state of mind, she might have supposed any young man of her brother's years, height, and girth, to be Philip were the suggestion made strongly enough. And the suggestion *had* been strongly made. The darkened chamber, the promises to secrecy, the offerings, the meaningless incantation—all would have been overpowering given Margaret's desire to believe it was indeed her brother she heard.

But Joan could not explain away so easily her own unnerving experience in the Waites' barn. It was not so much the mysterious whispering she had heard, the obscene image she had found, or the unsettling recollection of what had passed within on any of those nights when Ursula gathered her circle of intimates to show off her powers. Nor was it the brindled cat with its strange, hostile glare. It was rather a strong sensation—a kind of glimmering, as she called it. Since childhood Joan had experienced unaccountable moments of insight that came to her unbidden from time to time as warnings or assurances. This glimmering had been a particularly strong one. She had sensed a *presence* in the barn, something insidious and malevolent, and what she had sensed she felt sure was not of this world.

EIGHT

THE five men summoned by the magistrate had been ushered into the library of the manor and were now waiting for its lord to appear. Each man sat in a high-backed chair of sturdy oak, with walnut inlays and ornately carved legs and armrests, and quietly admired the other furnishings in the spacious chamber. All except one of them. The exception was the bailiff, a little transplanted Frenchman named Henry Moreau. With his long, sallow face and heavy-lidded eyes, Moreau seemed curiously indifferent to the splendor about him. His complacency suggested that he had been in the library on many other occasions—as in fact he had, being the lord's chief officer—and that he would not, like the simple burgesses around him, gawk at the splendid urns and amorini, the caryatids and heraldic beasts adorning floor, wainscot, ceiling, and chimneypiece in such profusion that one would have thought the artificers who had designed and decorated the chamber could not abide a plain, unpainted surface. Waiting with the bailiff were two somber-faced aldermen, Mr. Trent and Mr. Walsh; the parson, Mr. Davis; and Matthew Stock.

The magistrate entered, and the men rose. The magistrate was a stout gentleman of about fifty. He was dressed in a long satin robe of ash color, thickly covered with gold lace chevronwise, and a rather long cloak of black cloth, lined with velvet. On his head he wore a tall hat, adorned with a single jewel. In a voice rich with authority and awareness of place, he greeted each of the men by name, inquired of his health, and then invited him to be seated. The magistrate sat down at his desk, a massive piece of furniture with well-ordered stacks of papers and books, a large, leather-bound ledger, and writing materials at hand. The post had recently arrived and a bundle of letters lay before him with their seals unbroken. For a moment he examined the letters; then he looked up at the constable from under heavy brows. "Well, now, Mr. Stock, I have it there was some little broil in the town this morning, which thing I regret to hear and hope that it has since been made right."

"No broil, sir," Matthew said. "A gathering of sorts . . . at the Waite house. Some thought they saw a ghost at the glover's window and fled in great alarm and confusion, but the crowd has long since disbanded and the street is at peace."

"A ghost, you say? In broad daylight!" The magistrate seemed amused. "Pray, whose ghost was it supposed to have been?"

"Ursula Tusser's, sir."

"Oh, the witch," said the magistrate, more serious now. "But you say the crowd has disbanded?"

"It has, sir. I have posted a deputy before the house—just to be safe."

"Good. Yes, that's good." The magistrate leaned back in his chair and looked satisfied. A more relaxed atmosphere began to prevail. A servant entered with a decanter of wine and goblets, and while each man was served the magistrate spoke of the merits of civil order. He was a man of strong convictions, a bulwark of the law. He took his magistracy with great seriousness. The five men listened intently. Then the magistrate turned to the pastor. He wanted to know what the young cleric made of the supposed spirit. The parson admitted he had not been present. All he knew was what he had heard later, garbled stories made more so by the terror of the tellers. Of course, he did have his opinion nonetheless.

Before he could deliver it, the magistrate put the same question to Matthew. Matthew told him what had happened, what he had seen and what confirmed later from the lips of Brigit Able herself.

"But those in the street construed the face to be that of Ursula Tusser?"

"They did, sir. After that, there was no reasoning with them. A panic followed."

"To which they were all too prone from the beginning," the magistrate added. "Witchcraft has set all our teeth on edge, and since they had congregated at the house to see some wondrous thing, their fancies would not be appeased until such a wonder occurred. Tell me, did this Brigit Able resemble the witch?"

"They are of the same years—or were. Both were spindly. There the resemblance ceased. Ursula I would have called fair to look upon."

"Ha!" said the magistrate, slapping his silken-hosed knee. "Well do the ancients speak of the unruly multitude with contempt when one hysterical outcry can move an entire assembly to a delusion such as this."

"With all respect, sir," ventured the parson, who had been itching to have his say. "I would not too readily dismiss this remarkable occurrence as a delusion."

"How so, Mr. Davis?" returned the magistrate, regarding the cleric with an expression of mild curiosity.

"Some I spoke to swore upon their lives it was indeed the Chelmsford witch whose shape appeared at the window. I mean not to contradict our good honest constable, but is it not possible that it is he who is mistaken rather than the others?"

"It *was* Brigit Able I saw," Matthew insisted, not sure but that he ought to feel offended in having his word disputed. Had he not seen the girl with his own eyes? Had she not admitted to having looked from her window and then withdrawn her face again when the outcry began?

The parson made a conciliatory gesture with his hands and said, "But see, Mr. Stock, you have told us that the two young women were of the same age and figure. Is it not possible, therefore—"

"It is not possible," Matthew repeated, feeling his face flush. "I spoke to Brigit Able and her mistress afterward. Brigit said she had peered from the window and, seeing the noisy multitude below, had been startled by it."

"So says *she*," remarked Alderman Trent. He was a large-faced man of muscular build who had made his money as a butcher. "The Devil hath power to assume a pleasing shape, and if he has such power as the proverb holds, then it would follow his minions may do likewise. Who are we to say it was not the witch at the window?"

No one took exception to this principle, and there followed a brief account by the several persons present of remarkable incidents of supernatural metamorphoses, the most amazing of which was Peter Trent's story of a Norwich woman who regularly turned herself into an owl for the purpose of spying on her neighbor from an upstairs window.

"You suggest then, Mr. Trent," said the magistrate, "that the spirit of Ursula Tusser took possession of the living body of Brigit Able."

"Stranger things have happened, sir," said the butcher.

"Marry, one wonders what the witch could not do!" exclaimed Mr. Walsh, visibly shuddering at the very thought. "It is said she had the power to turn herself into a toad or cat, and *that* was while she *lived*. What powers can she have now attained, now that her soul is in hell, where it most certainly is."

There was a general agreement that Ursula Tusser's soul was in hell. Then the magistrate turned to the parson and asked, "But surely the Devil has no power to possess the body of a virtuous person?"

Looking pleased to have been asked for his opinion, the parson shifted in his chair and nodded shrewdly. He said the question was one that had been much written of. Fortunately he had made a study of the matter. The answer was not simple. "If we presume that Brigit Able's soul is virtuous, then that *would* preclude satanic possession. On the other hand—"

Trent interrupted with a cynical guffaw. "If we presume, if we presume. Now these are very good words indeed, these *presumes*. Surely they are wasted on Brigit Able. Why, she was one of the witch's confederates! She testified against Ursula to save her own neck. Is it not possible that she is as steeped in the black art as the creature that was hanged? And if so, then she has no more power to resist possession than did that herd of swine from which a legion of devils was cast, as the Scriptures speak."

"In faith, I have heard ill things of her," offered Mr. Walsh, shaking his head.

Matthew said Brigit had no evil reputation that he knew of, save for her part in the trial, at which he heard she had acquitted herself well enough, responding to the questions put to her and not denying her own attendance at Ursula's ceremonies.

"It seems Brigit Able has found a stout defender in our constable," said Trent archly. "Who undoubtedly knows her better than we."

"You hold then, Mr. Stock," said the magistrate, "that what appeared at the upper window of the Waite house was the serving girl and none other?"

"That is my opinion," said Matthew, at once irked with himself for labeling what he had seen as an opinion and not a fact.

"And you, Mr. Trent and Mr. Walsh and good Parson Davis, hold to the contrary, that it was the spirit of Ursula Tusser in the shape of Brigit Able?"

"We do, sir," said Trent and Walsh in unison.

The parson said he could not say what had been seen, since he was not present. He did suggest, however, that such manifestations were neither uncommon nor without scriptural precedent.

Matthew felt the urge to point out that in that respect the parson was very much like the aldermen. None had seen the alleged spirit, but each had become a great authority on the subject.

Trent said he thought it was a terrible shame that honest Christians should be subject to such enormities, and Mr. Walsh agreed. Trent suggested that Brigit Able and the entire Waite household be summoned for questioning. "Our cattle, our wives, our daughters, and our maidservants will all fall victim to this base hellhound, this secret and pernicious witch," Trent declared indignantly.

At this, the bailiff, who had sat quietly all this time with a superior air, joined the discussion, saying he thought this last suggestion a very proper one. "There's rarely one witch in a town," he said, "for they are like unto fleas, rats, or other noxious pests. Should you see one in a corner, be assured a multitude of his kinfolk make merry behind the wainscoting."

"It would ease the mind of many in the town were a jury impaneled," said Mr. Trent.

"Yes, a jury—that would do it," agreed the bailiff with enthusiasm. "These vulgar broils make us look very bad in London, I think."

For a moment the magistrate sat pensive, while the other men waited his decision. "Well," he said at last, "I don't know the origin of this tumult—whether it be from the sinful brain of man or the connivance of Satan—but I do know such unruly behavior as occurred today cannot be tolerated, and if an investigation will pacify the town, then you shall have one. Yet no jury, for I want someone I can hold responsible and direct. Constable Stock, I empower you to undertake such an investigation into these doings. Let your commission include the discovery of whatever dealings the Waites or their servants had or are now having that might reasonably require my warrant and the town its trial. All England will have its eyes upon us here to see how we acquit ourselves, so let us above all else be judicious in our proceedings and yes, Christianlike as well, neither tolerating evil nor persecuting the innocent."

The servant returned to remove the decanter and goblets and the magistrate rose to signal that the discussion was concluded. There was a quick exchange of farewells and the men were shown to the door. Moreau went off to see about some business of his master's. The parson excused himself to visit a parishioner who lived not far from the manor. Matthew and the two aldermen were left to walk back to town together.

They had gone about a half mile, conversing desultorily, when Trent brought the subject back to the Waite affair. "This is a great charge that has fallen upon you, Mr. Stock, a very great charge indeed."

Matthew assured the alderman that he understood just how great a charge it was, but Trent continued to discourse on the subject. Matthew suspected he regretted not having been appointed to the task himself. "This Brigit, this serving girl," Trent went on, glaring at the road before him, his voice contemptuous, "her reputation is stale. It would be well to speak to her, make her tell you all she knows of this business. Squeeze it out of her. The jury was too eager to hang Ursula Tusser—they should have examined Brigit Able more closely."

"I have already spoken with her," said Matthew, relieved to see the town ahead.

"I mean speak to her with *authority*," returned Trent. "Let her know your power. If she refuse to divulge what part Mrs. Waite had in this, she must understand we have ways of making her talk. You are in all things too softhearted, Mr. Stock. Hear now, the rigor of the law must serve or the town will be undone by these women."

Matthew bristled at the criticism but let it pass without rebuttal. Moulsham was at hand, the bottom of High Street. Within minutes the three men would part company.

Walsh joined in with similar counsel. He mentioned the names of several persons who he claimed had personal knowledge of Margaret Waite's witchcraft.

"The persons you name," replied Matthew stonily, "I know as well as you, and will consider whatever information they can give. Don't worry, either of you. I'll satisfy the magistrate's expectations."

"Well, sir," said Trent as the three men crossed the bridge, "it is not only the magistrate you must satisfy but the town. You saw the mood of the people. They are deathly afraid and beyond patience with this tribe of hellcats and their familiars. They'll brook no more, believe me. They will not be satisfied unless your inquiries uncover what their fear tells them is fact—that there is more than one witch in Chelmsford and of them Margaret Waite is chief. The serving girl is but a disciple, believe you me. As to what punishment awaits them, the law is clear."

Though Matthew sought to defend Margaret Waite of what he believed was an unfounded and malicious charge, the aldermen would not be persuaded otherwise but that she was a pernicious woman as these recent events made plain. They also made it clear they thought the less of him for disputing about it. "A fine investigator you will make, Mr. Stock, of this filthy business," said Trent. The three men stopped in the street. Trent began railing. "What? Does Margaret Waite already have you in thrall? Has she put a spell upon your cow and caused its milk to curdle or its teats to wither? Why else, pray, should you be so vocal in her defense, she who has been visited by a malign spirit, as a dozen honest citizens and more of the town are prepared to testify?"

"Ridiculous! It was Brigit Able at the window, I tell you. I saw her myself," answered Matthew, growing heated.

The two aldermen regarded him with the implacable countenances of men determined in their convictions and outraged that they should be questioned. "You are a fool, Matthew Stock, and as easily led about as a lamb," said Trent. "Watch that you are not served up for sacrifice."

"Would you have me arrest the woman forthwith?" Matthew asked caustically. "Or at least wait upon the magistrate's warrant? I have been commissioned to investigate. I shall do it, God help me. Let me remind you this is my commission, Mr. Trent, not yours."

"We well know it is *yours*," said Walsh, "but wish only that you carry it out. There are tests to prove a witch beyond reasonable doubt. Her body may be searched for the Devil's mark, or she may be dunked, for a witch cursed to scorn the waters of baptism may not sink in the water. God will aid the innocent, if Margaret Waite and her servant be so."

"Shall I then persecute the poor woman that grace may

abound?" asked Matthew, not bothering to hide his contempt for the alderman's suggestions.

"We ask you to persecute no man, nor woman either," replied Trent, whose flushed sweating face indicated his own temper was mounting. "We ask only that you do your duty. I hope you don't suppose that excludes inquiries at the Waite house just because you and the Waites happen to be old friends."

"I suppose no such thing," answered Matthew hotly. "But neither do I think my commission a license to undermine the reputation of a family just because some in authority in this town like them not."

"Just what are you implying, sir?" said Trent, glaring at Matthew. Trent was a big man, nearly six feet in height, with the broad heavy shoulders of a laborer. One of his thick black brows was lifted dangerously.

"I imply nothing," said Matthew, trying to keep his voice calm and assured in the face of these hostilities. "I do nothing more than answer the questions you put to me. I hope, my masters, that there have been no complaints abroad about my constableship. I am useless in his trust without your confidence and support."

"There have been no complaints we know of," said Walsh, apparently mollified by Matthew's soft answer. He glanced sideways at his colleague and seemed relieved that the larger man appeared ready to give over this quarrel, which by now was beginning to draw the attention of passersby.

"There have been no complaints," Trent agreed coldly. "See, now, we three are making a public spectacle of ourselves. I have said what I have said, Mr. Stock. A wise man need only once be warned of his duty, or of a peril. Let us be on our way, Mr. Walsh. Good day, Constable."

"Mr. Trent, Mr. Walsh."

Matthew watched as the two men proceeded quickly up the street. His heart beat rapidly with his anger and his mind raced with arguments and rebuttals, proofs and stratagems, so that there was no help in the sharp autumn air, in the familiar street, or in the thought that he would soon be at his own house and hearth. There was only frustration and determination. He knew what he had seen, and he would be damned if he would let any alderman, parson, or magistrate—if it came to that—tell him otherwise. Nor would he allow himself to become the instrument of another man's personal vengeance just because the present atmosphere of fear and danger gave occasion for it.

On his way home he stopped at the Waites'. He was relieved to find all as he had assured the magistrate it was, calm and ordinary. Arthur was still at his station. The young man looked very bored.

"Calm, is it, Arthur?"

"The usual comings and goings, Mr. Stock. Your wife paid a call on the glover's widow."

"Did she?"

"About four o'clock it was, sir."

"Is she still within?"

"No, sir. She's gone home now."

"Very good, Arthur. I suppose you'll want your supper too?"

"Yes, Mr. Stock." Arthur rubbed his right elbow and winced, as though an ague had settled there.

"Some trouble with your arm?" asked Matthew.

"It's been bothering me all afternoon," Arthur said. He cast a worried look at the house. "You know, sir, I was thinking about the glover's house and what has transpired there. Mr. Waite's death, I mean, then Ursula Tusser having lived right next door. They say a witch can curse a body and make the limbs shrivel up like a prune."

"That's what they say."

"My arm never hurt till now, sir," said Arthur.

"Maybe it's the cold weather," suggested Matthew.

Arthur shook his head doubtfully. Matthew patted him on the shoulder and told him not to worry. But the idea had wormed itself into the young man's brain and would not be dislodged by easy assurances. He had been on duty since noon and had heard all the stories, twice over. He wanted to know what the constable made of them. The whole town knew what had happened. Wasn't he in personal danger standing there outside the house the half day, exposed to evil eyes and God knew what spells from within? "They say she's a witch," Arthur whispered.

"Who?"

"Mother Waite."

So it was *Mother Waite* now. Not Mrs. Waite or Dame Margaret or any other name suited to her place as a freeholder's wife of a respected Chelmsford family.

"Only now you thought of these things?" asked Matthew.

"Oh, sir, I have thought of them since hearing that I was to stand here."

"Well, I am heartily sorry for your arm's discomfort, Arthur, but, as I say, I think it will be right as rain soon enough." Matthew told his deputy to go home to his supper, and advised him that his services might be needed on the next day at Malcolm Waite's funeral.

A worried look crossed Arthur's face. "The funeral?"

"Malcolm Waite's funeral, lad. A piece of churchyard fits every body."

Arthur cast an anxious look at his arm, which did not seem to hang as straight as before. "Yes, sir," he said without enthusiasm.

"And, Arthur . . ."

"Yes, sir?"

"Your arm will mend in God's time. Don't worry. Say your prayers when you get home and have a good supper. A full stomach and an easy conscience will set the worst fears to flight."

"Good night, sir."

"Good night, Arthur."

Matthew watched him as he walked down the street. Arthur moved slowly in the fading light, as a man does when the activity of the mind robs the legs of their strength and one foot shuffles before another out of mere habit. While he walked, his good arm held the other protectively.

N I N E

MATTHEW looked for his wife and found her at length in the garden, where she was watching the last glow of day far in the west under the mass of ragged, smoky clouds. He greeted her and asked if she was not cold standing there. She seemed to be meditating something. She returned his kiss but in a distracted way; her mind was elsewhere.

"I'm not cold," she said. "The kitchen was like a furnace. Betty has held supper. A shoulder of mutton."

"Arthur Wilts told me you had visited Margaret Waite."

"I did. A disturbing visit in every way."

"How so?"

Joan held nothing back, not even the alarm she had felt in the barn loft.

"You're sure it wasn't Brigit or Susan—or perhaps John, the nephew?"

"Susan was in the house, except when I saw her journey out to the privy. My oath upon it that she was never in the barn. When I returned to the house, Brigit was still out with the nephew at the tailor. No, I don't think it was John."

"The mare stirring . . . perhaps the cat you saw . . . Strange how it regarded you," he murmured, visualizing the scene.

"No," she said positively. "It was neither cat nor horse."

"I'm quite at a loss then," he admitted. "But they were just whispers—human voices—and footsteps and a creak and a thud, you said."

"The strangest feeling of dread came over me while I was in the loft, a horrid place. I found this wicked thing."

"What wicked thing?

She described the image, its grotesque parody of the human form.

"A wicked thing indeed," said Matthew, "but it was not that alone that frightened you, nor the whispers and noises."

"No, it was not those. It was a *presence* . . . a *presence* of something not of this world."

"A ghost?" he asked lightly.

But she was entirely serious. She looked at him reproachfully, with an expression that suggested her disappointment. As though to say, "I thought you would understand, but you do not."

He recognized her seriousness. It fell like a pall on them both as they walked back to the house and entered the kitchen. Betty was standing at the hearth. Joan told her to serve the supper. Husband and wife sat down at the table and waited before speaking again until the food had been served, Matthew had carved, and Betty was excused to other labors.

Joan broke their long silence with a question about his afternoon. Where had he gone?

"To the manor. I and Trent and Walsh and the parson."

"The aldermen?"

"To report to the magistrate. About the gathering in front of the Waites' this morning." He told her about the meeting and the walk home, how the two men had pressured him regarding Margaret Waite.

"A fine pair of birds," she said scornfully. "A pox on them. No wonder they spoke against Margaret. A fox will prove no harmless dog if it does take a dozen years. Trent is out to settle an old score against her husband. Him dead, the widow must serve."

"What old score?"

"Don't you remember? It's been some twenty years. Malcolm Waite served his time as town searcher, in the course of which duties he brought our good butcher, now alderman, to account for his tossing of bones and other filth in the river, a thing expressly prohibited by law. His transgression cost the butcher three shillings and some odd pence."

"A paltry sum," snorted Matthew. "I had forgotten the story, if I ever knew of it. But who would nurture a grudge like that for twenty years?"

"Peter Trent, our most revered alderman, that's who. The butcher has never forgot the incident. I myself heard his wife speak of it and claim the charge was all trumped up out of Malcolm Waite's envy. Now Trent bullies the widow. I'll wager it was Trent who was the most obnoxious on the way. Walsh is made of water compared to his fellow."

"It was Trent for a fact."

"He made threats, didn't he? He's a bully."

"I wouldn't call them threats," said Matthew.

"Not threats?" she exclaimed, her eyes flashing dangerously. "Why, husband, what else would it be called?"

"Strong admonishment," he said, pursing his lips to indicate he agreed it was something more.

"Marry, husband, well may you make such an antic face when you speak nonsense. Of course it was a threat. These are aldermen your plain honest dutifulness has offended, no mere town tipplers or errant knaves. Their displeasure might well be your undoing. Yet I like not their boldness. I would fain know where good Alderman Trent feels free to speak for me and the rest of the town. If I want the Waites persecuted for witchcraft or other high crimes and misdemeanors, I will tell him so myself and am not about to have such a clodpole upstart alderman as he is, who cannot rule his own house and lets that wastrel son of his haunt every alehouse in Moulsham until I know not what hour and—"

"Peace, Joan, peace!" Matthew cried, laughing despite himself, for her fury often had a comical side and it did now. Joan had worked herself into a dither, gesturing wildly and looking fierce. Suddenly she burst out laughing herself. Betty came into the kitchen to see what had provoked such merriment. Seeing nothing more than her master and his wife talking at table, she disappeared again.

"I concede to your wording, Joan," Matthew said, drying

his eyes with the napkin. But Joan made another face, mimicking Trent's glower. "Oh, stop, stop, for pity's sake," he declared. "I'll die of laughing."

"Let Trent be Trent," she said after her antic humor passed and she reached across the table to caress his face with her hand. "But pray tell me, how will you proceed in this business? I hope you will not burden poor Margaret in her time of mourning. It's true she was thicker with Ursula than we supposed, but it's over now. What's the point of raking it all over again to her detriment? Let her be, I say."

"Never fear," Matthew said. "We shall have no burdening of widows, no persecutions. But I must investigate, Joan, there's no help for it. The magistrate says I must, and if I do not, then Trent will. He wants my job as well as his own, and if he takes up the business, then you can say good night and amen too to the Waites and their kin. They'll all be charged and we'll watch them hang, one by one."

Joan shuddered at the thought. "Let us pray no more apparitions trouble us."

"Amen," he said.

"And if they do?" she asked.

"If they are nothing more than serving girls gawking from windows, I'll not care a groat, but if they go about causing deaths, then they must be looked into. In the meantime I'll speak with Thomas Crispin. Ursula was his servant. He may know more than he has told—certainly Margaret Waite did. What a careless affair Ursula's trial was is now made plain by these fresh discoveries."

"What will you ask of him?"

Matthew shrugged. "It's an ill mason that refuses any stone."

She considered the proverb and agreed.

"I'll do it after the funeral tomorrow."

"Ah, yes, the funeral," she murmured ruefully. "Would that Malcolm Waite's burial were the end of this business."

It was the night of the week when by custom the Stocks had their apprentices and servants in after supper for games and songs, for readings from Scripture and other edifying books. Betty now reappeared to ask if supper was done and the master was ready for such pastimes. In fact, neither Matthew nor Joan was in a mood for such lighthearted fare, but both felt duty bound by the tradition, and Matthew nodded his head. He no sooner did so than the servants and apprentices filed into the kitchen, talking noisily. Matthew directed them to their places at the long table as the talk subsided.

"What shall it be, young sirs and maids?" Matthew boomed with forced cheerfulness. "Japes or songs, riddles or some new thing learned at the street corner when your minutes might have been more profitably spent learning your trade?"

"The witch, Mr. Stock. Tell us of the witch that was seen today!" cried several young voices. Betty joined in the chorus, as did Peter Bench, his pale long face animated with interest.

Matthew was reluctant. Joan said, "Best satisfy their curiosity, husband, or they won't ask you to sing later on."

The apprentices laughed, and so did Betty. They encouraged him more strongly. He gave in.

"It was not a witch at all, but simply Brigit Able, the glover's serving girl, whom all of you know and see daily," said Matthew.

There were groans of disappointment and disbelief.

"But, sir, I had it from the baker's wife that it was a spirit indeed that was seen. Both at the window and elsewhere around the town," proclaimed the squeaky voice of the youngest of Matthew's apprentices.

"In the town they all say it was Ursula Tusser that was seen there," said Peter Bench. "The same that appeared to frighten Mr. Waite to his death."

"Aye, it's all true, Samuel," said the oldest of Matthew's apprentices to the youngest, making a terrifying grimace at the same time. "And she'll be coming for *you* tonight!"

Samuel's eyes grew round with horror, but the laughter that followed, touched even as it was with a certain nervousness, put the boy at ease.

"Here, now," said Matthew sternly. "Let's have no more of

witches. Mr. Waite will be buried tomorrow and it behooves us to speak well of him and his house."

"Will the shop be closed then?" asked Peter.

"During the hours of the funeral it will," answered Matthew. "Well, now, what is your pleasure?"

"Songs, songs!" cried they all.

"Very well," said Matthew, smiling. "What shall we sing?"

"'A Merry Maid Went Milking'!"

"'Summer Wanes Apace'!"

"'Follow Thy Fair Sun'!"

"Ah, I like the last. The verse is most fitting, I think. Someone fetch the lute who's a match for the strings and accompany me. On the second verse, all join in!"

The lute was brought. Peter Bench seized the instrument and tuned it with great care. When all was ready, Matthew began to sing:

> *"Follow thy fair sun, unhappy shadow!*
> *Though thou be black as night,*
> *And she made all of light,*
> *Yet follow thy fair sun, unhappy shadow!"*

By the time the rest of the company joined in at the second verse, the apparition of Ursula Tusser seemed all but forgotten. Matthew was quite caught up in his music. Indeed, all the voices blended sweetly. But Joan sat with a sad countenance, for even Thomas Campion's melodious songs could not dispel the shadow of her fears.

T E N

THE next day, under skies of such threatening hue that it seemed nature herself was grieved at the glover's death, Malcolm Waite was buried.

The funeral was well attended by the curious, who showed more interest in the now notorious widow than in her late husband. Every pew in the church was filled and—to the churchwarden's dismay—a multitude of gawkers kept watch and ward amid the gravestones in the churchyard, where they showed little respect for Malcolm Waite or the graves they trod on. Rumor had done her work. If there was a man in the shire who had not heard of the glover's strange death, he was blind and deaf and dumb too. Christmas and Easter would not see a tithe of the crowd.

The ceremonies began with a procession of mourners, who had come up High Street led by the undertaker's apprentice, a thin, sallow-faced boy fitted out in sable suit and carrying before him a standard draped in black crepe. The boy marched stiffly and self-consciously to some drumbeat in his head, looking straight on. Behind him appeared the gaunt, lean-jawed figure of the town undertaker, a man named Wynnyff, the very image of death himself, with his gray pallor and drooping mouth, and his eyes fixed on the cobblestones.

The undertaker led the horse at the front of the funeral cart, a four-wheeled conveyance with a canopy under which was the coffin. The coffin was crowned with sprigs of holly and myrtle, symbols of immortality. After came the handful of mourners for whom the glover's death had been more than a curiosity.

The widow was supported on both sides by her sons, who had arrived early that morning to see their father buried. Behind them John Waite and Thomas and Janet Crispin walked together, along with the Crispins' little girls, who were dressed like miniature adults. After the children came Joan, the only friend of the family who had dared to be seen in public with the suspected woman. At the end of the procession were the servants of the two families and a group of Thomas Crispin's apprentices and workmen from the tannery. Their attendance was obligatory and their faces showed it. Matthew, standing by the church door, spied Susan Goodyear among the servants, but not Brigit Able. He wondered where she was.

The funeral service itself was brief and overtly professional. The parson preached a sermon on the resurrection of the just and prayed earnestly before the mortal remains of the glover were carried into the churchyard and lowered into the ground, but it was evident that he did so without enthusiasm and with a certain amount of personal distaste. The great multitude of spectators and the subdued hostility they showed for the Waite family unnerved him, and he appeared relieved when his duties were done. The rain beginning to fall, the crowd fled for cover.

All during the long afternoon, a furious wind sent the rain dashing in sheets against the houses; the town seemed beleaguered by it. Everything dripped. The houses trembled with the gusts. After changing out of their wet clothes, Matthew and Joan spent their time by the kitchen fire, drinking hot punch. Their spirits had been much depressed by the funeral, and of course the miserable cold and wet made it the worse. Both avoided any further discussion of the Waites or their problems, hoping that with the burial of the glover more than a body had been buried. But both knew too that it was not so. The savage storm was ominous and would surely be interpreted in the town to Margaret Waite's disadvantage.

By four o'clock, although the wind persisted in its fury,

the rain had stopped and in the west the sun made a half-hearted appearance from between large mottled clouds. The cobblestone street was slick and treacherous, but Matthew decided to go out. He traversed the puddles and runoff from the alleys and ditches and arrived at the Waite house, where he found John Waite and Margaret's sons visiting quietly in the parlor.

In their thirties, the sons resembled the mother more than the father. They were men of middle stature with broad faces and wide-set eyes and mouths with fleshy underlips. Matthew remembered them as young boys, Edward and Richard—or Dick, as he was called. They had been quiet and well behaved as children, and had grown up to be serious men. Successful too, if their clothing was any indication. They greeted the constable coolly and exchanged reminiscenses. They were deeply grieved over their father's death but not surprised. They had been well aware of his ailment. They had not, strangely enough, heard about Ursula Tusser and had not learned until a few hours before of the slanderous accusations now being made against their mother. Their cousin John had explained it all. Outraged and defensive, they regarded the constable suspiciously until he assured them that he believed none of the gossip and would do all he could to clear their mother's name.

For the next hour, he provided his own account of what had happened since the death of Malcolm Waite, mentioning also his commission from the magistrate, just so they would understand the difficulty of his own position. During this time, John Waite listened intently and made no demur; Matthew assumed that his version largely confirmed what the nephew had told his cousins. Critical before of his aunt and uncle's credulity in regard to Ursula's powers, John Waite now seemed content to be silent, either out of respect for his aunt's bereavement or for fear that an incautious remark would provoke his cousins.

Margaret came down from upstairs, where she had been resting. Seeming slightly refreshed, she invited Matthew to join the family at supper, which had been laid out on a table at the end of the room and offered a pleasant array of meats, fruits, and cheeses. Matthew declined with thanks, and said he wanted to speak to the Crispins.

Margaret said, "Thomas was here—Jane too—and I hoped they would take supper with us, they and the children, but Thomas took my sister home. She was drenched to the bone and Thomas feared she would fall ill from it."

"She had a rheum and cough, I think," said John Waite.

The discussion turned to the weather.

"If ever some superstitious fool looked for a sign of God's disapproval, the frenzy of the storm was it," remarked the nephew in a loud voice.

One of the sons said he thought the very violence of the storm might purport nature's grief over the death of a good man.

They talked now about what the storm meant, the second son, Dick, observing that great inundations foreshadowed insurrections and the downfall of princes. Margaret clasped her hands together and prayed it was not so, for the family had had sufficient grief. Matthew excused himself, saying he would see himself out. But Margaret insisted that Susan show him to the door. As Matthew was about to step into the street, the serving girl touched his arm and asked him to wait.

"I must speak to you, sir," she said, staring up at him.

"About what? Where, by the way, is your companion Brigit? I missed her at your master's funeral. Pray God she's not in bed with some fever."

"She's gone," said Susan, her eyes brimming with tears. "That's what I had to tell you, sir."

"Gone where?

"I rose this morning and found her gone from our bed. She left no message and took what few clothes and possessions she had with her."

"She's run off, then," said Matthew, not surprised considering the temper of the town. "Does your mistress know?"

"I told her, but she is too mindful of her own grief to care. Now all Brigit's work must fall upon me until a new servant is found, which may not be soon, for who will work in this house with such horrible goings-on, spirits coming and going, and such a howling wind to put the fear of God upon us all?"

"That's just the weather—the wind's fury," he said in an effort to calm her. He wondered why she stayed herself, and was tempted to ask her. But he did not want to put ideas into her mind. Margaret Waite had enough troubles as it was. He asked her if she or Brigit had seen another apparition.

"*Another?*" Susan exclaimed with obvious dread at the very thought. "I don't think so—at least I have not seen it. When we slept, we covered the window and passed the night in each other's arms for fear. Brigit sprinkled our chamber with rosemary, which they say is wondrous effectual in warding off spirits. And none came. If at some moment when we were separated she *saw* . . . anything . . . face or form, I know nothing of it."

"You slept together all night long, then?" asked the constable.

"I slept like the dead," Susan said; her eyes grew wide and she shuddered visibly at the phrase that had tripped from her tongue so casually. "I did not wake," she said, amending her words and looking comforted at the rephrasing.

"Well, then," said Matthew, thrusting his hat on his head, "if she returns, will you come at once to tell me—or if you should see her about the town?"

"I will, sir," Susan said, "but I think not to see her again."

"Not again? Why so pessimistic? She isn't dead, is she?"

Susan stiffled a sob and rubbed her pale hand across her mouth. She was obviously disturbed by her own prophecy. "I don't know why I said *that*," she said. "I swear I do not. But as God lives, sir, I know it is true." She laughed feebly, a forced laugh. "Brigit won't be back. No, not ever."

Susan stared at him with glassy eyes. The laughter trailed off, but Matthew found both the stare and the strange laughter unsettling. That Brigit had run away seemed plausible enough It even showed a certain prudence on her part. Margaret Waite had a few friends left in the town, but Brigit was a mere nobody. He smiled kindly at Susan and reached in his purse to find a penny for her. "Here, put this in your pocket," he said. "Mind your mistress faithfully."

She continued to stare after him as the door closed. He went next door to the tanner's house, still thinking of her prophecy. He knocked and was shown into a well-furnished room on the second floor, where he found the tanner and his wife bundled up before the fire, Crispin in his shirt and hose, his shoes drying at the hearth, the wife nearly smothered in a woolen coverlet that hid everything but her face. She peered kindly at Matthew from the folds of the coverlet.

"You are most welcome, Mr. Stock," said the tanner, rising as Matthew entered and motioning to a stool near their own. Crispin called the servant to fetch more wood for the fire, which was well supplied already, and then settled back in his chair. Matthew observed the couple with interest. He had never known them well. His relations with them had been friendly but distant. They seemed an affectionate pair, alike in their tempers, their countenances displaying that similarity of expression which often makes others believe that husband and wife grow to look alike with the passing of years. They were obviously saddened by the loss of their kinsman and the distress of his widow, and affected too by the slanders now being circulated against her. But they seemed not only dejected but nervous. Crispin quickly made the cause plain.

"We found this nailed to our door when we returned from the funeral," Crispin said stonily, handing Matthew a fragment of coarse paper. It was a warning, scrawled crudely. The Crispins were advised to forsake the town and take their servants with them. Just what was to happen if they did not follow these instructions was not said.

"We thought all was done when poor Ursula was hanged," Jane Crispin lamented in her soft voice. "Now all is again astir with my brother-in-law's death."

"We have always led good lives," Crispin said with a tone

of injured merit. "Decent God-fearing lives. This falls hard upon us, Mr. Stock. Is there no remedy?"

"Time may heal it all," said Matthew feebly, not convinced himself that time would—or how much time; that was another question, too. A sense of foreboding hung dangerously over his own head. In this mind's eye he saw again the stark, horrified expression in the glover's eyes, heard the warning prophecy of Susan Goodyear, recalled his own wife's dread in the Waite barn. It was all adding up to something, pushing toward something. But what? He said, "Malcolm Waite's death and yesterday's panic in the street have given the gossipmongers and balladeers of the neighborhood stuff enough. Within a week, it will be business as usual. People *do* forget."

Hearing himself say these words, Matthew despised himself a little. He had chided Brigit for her pessimism; was he not more guilty still for a foolish hopefulness, a blithe disregard for the signs, all of which pointed to the prospect of things getting far worse before they would be better?

"Some forget," said Crispin, frowning thoughtfully. "There's a sort of meanness bred by long association. You take a town the size of Chelmsford. How many families are we—three hundred?"

The tanner did not complete his thought, but Matthew caught its drift. Crispin was right, of course. Unfortunately right, but certainly so. Intimacy, which was the sole and proper ground for love and friendship, made spaces as well for ancient grievances, inexplicable spite, murderous thoughts growing rank amidst the tender shoots of domestic felicity and civil order. Matthew doubted not but that the day would come when Chelmsford would require a small army to keep the peace—no more half-time constables with their mind on their trade, their accounts, but men whose sole husbandry was the management of this unweeded garden. The day would come.

Jane Crispin reached out for her husband's hand, murmuring softly. The fire in the hearth had brought out the color in her face and given her smooth cheeks a youthful glow. Her striking blue eyes were particularly intense, and Matthew could well understand her husband's devotion. Jane Crispin had a beauty above her station in life; her voice was soft and cultured like a gentlewoman's. "If the constable thinks all will be well," she said reassuringly, "then I am sure he knows whereof he speaks, for he watches the temper of the town the way a faithful physician does the heats and colds that trouble the body that is sick. Should the fever grow intense he will have a remedy for it."

She turned her radiant smile on Matthew, and he acknowledged the complimentary words with an awkward, self-conscious bow. A silence followed, during which Matthew thought of ways to broach the subject for which he had come to the Crispins. Finding no strategy and recognizing he must speak or take his leave, he blurted out his question without prologue or apology.

"At Ursula's trial, both of you gave the girl a good character. But surely you knew the mischief she was up to?"

Neither husband nor wife seemed disturbed by the directness of his question, the complete lack of reasonable transition from their former discourse. Without hesitation Jane Crispin said, "Ursula was with us over two years. We knew her very well, very well indeed. She had many good qualities, although about her work she was slow and deliberate. Her mind always seemed elsewhere. Of her . . . practices . . . we knew very little. To us they seemed innocent enough. The sort of conjury young girls are wont to practice while boys their age play rougher sports and games. In the course of her trial we discovered more. We were astonished but . . ."

Her voice trailed off; she glanced at her husband for help.

"We were asked at the trial about her work. We answered truthfully—she was a good servant," answered Crispin matter-of-factly. "We knew little of what transpired in the barn loft. Certainly we knew nothing of her that merited her death. It came to that—for us, at least."

Concluding his remark, Crispin looked at his wife, she at him. They seemed agreed. Ursula had done nothing to their knowledge that merited death. Matthew felt the solidity of their relationship. Shoulder to shoulder they were a formidable pair. Like the Stocks, he thought, and he felt a sudden warming surge of friendliness toward them. "Evidently," Matthew continued, "your sister had a different view of Ursula's powers."

"The testimony was my sister's," Jane said. "You must put that question to her. She undoubtedly knew of matters beyond our ken."

"I understand Ursula claimed to have a familiar. A brindled cat, I am told. I have heard it still haunts the premises. Ursula also promised to put your sister in touch with the dead brother of the two of you, Philip Goodin."

"We knew nothing of *that*," Crispin said, glancing nervously at his wife, who at the mention of Philip Goodin's name seemed visibly disturbed. Her cheeks, flushed from the warmth of the fire before, now grew pale and the expression in her eyes was one of sudden alarm. "Our sister was never reconciled to her brother's murder as my wife was," said Crispin, apparently sensitive to his wife's distress. "It was ever Margaret's desire to know of Philip's state in the next world. What was said betwixt her and Ursula regarding these matters is unknown to us. Surely we never sought to know forbidden things, or to communicate with the dead."

The tanner made a face to suggest the topic was as repugnant to him as the practice. He went on to say he thought the town had erred in executing the girl, that it had made too much of a lot of nonsense. He said he didn't want to think about it anymore. Certainly he had nothing more to *say* on the matter. Philip Goodin's death was also an ancient sorrow he saw no good in stirring up again.

"My brother died a long time ago," Jane said wistfully after staring into the fire for a long time. "He was greatly loved by us all, but by my sister Margaret the most. She never accepted his death, which acceptance came to me only through long prayer and meditation."

"Who knows God's will?" asked Crispin philosophically.

"We must have faith," Jane added, with a heavy sigh.

"Margaret Waite told my wife that her brother's spirit appeared to her in this very house," Matthew said, not content to let the subject die and eager to know whether the couple were aware of this apparition.

Their surprised expressions indicated at once that they were not. "What's this about an apparition?" cried the tanner incredulously. Jane moaned softly and covered her eyes with her hand. She seemed to lapse into unconsciousness and her husband was alarmed, but the fit was only momentary. She sat up in the chair, as pale as death, and searched Matthew's face.

Matthew repeated what he had said.

"I know of no such apparition," said the husband angrily. "This is some idle tale of the servants."

Matthew assured him the story had come from Margaret Waite herself.

"How could this have happened in my own house?" asked Crispin, glaring around him as though the apparition might have the effrontery to put in another appearance.

"I know nothing of this either," said Jane, finding her voice at last. "Surely my sister would have said something to me. Oh, my poor sister is distracted by her husband's death and does not know her own mind!"

"This transpired before Malcolm Waite's death," Matthew said. "It was with Ursula's aid that it occurred, the apparition. So says your sister."

"She says Philip Goodin appeared to her—his spirit, that is—in this very house?" Crispin asked, a dubious glint in his dark eyes.

"She said it."

"Well, then, pray what message did he have for her?" asked Jane.

"She said his spirit told her that he was in heaven," said Matthew.

"Pray it is true, but I doubt the spirit was anything more than the poor woman's fancy," said Crispin, who was obviously more comfortable with this explanation. "Tell us, in what likeness did he come?"

"According to her, in the likeness of Philip Goodin."

"Margaret swears to it?" asked Jane.

"She has taken no oath, but so says she," said Matthew.

"My sister wouldn't lie," Jane said, exchanging worried looks with her husband.

"I say not that she lies, but her mind . . ." The husband's voice trailed off. There was no need to finish the sentence. They had all observed Margaret's condition since her husband's strange death. She who had once commanded in her house with a sharp tongue and strong will now had been reduced through her suffering to a weak, helpless creature starting at every footfall, her head full of visions and memories, some of which had no more substance than a vain wish.

"This is a most wondrous thing, if it be true," said Jane, her doubtful tone suggesting that she shared her husband's fear that her sister was near mad for grief.

"My understanding of our Lord's teaching permits no such manifestation," said the tanner, shaking his head. "Although it is my dearest hope that Philip Goodin's spirit resides with God, my knowledge that it does must remain a matter of faith. No apparition can put it on surer grounds than that. Since the Apostles' time visions have ceased, save those which are illusory or of the Devil."

Jane murmured her agreement. The subject seemed to have run its course. Matthew's curiosity satisfied, he asked them about Brigit Able.

"Your sister's servant Brigit Able has disappeared. I fear some new manifestation has occasioned her flight."

"Another apparition, do you think, Mr. Stock?" exclaimed Jane.

"I'll wager she's with child and wants none to know it," Crispin mumbled beneath his breath.

Ignoring her husband's skepticism, Jane said, "I spent the morning helping my sister prepare herself for the funeral and did not see Brigit. I thought nothing of it but that she had been sent off on some family business. It was Susan who saw to my sister's needs. My sister was grieved but calm. She has accepted her husband's death as God's will, not the work of some sinister power, and seems consoled by the presence of her sons, who will remain with her the week until her affairs are put in order and the will is read. My greatest fear is the animosity of the town, as can be seen in this threatening letter."

Crispin gave a deprecating glance at the note, which Matthew still held in his hand. He said he had taken precautions against trouble and when Matthew asked him what sort of precautions he meant, Crispin said he had armed his menservants. He said he hoped there would be no troubling of his house or shop, or that of his sister-in-law, but if there were, he was ready for it. He owned several firearms, he said, and a half dozen swords and was prepared to swear by the loyalty of his servants. "I stand by them and they by me," the tanner said with a grim smile.

Matthew said he hoped no such violent defense of the house would be necessary, although he allowed that tempers were running high in the town. He briefly described his encounter with Alderman Trent.

"The Devil take him!" cried Crispin. "Peter Trent has been my brother-in-law's enemy for years. I am not surprised by the enmity he shows Margaret or me, for that matter."

"But how could anyone think *that* of my dear sister?" Jane exclaimed, as if only now recognizing the full significance of the accusations. "She's a sweet, decent soul, a most devout Christian woman. Why, she has ever given alms to the poor."

"It seems Christian living is not enough to stave off these scandalmongers and witch-hunters," said her husband hotly. He repeated his promise to defend his house, and even talked of bringing a lawsuit against Peter Trent.

"What has my sister said to have done—cursed a cow, conversed with toads?" asked Jane, her handsome eyes flashing with unwonted anger.

"The apparition of Ursula has created the suspicion that your sister is herself a witch who has raised Ursula's spirit from the dead," Matthew said.

"Marry, for what purpose?" cried Jane. "To trouble her own house, to frighten the foolish?"

"It is thought she brought about her husband's death by causing Ursula's spirit to appear at the window," said Matthew.

"A novel fashion of murder, then," said Crispin in a derisive tone. "What absolute drivel!"

"It is a wicked, outrageous lie," stormed Jane Crispin, rising from her chair and letting the coverlet drop to the floor. "My sister loved her husband with a sincere heart. Although her tongue was sometimes sharp and she overbearing, this was nothing more than her peculiar humor. No sin, certainly. Her love, I swear it, was as true and deep as is my husband's love for me or mine for him."

"This is the thanks we get for our good works," Crispin said when his wife had sat down again. "Shelter we provided for Ursula and her brother, honest employment to save both from the parish rolls. And what do we receive in return? Why, to be hounded and railed at as witches and their consorts. The Devil's brood they'll be calling us next, condemned on all sides and deserted by our friends. Is God in His heaven, or does He sleep that such injustice should be visited upon us?"

"Oh, husband, how can you speak so?" cried Jane reproachfully, her eyes brimming with tears. "God *is* just. He will preserve us in our ordeal, even as Job."

"Your relief of the poor and succor for these orphans has been noted and much approved," Matthew said. "It is wrong to think that God has forsaken you, or that the town lacks gratitude."

"Wrong, is it?" said Crispin, looking up at him under heavy brows. "I am heartily sorry, Mr. Stock, but at this moment I can think of but one wrong—that done to me and mine. Are we not most miserable who must barricade our door against our neighbors, who receive missives such as that you hold in your hand threatening our lives, who must defend our good names from the slanders of men like Trent and Walsh?"

The question hung in the air while the tanner smoldered, his anger now moving to dejection. His wife tried to comfort him but to no avail. He fell silent, staring into the fire as though he were imagining some vengeance. "Most miserable, most miserable," he repeated to himself.

Jane saw Matthew to the door. "Good night, Mr. Stock. We value your friendship."

"Good night, Mrs. Crispin," Matthew replied, still holding the threatening letter. He advised her to bar the door behind him.

The chill wind whistled down the street, driving against his face, and he pulled his coat about him and his hat down to his eyebrows. He started up the street to his own house, thinking still of the tanner and his wife. To him their prosperity seemed much deserved, their happiness in each other genuine and reminiscent of his with Joan. But now fortune had turned her wheel. Prosperity had become adversity, wretchedness, public scorn, and danger. What explained it? The tanner's question echoed in his head. Why had God allowed such misfortune to fall upon the good, while evil triumphed and escaped punishment?

Matthew had no answer. He was seized by a melancholy himself, the fruit of his troubled thought and his physical weariness. Suddenly he became aware of his surroundings as though, preoccupied before, he had paid no attention to where he was. He was the lone traveler on such a night. On each side of him, the tall houses whose painted fronts and signs were as familiar to him as his own face, and whose occupants he knew by Christian name and family name, had assumed a forbidding aspect. He felt himself a stranger in a strange town, with every door barred against him. He stared at the windows as he passed. He could see lights within, but they were pale, timid lights, quite overpowered by the darkness in the street. Doubt and fear clutched at his soul with an icy hand. The houses seemed now the houses of his enemies, and he fully expected dogs to come forth and bark at him. But on such a night even the dogs quaked beneath their masters' tables, judiciously ignoring whatever scratches and knocks might send them out-of-doors.

In the alehouses of Moulsham they would be saying Ursula Tusser's curse had fallen upon the town. Damp-footed and dejected as he was, weak from his missed supper and beset by weighty thoughts of God's unfathomable ways, Matthew could almost believe in the curse himself.

ELEVEN

THE wind rattled the windowpanes incessantly, the shop sign creaked on its hinges, but in the kitchen of Matthew's house there was warmth and security. Joan was waiting for him with his supper, and although he had been famished before, he was now so disheartened by his visit to the Crispins he could only pick at his meat like an old toothless man searching amidst the stew for something soft to swallow whole. His wife commented on his lack of appetite. "Come, husband, *eat!* There's cheese and pippins to come. What, don't you like my cooking? A cheerful look makes a dish a feast!"

But he was beyond cheerful looks. He was feeling very black indeed. "Thomas Crispin has armed his servants and prepares to defend his house against the town," he reported glumly. "He's had a threatening letter nailed to his door giving him and his family leave to take up residence elsewhere or face the consequences." He showed her the letter. She quickly read it over.

"Oh, I see," Joan said, softening. "What consequences are these, pray?"

"As you can see, the letter leaves that up to the tanner's imagination."

"Thus the armed servants. I don't like *that.*"

"Nor I."

"What a shame," she said.

"It is. I don't know them well, the Crispins, but they seem a perfectly admirable couple."

"Oh, they are notorious for it," she said, wiping her hands on her apron. She had been standing with her back to the hearth, enjoying the tingle of warmth penetrating the several layers of good cloth she wore. But it was too warm now; the tingling had become a roasting. She pulled away and joined him at the table. He began to eat, and this pleased her. "How are they notorious?" he asked, picking up the thread of her remark about the Crispins.

She laughed. "Why, he dotes upon her and she upon him."

"He seems a model husband," Matthew said between mouthfuls.

"Some would say so," Joan said, meaning of course her gossips, whose knowledge of the marital relationships of the town was prodigious.

He stopped chewing and laid down his knife. "Would *you* say so?" he said, a little jealous.

"I'd call him a paragon of husbandhood," she said. "He is most solicitous of his wife's happiness. They say her house is furnished like a gentlewoman's. That it has carpets on the floors and a German clock above the mantel that tells the hours. When an hour strikes, a little knight in silver armor comes boldly forth and then marches back again. They say her servants whisper in her presence for fear of speaking too loudly and that her husband buys her whatever her heart desires."

Joan smiled whimsically and watched her husband.

"I have seen the house," Matthew said with a slight note of disgruntlement. "Carpets it has for a fact, and the furniture is very fine for a tanner's house. As to the clock you speak of, I didn't notice it. It sounds noisy to me—the knight in silver a terrible distraction. Is the great clock upon the church tower not sufficient to know what hour it is?"

Deciding she had played with him sufficiently, she didn't answer his question about the German clock; the clock in fact meant little to her. She wanted to know all the Crispins had *said*.

He recounted the conversation, word for word as he was able to recall it.

"Tom Crispin is probably right. The slander touching Margaret Waite will blacken their own reputations, as this horrid letter proves. Do you think he really means to defend his house, or will he leave?"

"I think he will defend the house," Matthew said, "though when I left him he was most dejected, despite the patient encouragement of his wife, who, it seems, takes these slanders with greater forbearance than he."

"A man's pride," she observed, shaking her head. "It is both a thing of strength and a source of folly. Are these threats of violence real, do you think, or just the idle pastime of troublemakers?"

"They're real enough. There's fear in the town," he said grimly. "Already they're calling the apparition the Chelmsford Horror."

She shuddered, thought of the loft, and said, "Poor Margaret, poor Mrs. Crispin."

Matthew finished his supper. Then a knocking was heard. At first they thought it was the wind.

"Someone's there," Joan said.

"At this hour? Lord, what now?" He rose to see who it was this time; carrying the lamp through the darkened shop, he thought that at least *they*—whoever it was that knocked— had left him at peace long enough to fill his stomach.

"Well?" she said when he came back a few minutes later looking more grim than ever.

"There's a brawl at the Saracen's Head. Across the river in Moulsham—you know the place. I am summoned for fear the roisterers will break heads as well as the furniture."

"Oh, what a pity you must go out again," she said sympathetically. "And on such a night."

"There's no help," he said with an air of resignation. "What did I do with my hat and cloak?"

"Behind the door," she said.

"The wind's giving over, at least."

"A small blessing."

He put on the cloak and held his hat in his hand as he bent down and kissed his wife on the forehead. Her skin was smooth and warm to his lips and he wanted very much to remain. How weary of his duties he was, and how he desired the peace of his own house at this moment. But it was not to be his, he knew—not yet.

"When shall I see you again? Shall I wait for you?" she asked.

"No, go to bed when you please. I may be some time."

"Please be careful, Matthew," she said, adding that she hoped he knew how little she really cared for fancy carpets and German clocks.

He gave her his blessing and went out.

When he was gone, Joan prayed—for Matthew and for herself, then for her neighbors the Waites and the Crispins, and lastly for the town, plagued by its own fears and something more and even worse. She prayed that the forces of good might prevail over the horror, which she did not fully comprehend but felt deep in her being as a profound and murky pool that the light could not penetrate or human reason fathom. Her prayer, made fervent and desperate by her husband's being suddenly snatched from her, somewhat allayed her dread. But she could not rid herself entirely of her disquiet.

She tried to regain possession of herself by moving busily about the kitchen. Having sent Betty to bed earlier, to insure the greater privacy of her communication with Matthew, Joan now saw before her the dirty plates and cups, saw them with a kind of relief. Here was something, at least, to keep her occupied. But the dishes and cups were too quickly put away. She swept the floor. Twice. She resolved not to go to bed until Matthew returned. She found the stitchery she had been working on in odd moments for a week or more and went to sit by the fire. By a sheer effort of the will she plied her needle. It was a simple labor, virtually doing itself.

In time a warm, imageless sleep stole upon her, taking her without struggle or even awareness. Her stitchery dropped into her lap, then slid to the floor. Her head rolled onto her shoulder. But the oblivion did not last for long. The fire burned low in the hearth; it lay like a hundred hot red eyes on the blackened stones watching her sleeping. The gathering cold stirred her and she began to dream.

At first her dream was disconnected and static, like a succession of portraits. She envisioned the Waites, the husband alive and grim of expression, standing next to his wife, gaunt and cross. She saw the Crispins. Matthew. Her daughter Elizabeth, holding her child. The images, disconnected logically, had a unifying anxiety. She had a terrible sense of danger, enough to cause her mental pain but not enough to jerk her into waking.

At length her visions coalesced into a disturbing dream of unusual vividness in which were figured herself and her friend Mrs. Monks. The two women were standing before the door of the Crispins' house. Joan knocked and it was a very long time before there was a response. Finally the door opened and they were admitted by a serving girl, whose small pale features Joan dimly recalled. The girl's manner was not rude but it did inspire in Joan a certain unease that went with her up the stairs, where they found a bedchamber richly laid out and spacious—so spacious Joan was sure it must fill the entire upper part of the house. There was a great ornate hearth on one wall, and close-woven tapestries with perplexing allegories on the other. The floor was richly carpeted, and on the mantelpiece above the hearth no less than a dozen German clocks of exquisite design ticked loudly, although each showed a different time. The massive four-poster bed in the center of the room now drew her attention. The curtains had been pulled back, and Joan could see that the bed was occupied by an ancient woman taking rasping breaths, each so deeply and painfully drawn that it seemed to be her last. Somehow Joan knew this poor ailing creature was Jane Crispin, although there was no basis for the identification in the woman's ghastly appearance. Joan moved across the room toward the bed. The ancient woman wore a loose-fitting shift that exposed her bony yellowed shoulders and shrunken paps. The woman emitted a foul odor. Despite her revulsion, Joan went up to the bed and asked its occupant, who appeared to be sleeping, if there was anything she wanted.

At the sound of Joan's voice, the old woman's eyes opened slowly and turned in Joan's direction. Her eyes were blue and aqueous. Was it Joan's imagination that in the pupils she could see her own image, small and confined like a miniature in a locket? Surely she wasn't standing so close.

The woman's skin was mottled and drawn tight against the skull. She seemed wasted by some mysterious ailment, for the deterioration Joan observed, which both repelled and fascinated her, she was certain was something more insidious than the mere devastation of years.

The parched lips moved in response to Joan's question but made no sound. Joan repeated, "Dear Mrs. Crispin, is there anything you need?"

In her dream she heard her own voice small and distant, and it gave her the eerie feeling of being detached from herself, her body one place and her intellectual being farther off. Her body turned—she saw rather than felt it move—to see how her friend Mrs. Monks was taking in this piteous spectacle.

But Mrs. Monks, who Joan was sure had entered the room with her, had vanished.

Suddenly she was aware of how damp and cold the room seemed despite the large, crackling fire in a hearth large enough to roast an ox in. She turned her attention again to the bed and the old woman, and was now overcome with a terrible dread. Her dread was that at any moment the woman would rise from the bed and embrace her and she would feel the rotting body and unspeakably foul breath next to her.

The very thought made her sick, yet she was ashamed to think it. This was no leper before her, but her friend. And even if it were a leper or, almost the worse, a poor plague-inflicted stranger, did not Christian charity require more of her than abject fear of infection?

As she pondered the moral implications of her revulsion, it did not occur to her to ask the woman—whom she still believed to be Jane Crispin—how it was that she had grown so old and decrepit since their last meeting. Instead, Joan began to search the room for a vessel of water to relieve her friend's parched lips. This took quite a while. The room was so filled with *things*, more now than she had first noticed upon entering it. Everywhere she looked, there were *things*—statuary, plate, ornate chests, tapestries—multiplying by the minute, as though whatever Joan conceived of immediately materialized as a furnishing of the room. And on the mantelpiece—how grand it was!—there now appeared more German clocks than before, all still showing different times and ticking so loudly she could hardly hear herself think.

Then they stopped ticking. Joan heard a door open behind her and was about to turn to see who had entered, hoping that it would be Mrs. Monks, when she noticed the expression of alarm on the old woman's face. A yellow, bony arm was thrust out from the coverlet and a quivering hand was pointed toward the door.

Now Joan did turn, and saw that the serving girl who had admitted her had returned. The girl's face was lighted with a sinister smile, at once both mocking and vengeful. And Joan knew in that instant, knew in the depths of her being, that the servant was somehow responsible for her mistress's decaying condition. Joan knew this and she also knew who the servant was.

Suddenly all the things in the room—statues, plate, tapestries, everything—began to fly around the room like a flock of birds sent to wing by a sudden fright. And through this strange welter, she saw the servant's face.

It had been transformed into a grinning, mocking death's-head.

Joan woke, terrified. It took her some time to collect herself. The dream—it had been a nightmare of the first order—had left behind it a residue of nausea and shock, and she knew if she tried to rise from her stool her legs would buckle under her. She noticed that the fire in the kitchen had nearly died and a chill had settled in the room—the chill she had experienced in her dream. Her clothing was damp with sweat. Her heart still racing, Joan tried to compose and interpret the confused elements of her vision—Mrs. Monks's vanishing, Jane Crispin's aged appearance, the servant with the sinister smile, looking as though she understood full well what malady had infected her mistress. The awful odor of the charnel house. The odor of putrescent flesh.

Her effort produced only a deeper stupor of thought. She rose steadily, bracing herself by holding one hand against the wall, and reached down to put another faggot on the fire. She poked in the embers until the faggot spurted with a steady flame, and then she sat down again. She remained so for a while until her heartbeat returned to its regular pace; then she picked up the stitchery she had dropped to the floor, hoping to find solace in this familiar work, an emblem of the world of waking that she hoped to return to.

But it was a vain wish, the returning. It was as though the dream and its horrors would not confine themselves to sleep. She could not rid herself of the disturbing images or reckon what they meant.

She put her stitchery aside. She had no heart for it now. She sat staring into the fire, mesmerized by the flames' erratic dance. The heaviness of her ignorance and confusion was upon her, and it was some time before she became aware of the tapping, too insistent and regular to be the wind.

She turned to see from whence it came, the signal, and almost by instinct looked first at the window that gave a view of the back parts of the house. The curtains were pulled across it, and mechanically she got up and opened them.

She heard the tapping again. In the glass panes now exposed to the firelight, she saw her reflection move like a shadow, and then, merging with her shadow, materializing out of the darkness of the yard, a pale face pressed so close against the window that Joan thought she could feel the warm breath through the thin panes.

TWELVE

IT was nearly nine o'clock when Matthew arrived at the Saracen's Head. The rest of the town had gone to bed, but in this part of Moulsham lights could still be seen inside the windows of taverns and alehouses, and shouts and rude boisterous laughter could be heard. The dark streets and cartways of the neighborhood were inhabited by shadowy figures staggering homeward or to their next dissolute enterprise, or slumped helplessly in the filth of the street.

The tavern itself was a shabby affair with a bad reputation. Upstairs was a notorious brothel. The light and scene of confusion held Matthew in the doorway for a few moments, and if at any time he had wondered what had become of the great crowd of strangers that had flocked to Malcolm Waite's funeral his question was now answered. Elbow to elbow at the bar were as ill-looking a bunch of roisterers and winebibbers as Matthew ever hoped to see cursing some other town with their presence. The disarray of tables and stools, overturned benches, and glitter of broken glass made it evident the tavern had already been the scene of one brawl during the evening. The air, which was heavy with tobacco smoke, held the lingering pungency of fresh vomit.

No one seemed to take notice of his entrance; all attention was fixed upon two strapping fellows squared off in the middle of the room. One of these Matthew recognized as Will Simple, Thomas Crispin's foreman at the tannery. The other man was a stranger. Will Simple and the stranger were naked to the waist, and in the lamplight and haze of tobacco smoke their well-muscled shoulders and chests shone with sweat. The host, a short dumpy man named Snitch with a pocky anguished face, was wedged between them trying to settle the quarrel, whatever it was about. Snitch looked near to soiling his breeches for fear more ruin would come to his precious establishment, which was a scurvy filthy place to begin with. The other patrons egged their favorites on, told the host to let the two combatants have at it, and laid wagers on who should win and whether the loser should be killed or merely maimed.

Matthew surveyed the scene with disgust and apprehension and was about to elbow his way to the center of the room and stop the fight before it started when he saw someone else he knew. It was Ned Hodge, the unemployed handyman and carpenter with whom Matthew had spoken outside the Waite house the day before. Hodge was drunk. He had a queer look on his narrow ugly face and his bald pate glistened as though he had been anointed with oil. It was evident the recognition was mutual. Hodge wended his way toward Matthew until his hot garlicky breath blew strong in Matthew's face like the effluvia of a midden-heap on a hot day in August.

"Marry, heaven be praised!" Hodge proclaimed, in a high wheedling old woman's voice. "It's our constable. Come to the Saracen's Head to honor the company with his presence."

Matthew acknowledged Hodge's rude greeting coolly and made a move to get around him. Hodge blocked his way. "Tell me now, Mr. Stock, how is your good friend Mother Waite, she who gives the evil eye to her neighbors and knows how to rid herself of husbands when she puts her mind to it? She serves your needs, I warrant, since you and she are such great gossips?"

The mention of Mother Waite caught the attention of some of the men standing close at hand, and they turned to look at Matthew suspiciously. More might have followed from Hodge's question, shouted above the din in the same wheedling voice as before, had the two combatants not decided at that moment to commence battling in earnest. A flurry of blows and kicks savagely delivered to head, chest, and groin caught the attention of everyone, especially the more drunken of the men. His vision obscured by the onlookers who had pressed in tightly around the fight, Matthew glimpsed the bloody face of the stranger and then, maneuvering closer, he saw Will Simple let fly with a strong right arm that sent his opponent sprawling onto one of the tables, whereupon it collapsed with a huge crash.

"Kill him, Willy!" cried a harsh female voice from somewhere in the room.

"Hell and damnation," cried another voice, a man's. "He shall not, else I am no Christian!"

"Look out, he's got a dagger," shouted a blowzy slattern perched out of danger on the stairway.

Someone shoved Matthew from behind. He recovered his footing only by seizing the shoulder of a man in front of him. His effort to save himself was wrongly construed as an assault, however, and the man turned sharply, spat out an oath, and took a swing at Matthew's jaw. The blow clipped Matthew's ear, his vision blurred, and he felt unsteady on his feet. The stench of tobacco, which he detested, the sharp pain and ringing in his ear, the closeness of the room, and the rankness of sweat—all conspired to undo him. For a moment he stood wobbly, staring stupidly at the man who had struck him. Behind the man, the two fighters had resumed their struggle and seemed well on their way to mutual extinction. The man muttered another oath and turned around to watch the fight, while Matthew nursed his damaged ear and wiped from his eyes the tears of pain that momentarily blurred his vision.

When he could see again, he realized that the fight was winding down. The tanner's foreman had his opponent on the floor and was pummeling him severely in the face. Hoots and shouts of delight mixed with encouragement and praise for the victor. Matthew pushed forward, ignoring the throbbing pain in his ear, and seized Will Simple by the shoulders. In a loud voice he commanded him to stop. Someone— not Hodge but another—recognized Matthew and cried, "It's the constable!" The beating ceased, Will Simple got off the fallen man, and the crowd quieted.

The friends of the beaten man came forward, splashed some ale in his face, and got him to his feet. Holborn, as they called him, had two very swollen eyes and a red mouth devoid of several of its teeth. He was breathing with difficulty and clutching his chest. His eyes were ablaze with anger and humiliation. Will Simple, on the other hand, was in good condition, all things considered. While Holborn was being seen to, Will put on his shirt and jerkin, smiling with grim satisfaction. Some of the patrons patted him on the back and said he had handled himself well. The host gave him a cup, which he drained, wiping his mouth on his sleeve.

Matthew knew the tanner's foreman to be an industrious, well-behaved young man who had always managed to avoid this kind of trouble. His first question, now that the fight had stopped and the room had grown quiet enough for him to hear the sound of his own voice, was what had caused the quarrel.

"It was *him,*" said Will, thrusting an accusing finger in his adversary's direction.

"What did he do?" asked Matthew impatiently.

"It was what he *said,* sir. He told a devious lie, sir."

Matthew looked at the other man, at Holborn. Holborn was holding a bloody handkerchief to his mouth and glaring at Will Simple with intense hatred. "Very well, what did *you say?*" Matthew asked Holborn.

"I said his mistress practiced the black arts, that she was a very she-devil herself, and them that served her was no better than she." Holborn spoke with a northern accent, and Matthew asked him where he was from. Holborn said he was from Norwich; he had come to Chelmsford to see the witches hanged.

"Have you no witches to hang in Norwich, then, that you must come to Essex to make trouble?" Matthew asked dryly. Holborn did not answer. He kept daubing his mouth with the handkerchief. Someone handed him another and he thrust the bloodied one away, revealing for a moment the extent of the damage to his mouth, a swollen mass of red tissue.

Matthew turned back to Will. "And, hearing this, you flew to your mistress's defense?"

"I did, Mr. Stock," said Will Simple.

"I grant this fellow's words were a powerful provocation," said Matthew, looking first at Will Simple and then at Holborn, "yet while defending your employer's wife is a virtue indeed, you are both guilty of breach of peace and, considering the state of things here, the host may have a complaint against both of you for damages."

"Aye, I will indeed, Mr. Stock," said Snitch, wiping his hands on his filthy apron nervously. "A half dozen of my stools lie beyond repair—and look at that table! The legs are flattened like a spider's legs. And this mess upon the floor, the blood and gore—"

"That will clean up fast enough," said Matthew, interrupting the host's inventory of damages. "The broken stools, I grant, are another matter."

"Why, what must a man do when his mistress is defamed by such a dunghill mouth as this fellow is?" proclaimed Will Simple, growing heated again. "Say, 'Thank you, sir, that's all well and good'?"

"Why, turn the other cheek," cried the high-pitched railing voice of Ned Hodge as he came forward. "That's what our good honest constable recommends for the town as well, while we poor Christians are forced to endure the enormities of witches and their minions."

This remark incited the approval of many in the crowd, and Matthew had to take a barrage of complaints from perfect strangers. They maintained that no decent constable spoiled the fun of some stout fellows having a good time when he should be pursuing malefactors and traitors such as witches. Matthew had hoped Hodge had gone home. His continued presence and loud mouth were ominous.

"In faith, Constable," cried a big-bearded man, glaring at Matthew from red, watery eyes, "why are you here when

Mother Waite makes merry with the Devil and mocks the sacraments by giving the wine and wafer to her dog?"

"Oh, Lord!" exclaimed the slattern on the stairs, "Oh, tell me not that she does *that!*"

"Aye, she does," replied a third man, whom Matthew vaguely recognized as one who had spent a day in the stocks last summer for urinating in the street. "For I have seen it with my own two eyes."

The man, who wore a tattered leather jerkin and dirty cloths bound around his feet for shoes, came forward to the center of the room. He strutted around like a cock, proclaiming, "I have seen it with my own eyes and shudder to tell of it."

The crowd grew attentive, and the brawl and the host's complaints were immediately forgotten.

"I was walking in the street, I was. There she were, sitting in the window. It was Mother Waite herself, upon my oath. 'Good morning, Mistress,' says I in a friendly way, expecting no more from the woman than a Christian greeting in return. But does she speak to me? Nay, not a word she says. Instead, she screws up her face like a bloody mackerel." The man twisted his face into a grotesque scowl. "Then she takes a cup and pours it and gives the same cup to her dog."

"Pray, what color was the dog?" called the slattern on the stairs in a harsh, guttural voice.

"Why, it was black, black as night."

"Ah" went the crowd, and some blessed themselves.

Matthew started to say that Margaret Waite kept no dog, but he knew the denial would be useless. The crowd in the Saracen's Head, restless for some new novelty, had become quite caught up in the shabby man's story. He was urged from all sides to continue, by drunken, drawling voices hoarse with impatience and too much use.

"She gave it to her dog to drink," the shabby man continued. "Then she takes a bit of bread and breaks it. I heard her mumble something."

"What was it, fellow?" asked Will Simple skeptically "'Come, beast, drink this milk, eat this bread'?"

"Nay, it was not milk she gave the creature but wine, and the words she spoke were in the Latinish tongue."

"Oh, in Latin," moaned the slattern on the stairs. She hugged her bony knees and tipped from side to side. "Lord have mercy upon us!"

"What meaning had her words?" asked Hodge, looking more sober now and thrusting himself to the forefront of the discussion.

"It was the Mass, such as Papists say. *Bonum, bonorum, honororum, sic,* and so forth," entoned the man.

"Why, that's the Paternoster backwards!" exclaimed the bearded man.

Matthew knew a little Latin, enough to know that what the man had said was perfect gibberish, but the rest of his audience was obviously impressed.

"It was Mother Waite who did it, you say?" asked the host, a note of concern in his voice. "She who lives on High Street . . . the glover's wife?"

"Where have *you* been, host?" growled Hodge, regarding Snitch as though he had just said a most foolish thing. "Is there anyone who doesn't know she buried her husband this very day—and in the churchyard too? Some say she killed him with a dreadful curse that made his bones and heart dissolve the way a waxen figure melts in the fire to a shapeless puddle. Others that she raised the spirit of Ursula Tusser— that famous witch—from its grave and caused it to appear to her husband, so that his heart would stop from the sheer horror of the spectacle. Oh, he was a good man, Malcolm Waite was. A decent man. Now his wicked widow makes merry with his money." Hodge's voice trailed off and terminated in a stifled sob of sorrow. The crowd murmured with discontent and horror.

"Malcolm Waite was out at heels when he died," said Matthew, unable to restrain himself any longer. "And I have seen the widow both the day of her husband's death even until now. A more grieving widow you will not find—no, not in Christendom."

"See, friends, how our constable speaks the witch fair, defends her boldly in the face of such powerful testimonies!" cried Hodge. "Mother Waite's husband lies in his grave, hardly cold, while *she* lives—*she* and her sister, corrupt both, to work their spells on the rest of us brave enough to denounce their wickedness."

The temper of the crowd had now turned dangerous again and Matthew was berated all around. Holborn, his bleeding staunched at last and feeling himself vindicated, joined forces with Hodge to denounce Matthew. The whole room seemed to be against him. They yelled in his face; they pushed close with their bodies and shook their fists, defying him. In all the room, Matthew's only ally was Will Simple, who was also enduring the onslaught of insult and complaint. Now the little carpenter leaped upon one of the tables and commanded the attention of all by commencing a diatribe against the freemen of the town. His speech was rough but effective. He claimed the only honest ones among them were those of modest means. The freemen lived upon the backs of the poor and kept them in the dirt for the benefit of the rich. He stormed on, his eyes flashing wildly: "See this merchant-constable before you with his brave worsted hose and fur-faced gown. Why, attired as a gentleman he is, though no better a man than the rest were he laid bare to the buttocks. Comes he to spoil the innocent pleasures of the poor—those among us who must sweat for our bread—charging us with disturbing the peace. Whose peace? ask I. Why, the bread-and-butter peace of the constable and his friends. Yet will he do nothing about the real evil that threatens us, threatens us all, every soul here?"

The crowd cheered. They glared at Matthew menacingly. "We'd best get out while we can," Will whispered to him.

"Is there an honest Christian who will abide such wickedness," Hodge continued, fully sobered now by his own rhetoric. "Who will not take up his cudgel or staff, his torch and sheaves and come with me to burn this wickedness away? When Ursula Tusser was hanged, I heard our parson, Mr. Davis, say, 'Thou shalt not suffer a witch to live.' The words were from the Holy Book. What, shall we dispute with God? Shall we deny His Word?"

"No, no, no!" answered the crowd in a raucous chant that seemed to shake the house on its foundations and drown Matthew and the tanner's foreman in a flood of hostile noise.

Matthew nodded to Will, trying to remember if there was a back door to the tavern. The signal was effective. A moment later, the chanting subsided when some men who had gone out a few minutes earlier to fetch torches came stomping into the tavern to the welcoming cheer of their comrades. For a brief period all heads were turned on the newcomers. It was enough. Will plucked Matthew by the sleeve and mouthed the words "Follow me."

Will thrust his way toward the stairs, Matthew following. The movement was unexpected and caused more surprise than organized resistance. They pushed by the slattern. Matthew stepped on her foot and she cried out in pain.

"Oh, you devil!" she screamed. "What, trying to get away, are you?"

At the top of the stairs Matthew paused to glance below. The woman's scream had now alerted the mob to the escape. Hodge was pointing his finger and yelling, "Stop them! Stop them!"

"Come, Mr. Stock, for God's sake!" shouted Will, pulling Matthew down a dark passage off which were several rooms. One door was unlocked. They flung open the door and saw a man and a woman in bed. The couple, illuminated by a single candle, sat up at once, too amazed by this sudden invasion of their privacy to speak. The man was in his shirt but the woman appeared to be naked. Not bothering to apologize for their intrusion, Matthew bolted the door while Will used his strength to shove the bed with its startled occupants against it for added support. As he did so, Matthew could hear the sound of angry voices in the passage, then a terrible pounding and cursing.

"Come forth, you friends of Satan!" screamed Hodge.

The man in his shirt, trusting in some vague sense that his advantage lay with the defenders, now leaped from the bed to lend his strength to the cause while his terrified female companion hid beneath the covers.

"Break it down, put your shoulders to it!" barked another voice.

Now came the assault. The door shook but held. It was of solid oak, but with every blow Matthew's heart sank and his pulse raced madly. Soon the mob gave over, and the carpenter's voice could be heard commanding his followers below, urging them to put their muscles to a different purpose. Stamping and scuffling could be heard as the mob retreated down the stairs.

When they were apparently gone, Matthew left his post at the door and rushed to the window. He threw open the casement and looked out into the darkness. The crowd that a few moments before had laid siege to the door was streaming into the street, hooting and howling as it went.

"Where are they bound, do you suppose? Will asked, coming up behind Matthew.

"To the town," said Matthew, watching the last of the rout emerge into the street.

"New mischief, I warrant," said Will.

"Without a doubt," Matthew answered. He turned sharply. "Fly, Will Simple. Make haste and redeem yourself for your ill behavior this night. Raise the town. The mob is headed for the Waites' for sure, and will doubtless give trouble to your master as well. If you cut across the meadow, you can be at the church before they get to the tanner's house. Have the parson ring the church bell. With all those torches in the hands of drunken men there'll be a fire at best—at worst a murder. Go now, lose no time."

Matthew helped the two men get the bed away from the door, and Will Simple went off at a run. Matthew lingered only long enough to thank the bewildered fellow whose amorous evening they had interrupted for his assistance, and then went out himself.

On the way downstairs he encountered the slattern, who had been too drunk to go with the others. She looked up groggily, recognized him, and cursed him. "Witch's bawd," she hissed.

Ignoring her, Matthew dashed into the street.

THIRTEEN

Beset by fears of fire and concerned for his wife's safety, Matthew pursued the unruly mob into Chelmsford. The mob moved slowly and noisily, gathering strength as it went. Along the way, householders, awakened by the angry cries of the rioters, the glaring torches, and, presently, the hysterical clamor of the church bell, poked their heads from their windows and doors to ask what all the uproar was about. Told that justice was to be done to the Chelmsford witches, some of the householders hurriedly dressed to join the mob, bringing with them more torches and an array of bills and pitchforks, swords and cudgels.

The street before the Waite and Crispin houses was filled to overflowing by the time Matthew arrived there. Some of the mob had begun pelting the house with stones wrenched from the street, with turnips, eggs, and trash. Matthew could hear threats and curses hurled at the two families, punctuated by shattering glass and the clatter of missiles aimed at the timbered walls and doors. The size of the crowd and the narrowness of the street prevented him from getting close to the front of the action. From what he could see, it was apparent that the besieged families had not been taken by surprise. The upstairs windows of the Crispin house had been shuttered, the house turned into a fort. Matthew surmised that Margaret Waite and her family had also taken refuge there, a supposition presently confirmed by several of the rioters who burst from the glover's shop door to complain that Mother Waite and her wretched brood had got clean away.

Suddenly, in the midst of a din of angry voices, an upstairs window of the Crispin house was thrust open and the tanner's face could be seen. He looked dark and devilish against the glare of the smoking torches below. For a moment the hurling of objects and shouting stopped as the crowd, many of whom were strangers and did not know the tanner from any other fellow, restrained their fury to see what the man at the window had to say. He had nothing to say, however. He thrust a pistol out the window, aimed it at the crowd, and fired. There was a puff of smoke and a thunderous report; then a shrill cry of pain came from somewhere in the crowd.

The use of a firearm against a mob armed only with pitchforks and old swords was unexpected and caused the crowd to disperse in terror. There was a mad rush for the side streets and cartways, a bedlam of screams and curses. Another explosion was heard, but whether or not the ball found a victim was impossible to tell for the confusion. Matthew, pushed violently against a wall by the press of fleeing rioters, had the wind knocked from his chest. He dimly saw a wounded man being carried off and up the street, while a half-dressed serving man racing past him shouted out that the tanner's house was possessed of devils. Still another shot rang out. The street before the houses was now cleared, and Matthew himself would have approached had he not been afraid of being fired on. The tanner had been true to his resolution. He seemed to be firing indiscriminately. Matthew could smell the gunpowder in the cold air.

Then Matthew saw someone sidling along the housefronts in his direction. It was Will Simple.

"I told the parson. He's rung the bells," Will gasped, breathing heavily and eyeing the dark fortified house.

"You did well," said Matthew.

"The parson said he would send word to the magistrate too."

"Very good."

At both upper and lower ends of the street, the rioters had

gathered under their blazing torches, and these cast a dim light on the houses of the two besieged families. Matthew could see that the upstairs window had been shuttered again.

"Was anyone killed, Mr. Stock?" asked Will.

"Wounded. Dead by now, perhaps. I saw no others fall. Your master knows how to handle his pistol."

"Aye, he does," said Will, grinning. "He does for a fact."

"You want to join him?"

"Yes, sir."

"Go, then, but make your identity known."

Matthew watched as Will Simple hurried across the street and knocked at the door, calling out his name at the same time. Presently, the door opened, Will was admitted, and the door was shut again.

Down the street the mob was beginning to move toward the house. Matthew could see them. They stopped about twenty paces from the tanner's door and the shrill voice of Ned Hodge could be heard.

"Come forth, Thomas Crispin, you sink of inequity! Surrender yourself and your wife and sister too, or we'll burn down your house and all souls therein!"

Behind him, the unruly crowd cheered and raised their fists threateningly. The upstairs window opened again and Crispin's head appeared. "I know you, Ned Hodge, and may God help me to place a ball in your black heart if you take another step toward my door."

"What?" shouted the carpenter, "will you murder us all, then?" Hodge could be seen moving about busily in front of the mob. "Perhaps your wife will bewitch us with one of her spells that you may return to the comfort of your bed."

This remark brought a few derisive laughs from the onlookers, but it was evident that for the majority of them the prospect of Jane Crispin's curse was more dreadful than amusing.

Matthew thought this as good a time as any to come forward. He walked into the center of the street and approached the carpenter Hodge.

"Go home! All of you! Go to your beds!" Matthew

shouted. "I charge you, in the Queen's name!" His words were lost in the night. Even to him they sounded powerless, fatuous. He might well have kept silent for all his commands accomplished. The little carpenter had wrought the crowd up well. Their fear was at a fever pitch and knew no help but the destruction of the tanner, upon whom all their wrath was now heaped. The crowd roared, and when the roar subsided, Ned Hodge spoke again in his shrill voice.

"Crispin and that family of his will pay the price, Constable! Fire at us, will he? I'll be damned in hell but I'll find cannon of my own to pepper his beard with!"

"The law will answer your complaints," Matthew said.

"The *law?* The law, say you? Why, the law is a toothless hound with a broken back!" snarled Hodge contemptuously. "It will do nothing but yelp and yelp." He spat in the street.

Matthew attempted to arrest the carpenter, but as he advanced he found himself surrounded by Hodge's drinking companions from the Saracen's Head, made sober now by the chill air and the excitement of the riot. Nor was there help elsewhere in the street. A large part of the crowd, many of them friends and most certainly acquaintances of the constable, were as confused as they were fearful. In their panic they had accepted Hodge as their leader, if only because his loud, strident voice spoke of their own grievances and fears.

The crowd surged forward as one of its number hurled a burning torch at the tanner's house. Landing short of the walls, it burned itself out on the damp pavement. Matthew's authority was nullified by the sheer number and force of bodies.

At the same moment, a new alarm was raised. From down the street toward Moulsham a clatter of hooves could be heard, and quickly thereafter a dozen or more horsemen came thundering up, yelling and waving their swords above their heads. Fearful of being trampled, the crowd rushed again for the walls of houses, found refuge in doorways and alleyways. For a few minutes all was terrible confusion. Matthew wedged himself in a doorway to avoid being crushed by the stomping horses. All about him there were screams, cries, curses, threats. Through the melee Matthew could see that the leader of the band was the magistrate. He was dressed in breastplate and helmet and giving out orders like a seasoned commander. He deployed some of his men in front of the house and sent others to the opposite ends of the street to confront the few rioters who had not found cover. Within minutes the street was empty except for the magistrate's men on their horses. Matthew came out into the street, and the magistrate advanced to meet him. "How now, Mr. Stock?" the magistrate asked, peering down at Matthew with a glare of obvious disapproval. "I came in good time, I see. Could you not bring order here with your authority?"

"I did what I could—for a man alone, sir," Matthew said, his heart still pounding from the angry confrontation with the rioters. "I charged them to disperse in the Queen's name, but none would obey." He told the magistrate all that had taken place at the Saracen's Head and since, explaining too how the bellicose little carpenter had become the leader of the rioters, whipping them into a frenzy with his rhetoric, and how Thomas Crispin had fired his pistol in defense of his house.

"Jesus save us all from politicians," murmured the magistrate when Matthew had concluded his report. "This is a fine mess here. London will surely hear of it and to the advantage of neither of us." One of the magistrate's men, on foot, came up to take the reins of his master's horse while he dismounted. The magistrate pointed to a house across the street and asked Matthew whose house it was.

"Simon Markham, pewter-maker," said Matthew.

"We'll use it for our headquarters while I decide what to do next," the magistrate said. The two men walked toward the house, knocked until there was an answer. The pewtermaker looked out. He was a small, bald-headed man with a smooth-shaven face. He had been very frightened by the uproar and was still trembling.

"I'll ask for your hospitality, Mr. Markham, if you'll give it. For me and my men this next hour," said the magistrate, crossing the threshold before the man had time to answer.

Intimidated by his important visitors and abashed at being found in his nightclothes—although it was well on to midnight—Markham ran to fetch a lamp. Four of the magistrate's men came in and stood quietly watching as Markham, having returned, lighted the lamp. Then the magistrate told the pewter-maker to find work for himself elsewhere, and Markham, correctly interpreting the magistrate to mean that he wanted the little room in which they stood for himself, went upstairs, wishing all the gentlemen a very good night in a voice quavering with terror.

The magistrate now began to vent his fury against the rioters. "Besotted knaves and traitors!" he exclaimed. "They are more ready to fear the abomination of witches than the wickedness of their own incontinence. Has the Queen's name no authority here, then?"

"They're frightened beyond reason," Matthew said, feeling some obligation to make excuse for his fellow citizens.

The magistrate was about to respond when Moreau, the bailiff, came stamping in, much out of breath from the ride. He too was vested in armor but, lacking the stature or martial bearing of the magistrate, the Frenchman cut a somewhat ridiculous figure, and his heavy-lidded eyes showed more anxiety than courage.

"Here's our bailiff," said the magistrate, "Come, Mr. Moreau, let us have your counsel. We've a riot in the town, as you can see, and half the men we require to quell it."

"Why, arrest the lot of them, sir," said Moreau. "And hang the leaders."

"That would expedite matters," remarked the magistrate ironically as he sat down on a stool. "But in the meantime the rout will in its own defense set the town afire. You saw the torches as you rode up, doubtlessly. Already the flames lick at the housetops. I'm a practical man who likes practical means. We may all shout ourselves hoarse, as good Constable Stock has done, yet if there are no ears to hear . . ."

"I recommend that we parley with the tanner," said Matthew, advancing into the lamplight.

"To what end, Mr. Stock? He's probably gone to bed by now. Would that his neighbors would do likewise."

"To secure his surrender, sir," said Matthew. "With him and the women in custody, the mob will have no further reason to complain, for the burden of their dislike at the moment is that the tanner's wife and her sister are at large, despite the outcry against them."

"I see," said the magistrate thoughtfully. "But *will* he surrender? You say the house is fortified?"

"Crispin's a reasonable man, sir—and an honest one. If he is made to understand the situation—the fact that he is in no less peril as he is, than as he might be, protected by your authority. If he sees that peace is as much to his advantage as it is ours and that the only resolution to his difficulties is a full hearing in court. If he understands all this, and I think he does—well, then, sir, I believe surely that it is worth an effort."

The magistrate mulled this over, then said, "Your patience runs somewhat counter to my own inclination, which is to send the mob cackling home by force of arms. The trouble is I don't have the men I need for such a campaign—or won't have until morning. By that time God only knows what damage may be done to property and yes, to lives too. The mob will regroup presently. They scattered because we had the advantage of surprise and they were in the open. Concealed in houses and alleys or climbed up on rooftops, they will wreak havoc enough. Let us parley, then, with this tanner and see if he will surrender with the women. At the same time we'll make sure this carpenter— What's his name?"

"Ned Hodge, sir," said Matthew.

"Yes, this Hodge—curse him—knows of our intent. It may hold him at bay for the moment—at least out of curiosity to see the outcome. We'll give him what he and the mob wants if we can, and when the town is quiet again and he has no maddened citizenry at his back, we'll make him pay for his sedition."

Another of the horsemen came in to report that there was a

great multitude of men and boys in the back parts of the houses, trampling down the gardens and scattering the chickens and ducks. Also, the Crispins' privy had been overturned and set ablaze.

"We must act quickly or there will be no controlling this mischief," said the magistrate upon hearing the news. "Mr. Moreau, you go find this rancorous carpenter, this Hodge, and tell him that the magistrate has come to arrest the tanner and the two women. Tell him I am arranging a parley—that there will be no more firing of pistols. My purpose is to secure the surrender of the house. Tell him the women will be charged with those crimes he speaks of and taken into custody forthwith. Tell him I promise they will be speedily tried—and if found guilty, hanged. Tell him that I order him to put down his weapons and cease his threats until the present business is resolved. Tell him he shall find the law is a dog with fangs, after all."

"Yes, sir," replied Moreau doubtfully. "But, sir, what if he will not comply?"

"Not comply!" boomed the magistrate. "Are you not the bailiff of the town, the magistrate's chief officer? Let it be on his head if he does not comply! Here, take Hodkins and Martin with you for company."

The magistrate nodded in the direction of two of his men who had been among the four waiting patiently for their next instructions. The pair came forward and accompanied Moreau outside. The magistrate turned to Matthew.

"You, Mr. Stock, will also be my ambassador. Go now to the tanner's door and tell him I will speak with him. If he asks the reason, as he may well do, tell him it is to find out for myself the cause of this broil. Speak him fair. If he is as reasonable and honest as you say, he will respond in kind and we may all get some sleep this night."

Matthew acknowledged the magistrate's order and the timid pewter-maker was summoned from above and asked to fetch a white handkerchief to be used as a flag of truce. When he returned, Matthew took the handkerchief, which was a piece of good quality, and tied it to the staff of one of the officers. Then Matthew went out into the dark street, his heart beating with apprehension and excitement. Carrying his flag, he walked slowly toward the tanner's house, in which no light showed or sign of life was visible. But since he knew well what danger to him lay behind the shuttered windows he said a prayer to himself that the doughty defender of the house would recognize the symbol of parley, if not Matthew's own form, and not shoot him with that devilish pistol.

He was within a dozen feet of the tanner's door when Matthew heard Crispin call out, asking who approached and for what purpose.

"It is I, Matthew Stock, your friend and neighbor," replied Matthew in as confident a voice as he could manage under the circumstances.

"Go away, Mr. Stock!" cried the tanner.

"I am come at the magistrate's orders, sir. He desires to speak to you."

"I have nothing to say to him or to any man. I ask only to be left in peace."

"Peace? Impossible now! Be reasonable, Mr. Crispin. Your salvation rests with the law."

"The law is my accuser."

"It can also be your protection if you will allow it."

"How's that?"

"Agree to let the magistrate come in."

Crispin thought about this for a few moments and then said he would talk, providing neither the constable nor the magistrate carried weapons.

Matthew paused before responding. The condition exceeded his instructions, but he hoped the magistrate would agree. "No weapons, sir. We will be unarmed and pray you will be also."

"Very well," called the tanner.

Matthew turned and walked back to the pewterer's house.

"He will talk, then?" asked the magistrate as Matthew entered.

"He's agreed, sir," said Matthew, "but asks that we come unarmed."

"Unarmed? That's what he wants, does he? That's hard, Mr. Stock," said the magistrate, stroking his chin thoughtfully. "He's already fired on his neighbors once tonight. What guarantee do we have that he will not fire upon us when we are in his house?"

"I don't think he will do that, sir," said Matthew. "I think he agrees that his best interests are with the authorities now."

"*Think, think, think,* Mr. Stock, all thoughts. But what of certainties?"

"None, sir. I admit it's a chance. But the odds are surely in our favor. Crispin is not by nature a violent man. If we offer no violence to him, why should he offer any to us?"

"Well, you put my faith to a test. Let us pray you're right and that we both live to see the morning."

Moreau now returned to say that he had spoken to Hodge and the carpenter was content to wait the outcome of the parley.

"He's content, is he?" remarked the magistrate. "Already he talks like a great captain, but I shall prove him nothing but a knave at last. Come, Mr. Stock. Let's go speak with the tanner."

Crossing the street, Matthew walked slightly forward of the magistrate, holding a torch above his head so that the identities of both men could be plainly seen from the house. While he walked, Matthew prayed again, this time that Crispin would prove true to his word, for the lives of two men depended upon it now.

When they were not far from the door, the window in the upper story opened and Crispin's face appeared. The tanner called out halt, and Matthew and the magistrate stopped. Matthew held the torch aloft. "We come unarmed," he called. The magistrate opened his cloak to show Crispin he concealed no sword or pistol. Then the magistrate held the torch while Matthew opened his cloak to demonstrate the same.

"You've no knives or pocket dags about you either?" asked the tanner from the window.

"None. We said we were unarmed," answered the magistrate.

"Come forward, then," said Crispin.

He shut the window and the two men approached the shop, the front window of which had been badly shattered by stones hurled by the mob. Momentarily, they heard the door being unbarred. It opened and Crispin appeared. Matthew extinguished the torch and he and the magistrate went inside.

When the door was shut and barred again, the tanner lighted a single taper that cast a dim yellow light around the shop. The floor was covered with broken glass and with stones, turnips, and other debris. With Crispin in the room were two sons of Margaret Waite, her nephew John, and two of the tanner's workmen. The workmen were armed with swords and the elder son of Margaret Waite held a pistol, which he pointed to the floor. Matthew assumed the women were upstairs.

"We have come unarmed," the magistrate said, looking about him at the grim-faced men. His eyes rested on the tanner, who was leaning against the counter. "Thomas Crispin, would I could wish you a more pleasant evening. This is the hour that honest men sleep. Pray we do not incur heaven's wrath for what has transpired this night."

"I welcome your honor to my house," said Crispin. "But I know you have observed the state of things. A man must defend his house, his wife. I have two young daughters upstairs who are beside themselves with terror and confusion. I have broken no law, sir."

"May I sit down?" asked the magistrate calmly.

Crispin made a sign with his hand, and one of his workmen brought a stool forward and placed it before the magistrate. Then the workman looked at Matthew as though to ask if he wanted one too, and Matthew shook his head and said he preferred to stand.

The magistrate sat down and crossed his legs. For a moment he gazed at the tanner as though he were assessing the man; then he said, "This insurrection has put the whole town in jeopardy, both from the rigor of the Queen's law which forbids such riotous assemblies and from its very self, for with so many torches there's a clear and present danger of burning down the town. I desire to see no man taken from his house by violence, yet I would have peace and order and, by God, I will have it or more than one will suffer for his ill behavior."

As he spoke these words, the magistrate's voice rose; he had begun softly and ended in a carefully controlled anger that caused every countenance in the room to pale before it. Crispin's workmen looked uncertainly at their master. John Waite seemed horrified by the power the magistrate was about to unleash upon him, and even the tanner seemed cowed.

Crispin answered defensively, "I was asleep in my bed when the riot began. Had I not put two of my servants on guard because of the threats against me earlier made, the mob would have broken down the door and taken us all in our sleep."

"Very likely," said the magistrate, calm again. He looked around the shop, surveying the damage. "This is a bad piece of work. The question before us now, sir, is what is to be done?" The magistrate turned to Matthew and indicated by a slight nod of his head that it was the constable's turn to speak. Matthew advanced toward the tanner.

"Our first purpose is to secure quiet in the town," he said in the same soft voice that the magistrate had used and that seemed to be having a telling effect on Crispin, who looked less belligerent than before. "There must be no more riot, no fires." Crispin nodded. Matthew continued: "The leader of the riot says he will stir up no more trouble on the condition that we take you into custody—you and your wife and her sister."

"Surrender!" exclaimed Crispin angrily.

"There's little alternative," said the magistrate. "It's the only thing that will pacify the mob. Of course sufficient force will restore order—for a time, at least. But I can't have reinforcements brought down from Colchester until morning, and God knows what damage will be done by then. At present you are at the mob's mercy, and your weapons will be to no avail if they decide to set fire to the house. They're in an angry mood, angry enough to burn you out."

"But your men—on horseback. Surely the mob wouldn't—"

"Don't underestimate them. We had the advantage of surprise, but we've lost that now. They've regrouped and we're outnumbered."

"If they see you're under arrest," Matthew said, "it will take the wind out of their sails and they may be content to row themselves home again."

"I have made note of their leaders," said the magistrate. "They'll get their punishment. In the meantime you and your wife and her sister will be housed in the Blue Boar. They'll be under arrest, but secure from the mob's wrath. In your present state I can guarantee nothing but blood and fire if these things must be done by force of arms."

The tanner shook his head and frowned, yet he seemed to be considering these proposals. "But you have said you couldn't protect us *here*," he said, looking first at Matthew and then at the magistrate. "Why should I think you could do so were my wife and sister-in-law in custody at the inn?"

"The light of day will put the majority of those assembled outside in a better frame of mind," the magistrate answered. "They will recognize the dangers to themselves if this civil broil continues. A troop of horsemen from Colchester will show them the wisdom of going about their business."

But the tanner continued to look dubious. At that moment his wife came down the stairs. Looking about her at the men and the debris in the shop, Jane Crispin shook her head sadly. Then she said she had overheard the discussion and was of the mind to surrender to the constable as had been suggested. "If it will save souls," she said. "I would much rather stay with my husband and poor wretched children, who must bear the brunt of these proceedings. But my liberty puts *their* lives in greater danger. For what shall we do if the house is set afire or the mob comes raging in? Whom will they spare in their rage?"

For a moment they all were silent. Then Crispin sighed and said he would agree to the surrender. "What would the charge be . . . against my wife?" he asked.

"Nothing more than breach of peace, for the present," answered the magistrate, who seemed pleased at the prospect of an end to the riot. "The mob will think it more serious, and for the time being we will allow them to."

"Very well," said Crispin. "I surrender, then." He handed over his pistol.

"I do as well," said his wife.

John Waite went upstairs to fetch Margaret, who presently returned with him. The arrangements were quickly explained to her and, seeing that her sister and her husband had already conceded to the plan, Margaret made no objection. She was terrified and exhausted by the night's events. "My trust is now in God, who alone has power to save the innocent from such abuse," she said.

Then her sons asked if they could accompany their mother, and the magistrate said no. "It must look like an official arrest, not a family expedition. You were best to stay and watch your mother's house."

One of the Waite sons opened the door and the little company stepped into the street. The parley had lasted for nearly an hour, and when Matthew emerged he could see that a large number of the mob had again approached the house. They were held back by only a half dozen of the magistrate's men, who formed a line against them. At the head of the mob, Matthew could see Ned Hodge. The appearance of the truce party caused the crowd to murmur angrily. Hodge shouted, "There's Crispin and the witches! See what you have in your own town, friends and countrymen. Why, look what the tanner has done to honest Stephen Binding."

Binding, who was the man Thomas Crispin had wounded, stood supported by a staff. His right thigh, where the ball had struck, was bound with cloth. At the carpenter's cry there were expressions of sympathy all around. Somebody said the poor man was like to lose his leg and there were cries for vengeance and a hail of curses. Out of the night came a cobblestone someone had hurled. It whizzed past Matthew and struck the tanner's sign with a sharp crack.

"I have issued my warrant and taken the prisoners into custody, as you can plainly see, good people," the magistrate called out sternly. "There is no need for you to remain in the streets. Go home! Go to your beds! I charge you, in the Queen's name!"

But the crowd seemed unwilling to move. Hodge continued to rail against the prisoners, especially the tanner. The magistrate threatened to clear the streets by force if the mob did not go home, and his men drew their blades and prepared to execute his order. For a few tense moments it seemed the strategy of surrender would fail. But then the crowd's courage began to waver. Some of them, mostly citizens who had been caught up in the initial wave of hysteria and were now shuddering in the cold and losing heart at the prospect of a pitched battle, begain to trail off to their homes. Soon only the hard core of troublemakers from the Saracen's Head remained clustered behind their self-appointed general.

The magistrate turned and whispered to Matthew, "See now, Mr. Stock, cold hands and hearts have done their work. We're more than a match for them now. Rebellious knaves to stir up such trouble! By God, fortunate they are that it is I who am magistrate here and not someone like Sir John Popham, who'd dangle a hundred of the worst of them from every tree in the parish." Having said this, the magistrate ordered his lieutenant to advance upon the remnants of the mob and seize its leader, which they presently did, or at least attempted. Hodge, nimble-footed and seeing himself abandoned by his friends, was able to escape in the ensuing retreat.

The magistrate was not pleased when he heard that the leader of the mob had escaped, and Matthew and his prisoners had to remain standing in the street while the gentleman berated his lieutenant. Then he said to Matthew, "Constable, these people are in your charge. See that they are properly housed and protected. I charge you to commission as many deputies as are needful to keep them safe until their trials. In the morning I want you at the manor house by ten o'clock. There we will determine what additional charges are to be levied against them."

"Additional charges!" protested Crispin, overhearing the magistrate's instructions. "What additional charges do you mean? Surely I am not be held accountable for blasting the leg of the abominable villain who would have spoiled my house had he had his will?"

Jane tried to calm her husband, who was glaring fiercely at the magistrate and at Matthew too. Finally he had to be subdued by two of the magistrate's men. They handled him roughly.

"Take them away, Constable," ordered the magistrate, his patience seemingly gone.

The women began to cry. They were shivering with cold, having stood so long in the street. Matthew took them to the Blue Boar, which was only a handful of houses away. There he found quarters for them, waited until a proper fire had been laid and a guard appointed them, and then returned to where the magistrate was still supervising the dispersal of the final mobbers.

"The prisoners are at the inn, sir, and bedded down for the night," Matthew reported to the magistrate, who was standing in the street beside a bonfire that had been made.

"Very well, Mr. Stock. There remain a few troublemakers about, but presently we can all go home to bed, I think."

The magistrate had no sooner said this than there was a fearful cry from the back part of the Crispin house. Will Simple came rushing from the door of the tanner's shop to report that he had seen flames shooting out of the roof of the Waite barn.

The magistrate ordered what men stood by the bonfire to assist in this new emergency while Matthew ran up and down the street shouting "Fire!" at the top of his lungs. Once more the citizenry came streaming into the street, most still dressed from the earlier broil, but more bent to cooperation now that a familiar peril threatened, not a supernatural one. Having given the alarm, Matthew ran to help, mindful of the danger a single blaze presented to the entire street. He arrived on the scene and saw that the fire in the barn had already become a conflagration. Bright licks of flame could be seen from the cracks in the walls and clouds of black smoke bellowed from the sodden rotting thatch. Crispin's household servants were running to and from the well with buckets of water to douse the flames, but the fire was too intense. From inside the barn could be heard the shrieks of the mare, whom no one had thought to let out. Now it was too late. The men who tried to do so staggered into the open air coughing and gagging. Matthew helped with the bucket brigade, but the effort was soon seen to be futile. With a great crash, the barn collapsed in a heap of burning rubble and the air was filled with cinders and sparks. This started smaller fires, which were quickly extinguished. Several people who had fought the blaze, particularly the tanner's servants, sat down on the bare cold ground and wept from sheer exhaustion. The absence of wind had saved the house and probably the neighborhood, and there were expressions of gratitude for that. Matthew thought it was just as well Margaret Waite had not seen this new misfortune. How much misery could a person stand in a single day? Her husband buried at noon, her house invaded in the evening. Now this.

Onlookers began to drift away. The danger was past. Someone remarked, in a voice loud enough to carry for some distance, that the fire had been arson plain and simple. But another voice said no, the fire was the judgment of God upon the Waites for their entertainment of the Devil. Matthew heard no third voice denying it.

F O U R T E E N

WELL after midnight, numb with exhaustion, Matthew returned to his house and was amazed to find the lights still burning in the shop and the kitchen. He knocked twice and called out. The door opened and Joan admitted him; she was still dressed as he had last seen her, in her apron. Her face was drawn; she seemed to be in the midst of a strange waking dream, only half aware of his presence, but she clutched at his sleeve and would not let go until they had passed through the shop, he had extinguished the lamps, and they had gone into the kitchen where there was a great roaring fire to warm him.

"Thank God you've come home," she said, her voice quavering.

"The Waites' barn was set afire," he said, embracing her. "Margaret Waite and Jane Crispin and her husband are all conveyed to the Blue Boar under arrest. Tom Crispin shot a man with that pistol of his, but the fellow will live."

She said she had heard all that. The riot had drawn her out-of-doors—at least far enough to satisfy her curiosity about what was going on.

"You look tired," he said. "More than tired—you look as though you've seen a ghost."

"Faith, I think I have," she said. They sat down at the table and she poured them both a hot drink. When they had drunk, Matthew waited for her to explain herself. He could tell by her expression that she had not been joking about the ghost.

She told her tale rapidly and concluded breathless. She told him everything—her terrible dream, her sudden awakening, the dread, and then her terror as she saw the face peering in at her.

"And this visage at the window. It was—"

"Ursula Tusser, to the life," Joan said, looking at him directly as though challenging him to deny it. "It was the face in my dream too. The serving girl. She looked familiar to me then . . . in my sleep. Strange that I did not recognize her at once. My blood ran cold."

"But how can you be certain it was she and not one of the mob—or some innocent passerby, for that matter? They were all about the back parts of the houses. Some of them might have drifted on up the street. Observing the light, they might have supposed—"

"No, husband. It was no passerby—no mobber, either. Besides, this happened before the riot. It was within an hour or so of your leaving. Later I heard the clamor of the church bell."

"Some passerby, then, or neighbor come to beg sugar or salt or—"

"I know the girl's face," she insisted. "It was her very eyes, her nose, her mouth."

Joan's face was hard with certainty; he dared dispute with her no further, nor did he care to. He was satisfied; he believed that she had seen the face. But whose?

"What happened then?" he asked.

"When?"

"When you saw the face."

"Nothing. For a moment the face was there, looking in at me, breathing against the glass."

"Breathing you say?"

"Yes, it was breathing. I think I could see the breath."

"No ghost *breathes*, Joan," he said quietly.

She reflected a moment. "That's right," she said. "It

breathed. Therefore it was not dead, yet it was she, my life upon it."

"A mystery, then. Tell me, when the face appeared you were startled?"

"Yes, and then the face vanished. I didn't even have time to scream. The scream lodged in my throat. I felt I was choking."

"So the face must have appeared to Malcolm Waite the night he died," Matthew said. "Did you go outside to see where the apparition went?"

She looked at him incredulously. "Are you in jest? What woman or man either, seeing such a sight, would pursue it?"

Since he was not sure he would have followed the spirit himself, he did not contend with her answer.

"Which window was it?"

She pointed to the window next to the postern door. It was a small rectangular window with leaded panes. He picked up the lamp that sat between them and carried it outside. Joan followed, asking him where he was going.

"You'll see anon," he said, lifting the lamp so it illuminated the area beneath the window. In the spring and summer the patch of earth was a bed of hollyhocks and marigolds. Now it was covered with a thin layer of moist leaves. "I'm looking for footprints," he said, crouching for a closer inspection of the ground. He poked around in the leaves and stood up and tried to peer into the window. He was just able to see inside, but only by standing on his tiptoes. "How tall was Ursula?"

"Tall? Oh, I think of middle height."

"Taller than you?"

"I don't think so. About the same."

"And her feet—were they small or great?"

"Small, I think. She seemed most daintily made in every part." She sighed with exasperation and weariness, her arms akimbo. "Husband, what mean all these questions?"

"There are prints here—impressions in the soft moldering leaves. As though someone *stood* at the window." He held the lamp so she could see for herself. "A spirit that *breathes* and *stands*."

"I know it *was* Ursula."

"Ursula is dead. I saw her die."

She did not respond. They went back inside.

"Don't you believe me?" she asked in a small voice as they climbed the stairs.

"I believe you," he said, but his suspicions were deep and disturbing. He did not know how to explain what she had seen.

He slept until nearly six and then awoke with a start. By his side Joan moaned softly and rolled onto her back, her own repose as peaceful as a child's. Deciding not to wake her, he dragged himself from bed, dressed hurriedly, and left the house to go at once to the Blue Boar to see how his prisoners had spent the night.

His own sleep had been restless, full of vague disturbing shapes and noises, eerie wails, and the terrified stomping and shrieking of the Waites' mare suffocating in its stall. Now as he walked briskly down the street, the short night's disquiet remained with him, mocking the distinction between sleep and wake and discoloring the images of the day.

At the inn he found his prisoners secure but agitated. Their sleep had been no longer or sounder than his own; they were disheveled in dress and their faces bore the pallor of the infirm. Crispin paced the floor nervously and answered curtly when Matthew asked him how he did. Margaret wailed like a child. She wanted to go home, she said, and looked pleadingly at Matthew as though permission were fully within his power. Matthew assured them that their safest course was to remain where they were. Breakfast was served, but they ate little and the boy who brought breakfast looked at the prisoners with a mixture of fear and loathing, although a few days earlier he would have tipped his hat respectfully as the tanner passed.

"So we are secure here," said the tanner with a scowl on his face. He leaned against the windowsill. "Some security it is when we are treated no better than common felons. Come, tell us, what are the new charges to which the magistrate referred?"

"They will be determined this morning," Matthew replied not unsympathetically, for he too felt that new and more serious charges had not been part of the tanner's reckoning when he agreed to lay down his weapons and submit to arrest. Matthew couldn't help feeling himself a participant in the betrayal.

"This is a fine mess," Crispin said. He turned to look out the window. "See now," he said, his voice breaking, "I can almost see my shop." The tanner's muscular shoulders shuddered, betraying his silent grief. Matthew, finding Crispin's sorrow difficult to look upon, turned to the two women, who were seated on the bed. They too aroused pity in his heart. He was doing his duty as he saw it, yet if it was his duty he did, why did he now feel a persecutor of the innocent rather than a friend of justice? For a while it was very quiet in the room. Crispin had regained his composure but remained staring into the street. The women waited, and Matthew watched them. He thought about Joan's terrible vision and remembered that Margaret too had seen it. What did it mean? The question assumed a center place in his consciousness. The apparition had been real, and the evidence was that it was mortal still—a corporeal spirit, then. He was sure it had been real. And Joan had said so. But what did it want? Why had it come to his house?

He returned home in a gloom of dark thoughts. Joan was in the kitchen, the breakfast on the table. His uneasiness persisted. He felt like a man wandering in a thicket; whichever direction he took he was cut and scratched. Was he victim or victimizer? Were the sisters innocent or conjurers? He could not hide his gloom from Joan.

"How are the sisters?" she asked.

"Tired, confused. They want to go home. Even Jane now. They still don't understand the danger they face—from the law and from their neighbors."

"Poor Margaret, poor Jane. So dreadfully wronged."

Her expression of sympathy surprised him, given what had happened the night before. Did she hold the women blameless even though she was convinced the apparition had pressed its face against *her* window? He asked her about it, wanting to know how she had clarified in her mind what was in his a muddle of conflicting facts and agonizing doubts.

There were dark circles of fatigue beneath her eyes, and he realized at that moment that he was seeing her as she would appear to him in—say—ten or fifteen years. But she spoke in a plain sensible tone. "I saw the shape of Ursula Tusser, just as Malcolm and Margaret Waite saw her. I cannot deny it, I will not—no, not if put upon the rack. Yet whether the apparition manifested itself at the Devil's behest or came of its own accord, I cannot say. It does not follow in my mind that either Margaret or her sister beckoned that awful spirit from the grave, if that is the doubt in your heart. It could have been someone else who conjured."

"Who else?" he asked dubiously.

"The Devil never wants for helpers," Joan answered. "Keep an open mind, husband. Don't condemn the poor women out of hand. There may yet be an explanation for these strange occurrences."

"Which explanation I pray soon comes to light," he said, "for them and for us all."

He stroked her cheek affectionately. She grasped his hand. "God keep you, Joan," he said.

"And you," she answered.

Matthew felt the blessing was much needed.

FIFTEEN

AT the manor house, Matthew found himself in an impressive gathering of gentry and public officials. There were several knights of the neighborhood, the aldermen of the town, the bailiff Moreau, various clerks and secretaries of the assize court, petty constables from surrounding villages, Parson Davis, and two gentlemen from London who had come at the behest of the Privy Council to observe the proceedings. The magistrate wasted no time in getting to the business at hand. He quickly summarized the strange and dangerous events that had occasioned the meeting, although few present had not heard of them. When he was finished, he announced that he had decided to charge both Margaret Waite and her sister with witchcraft.

"The evidence is more than sufficient," remarked Alderman Trent, flushed with pleasure at finding himself in such distinguished company. Words rolled off his tongue in a fluent baritone. "A hundred witnesses will testify if need be to their conjurings, their intimacy with familiars and like spirits, their practice of necromancy, as evidenced by the hideous and dreadful apparition of Ursula Tusser."

When Trent had given this opinion, Matthew was asked for his views. Intimidated by the size and importance of his audience, Matthew struggled with his own contradictory impulses and what proceeded from his mouth was a testimony to how far he was from settling his doubts about the two women. "I have known both sisters for years," he said quietly but firmly. "I am reluctant to think of them as anything other than decent Christian women who have been much abused by gossip and the malice of their enemies." As he spoke, Matthew noticed the scorn on Trent's face, the disapproval on the magistrate's. "Yet this past night, while I was away, my own wife saw the apparition of which Alderman Trent has told us."

That Matthew had spoken the truth gave him no satisfaction now that he had said it. Across the room he could feel the approval of Trent and the magistrate, and he flushed because he was disgusted with himself. He could not abide Trent, but suddenly he had joined his camp, or had seemed to. He had conveyed to the persons present more evidence to condemn the women, his friends.

"What did this apparition say or do?" asked the magistrate when Matthew made no effort to elaborate on his wife's experience.

"Nothing was said. The shape appeared at the window. It only peered at my wife."

"It was by such seeming innocent eavesdropping that the witch Margaret Waite murdered her husband," declared Trent. "Perhaps that was her intent in sending this horrible shape to your wife, Mr. Stock, to scare her to death." Offering his suggestion, Trent smiled mockingly and moistened his thick lips with his tongue. Anger raged in Matthew's heart; gladly would he have killed the butcher-alderman at that moment, but he held his peace. Nor did he say anything to deny Trent's suggestion, which others in the room were evidently taking with some seriousness. He could not deny what *might* be true, but he hated Trent for being the one to utter it and he understood the insidious pleasure the alderman was taking in Matthew's confusion and fear.

Then one of the London gentlemen remarked that the shire seemed to be cursed with witches. A local knight admitted this was so, and recalled several earlier trials that had achieved widespread notoriety. There followed a discussion of witches and their methods, during which the parson described a learned book on witchcraft he had recently read, written by the Scottish King, wherein the royal scholar confounded the damnable opinion of a certain Englishman that there was no such thing as witches.

"He who would deny that witches be must needs be of the Devil's party," asserted the knight hotly. This knight esteemed himself a theologian and had accumulated a considerable library of books and tracts relating to the occult. His position was generally approved, and the London gentleman pointed out that the resolution of these matters was essential, since witchcraft was a kind of treason.

Then the magistrate announced that he had heard enough and thanked all those assembled for their very good counsel. The women, he said, would be charged as he had indicated.

"With what specific charge, sir?" asked the clerk of the court, preparing to draft the warrant.

"According to the Act of 1563," the magistrate answered solemnly, "against conjurations, enchantments, and witchcrafts. Margaret Waite will also be charged with the murder of her husband, for it now seems it was to that end that she conjured Ursula Tusser's spirit."

Peter Trent wanted to know what was to be done about Thomas Crispin, whom he characterized as a notorious ruffian and seditionist, as his violence on the previous night made plain. But several of those present spoke up on the tanner's behalf, including Matthew, pointing out that the man had acted in self-defense, and who could be blamed for that? Besides, the man he shot had only been slightly wounded and was one of the leaders of the riot as well. The magistrate considered the various arguments and then decided that he would bind the tanner over to the next quarter sessions on a charge of breach of peace—a charge that, were the tanner found guilty, would occasion only a small fine.

"The trial of the witches must take place as soon as possible," the magistrate went on. "At a special session." He looked in the direction of the clerk of the court, and the clerk nodded indicating that he had understood. "We cannot wait until the next assizes, not with the fear that exists in the hearts of the town."

One of the London gentlemen suggested a certain famous witch-hunter as prosecutor.

"Who is this man?" asked the magistrate.

"His name is Roger Malvern," said the gentleman. "He is a lawyer of note, much practiced in these matters."

Moreau said he had heard of Malvern, and others in the room said they had too. All the gentry then approved the motion, and the magistrate said it was as good as done. "We shall send for the man, lay the facts out before him, and see what he shall make of them. An expert is what is needed here, no novice. In the meantime the women will remain confined under the watchful eye of our good constable. Until this business is concluded, I order every man to keep the peace and render whatever assistance might be needed to maintain order in the town. Be these women witches indeed, or merely victims of calumny, we shall have no more riots."

And on that note the company said their farewells and went about their business.

Matthew returned to town determined to shake off his black mood and settle his nagging doubts about the Chelmsford witches once and for all. He stopped at the Crispin house to see how matters stood there. The shop was closed and the shattered windows had been covered with boards and oilcloth. Sometime during the night—probably on toward morning—a vandal had scrawled the name Satan on the tanner's sign with bright red paint. The tanner's servants were sweeping up the rubble in the street, and Matthew thought he could hear one of Crispin's little daughters call out for her mother from an upstairs window.

He went around to the back of the house, where he saw next door the charred smoking remains of the Waite barn. The poultry pen still stood, but it had been ravaged during the night and not a hen or a duck remained. The garden had been thoroughly trampled. Crispin's servants followed Matthew; they wanted news. He told them that their master would presently return. They asked about Mrs. Crispin, to whom they were devoted. "She's been charged with witchcraft," he told them. "She and her sister too."

They nodded their heads and returned silently to their work—except for Will Simple, who said beneath his breath, "Damn them all," and continued to stare disconsolately at the ruins of the barn.

Matthew went next door. Susan let him in. He asked her if there had been any word of Brigit, and she shook her head but showed no pride in the fact that thus far her prophecy had been fulfilled. She said the remnants of the family were holding some sort of council in the parlor and she was not to disturb them, but she thought the constable would be welcome.

He went into the parlor and was coldly greeted by Margaret Waite's sons and nephew. Matthew told them the ill tidings, which occasioned no surprise. The Waites' original anger at the slanders levied against the family had now given way to a fatalistic sense that if it was not all God's will that they suffer, the suffering was at least more to be borne than protested.

"We feared the worst from the beginning," said Dick Waite stoically.

Edward Waite communicated his grief with a heavy sigh, while the nephew John, whose superior air seemed much diminished since the family disgrace, said he doubted his aunts would have a fair trial in Chelmsford. "The town has the scent and will not quit its baying until the prey is well chewed." But he had also a word of censure for the accused women. "This is what comes of flirting with this foolish witchery in the first place. Aunt Jane should have let the damned girl go to hell before she allowed her to play the fool in her house, and Aunt Margaret should have shut the barn door against her. Now the barn is burned and my aunt's imprisoned, and God only knows what shall be the end of it."

"When will the trial be?" asked Dick Waite.

"Within the week, or so says the magistrate," answered Matthew. "He's called a special session."

"A special session, is it," remarked John Waite. "I trust it will be very special indeed."

They regarded Matthew with hard, accusing faces. It was obvious they blamed him too for their troubles. He wished them well and left, more melancholy than ever.

During the next few days, there were no more disturbances in the town. The date of the trial had been firmly set and the witch-hunter Malvern had written to say he would gladly come to Chelmsford, weather permitting, and so there was great excitement in the air. The jury had been selected from the freemen of the town, and the citizenry was divided between those who, like Peter Trent, believed the sisters guilty beyond question and those—an embattled minority now—who, while not quite willing to proclaim the sisters' innocence, were at least willing to grant them the benefit of the doubt. Meanwhile the families of the accused kept to themselves. Crispin's tannery remained closed and his workmen idle, for it was clear that no business would come his way until the matter of the witchcraft was resolved. The only event that marred this peaceful interim was reported by John Waite, who came to the constable's house early one morning to complain of a prowler.

"What sort of prowler was it?" Matthew wanted to know.

"A thief, I think, but he's a fool if he thinks there's anything left to steal. The mob made off with our chickens and ducks, and the horse, as you know, died in the fire."

All the neighborhood was aware of the dead mare. Covered by rubble, the decaying flesh had been potent all week and was much complained of, but it was impossible to find anyone willing to do the work of uncovering and burying the animal. The Waites had only Susan to keep house for them, and almost all the Crispins' servants had stolen away. Warmer weather coupled with frequent rains had made matters worse.

"Tell me if you see this prowler again," Matthew said.

On Thursday of the week, Mr. Roger Malvern arrived in Chelmsford, bringing with him a scrawny boy whom he introduced as his assistant. Malvern was a corpulent man of about fifty, with ruddy smoothly shaven cheeks and bulging eyes that gave him a threatening, belligerent appearance. He limped slightly and spoke with the deep, resonant voice that finds a happy home in a court of law. The magistrate offered him the hospitality of the manor house, and there for the next few days he was frequently called upon for his views. He counseled with potential witnesses and became acquainted with the various clerks. He memorized the facts in the case and generally gave the impression of being steeped in Devil lore. When he met the constable, Malvern asked first whether the accused women had been examined for the Devil's mark.

"Why, no, sir, they have not," Matthew answered.

Malvern made a face of exasperation. "That's the first thing to be done in such cases," he said. "A jury of women must be appointed to do it."

To Matthew fell the task of recommending reputable women to perform this function. He included the name of his wife, but Joan was far from pleased.

"What! How could you serve me so, husband? Should I betray a friend by such service?"

"You will insure that the jury conducts itself honestly," he argued. "The court will want marks, no pinch marks or moles to build its case. You'll be doing the sisters a favor."

Joan thought about this for a while and then agreed.

The next day, the jury of six women convened at the Blue Boar, where the examination was to be conducted. Joan later told Matthew what happened.

"Margaret was first taken and helped off with her clothing, which was laid out upon the bed and examined carefully. It was humiliating for her. The poor dear was near unto death with shame and fear, quaking and mumbling prayers all the while she was eyed and probed and talked of as though she were not present at all. Her body and most specially her foreparts had many moles and wens, so that among the jurors a dispute commenced as to which made plain her commerce with Satan and which were mere imperfections of the flesh. Then Jane was stripped and examined after the same manner. Now, her body was very white and lovely to look upon, and I could tell some of the women were more envious of that body than curious for her soul's health, and wished they had skin so fair and breast as high and full at her age."

"How did Mrs. Crispin take this?" Matthew asked.

"Even as her sister. She was much mortified and she upbraided the women for their prying and prodding, which several of them—though not I—declared to be their Christian duty. To me it was plain meanness. I wish I had never consented to serve. I was too disgusted to speak."

"Well, what, if anything, was found?"

"On Jane nary a mole nor mark. Her body was as smooth as a babe's, yet even this caused suspicion amongst the women, who said only Satan could so preserve the flesh in a woman of middle years. Oh, Matthew, I wish none of this had ever happened!"

Matthew said he was sorry he named her to the jury, although he defended his intentions.

"You should have seen the husband's face when he returned and saw what condition his wife and sister-in-law were in," Joan continued. "At each of us he glared. If looks could kill! You know he's been staying with them at the inn. By his own request. With hardly a servant left at home, he has sent the two children to stay with his sister in Brentwood."

Matthew of course knew that Crispin had been staying with his wife. He had seen no harm in it, and the truth was he felt very sorry for him. The tanner seemed little deserving of these miseries.

"What will happen now?" she asked.

"The trial is tomorrow," he said.

"Oh, that *trial*," she said with disgust. "A fine fair trial it will be, with the sisters already condemned in the public mind and Peter Trent doing everything in his power to convert those few left in doubt."

"I know," he said, thinking of the women. Of their guilt or innocence he remained uncertain, but of one thing he was sure. Neither would have a fair trial in Chelmsford.

SIXTEEN

EVERY inn in town was full, and on the morning of the trial the wide place on High Street before the Sessions House was crowded with townsmen and strangers. Frustrated at not gaining admission to the upper rooms, they were obliged to wait in the street for intermittent reports fetched for them by the clerk's boy, who was tipped handsomely for the service. Promptly at eight o'clock, Matthew drove his cart to the front of the Blue Boar, and with the assistance of Arthur Wilts and two other men deputized for the nonce, he put his prisoners in the back of it. The women were bound, as was the custom in transporting prisoners, and looked humiliated and dejected to be so treated. Yet they spoke without rancor to Matthew and did not appear, like their kinsman, to hold him to account for their arrest. "God must be our help," Margaret murmured, "now that we are forsaken by our friends."

Matthew drove the cart slowly up the street. As he approached the Sessions House, he was recognized and he and the women and his deputies were subjected to a storm of crude insults and threatening gestures. He tried to ignore the crowd, but it was not easy to do. He felt he himself was being incriminated, and many insults were indeed aimed particularly at him: "Witch's bawd!" "Satan's minion!"

There was a side door to the Sessions House and this Matthew used as an entrance. The prisoners were led up the stairs into a large dusty courtroom furnished with long benches and a table for the judges and other court officials. There was also a special row of stools for the jurymen and a stand for the witnesses and prisoners. All were presently filled except for the judges' chairs. Every bench was crammed, and at the back of the room those standing wrangled for positions affording a better view of the proceedings to follow. There was much noise of conversation but this stopped as Matthew led the women up the aisle to their seats. He noticed Joan sitting toward the back of the room and nodded to her; then he rose with everyone else when the clerk of the court announced the entrance of the three judges.

The three robed men, one of whom was the magistrate, filed in and took their seats. The jurors and spectators sat down, and the two women were made to stand while the clerk read out the charges against them. When each was asked how she pled, she answered innocent, and when Margaret had spoken, someone in the back of the court said, "Yea, innocent as Judas was, by God!" The magistrate reprimanded the person who spoke, although just *who* had spoken had not been determined, so crowded was the room. Then Roger Malvern, the prosecutor, rose at his place opposite the prisoners' bench and said that he would prove with incontrovertible evidence that the two accused women were witches indeed, foul conjurers and necromancers, and that Margaret Waite was a murderess as well. He reminded the jury that the offense was a capital one, for witchcraft was not only a crime against God, but treason to the state; he then handed a list of witnesses to the clerk, who proceeded to call out their names. When it was evident that all named were present in the court, the clerk called the first witness.

To Matthew it was immediately apparent that while all the witnesses had had some association with the two women, none had been particularly close or friendly with them. Most appeared to be nursing some ancient grudge that the trial had given them opportunity to vent in a socially approved way. All but one were female. The first, Mary Bowen, was a frail woman of about thirty-five whose husband was a tailor and suspected Papist. She testified that both Margaret and her sister had cursed sheep and crops, frequented with cats and familiars, and exchanged letters that consisted of nothing but strange symbols, which she claimed were satanic in origin. Mrs. Bowen spoke with great earnestness and detail, and could even recall the exact day of the week it was when she had heard Jane Crispin tell a neighbor boy that if he bounced his ball against her window another time she would cause his arm to wither. Matthew listened intently to Mrs. Bowen's testimony but dismissed the business about satanic messages, for he knew very well Mrs. Bowen could not read plain English and therefore that fact put her scholarship in grave doubt. Besides, he had heard of no boy in the town with a withered arm. He was amazed when no one else in court showed signs of being disturbed by these inconsistencies.

Two other females—an aging widow sometimes thought to be a witch herself, and a young girl of about thirteen—testified that the sisters were wont to converse in an unintelligible tongue, to exchange mysterious glances, or to fix with a menacing stare passersby who would not enter their husbands' shops. A man, Harold Lightfoot, who had once been employed in the tannery, said he had seen his former employer's wife in deep conversation with a crow. He said that he believed the crow to be the Devil in disguise and that after this conversation was terminated the bird vanished into thin air.

Upon hearing this, Crispin, who was seated two rows behind the prisoners' bench, jumped up and called Lightfoot a liar and thief, for he had stolen two calfskins and a doeskin from the tannery and that was the reason he was sent packing. "His abuse of my wife is nothing more than revenge!" proclaimed Crispin.

"Mr. Crispin!" shouted the magistrate, rising imperiously. "You are already under bond for disturbing the peace. You will keep quiet in my court or I'll have you thrown out the door!"

Crispin sat down. After the magistrate's reprimand the court was very quiet. The magistrate motioned to the prosecutor that the testimony should continue.

Next to testify was the baker's wife, Priscilla Roundy. She was a plump, red-faced woman who wore a little white cap that crowned a tangle of blonde curls. Of the witnesses so far, only she had seen the shape of Ursula Tusser. She said she had come upon the spirit while dumping trash in a pit behind her house. It had startled her and she had thought at first that it was no more than some stranger hunting among the refuse for scraps. She was about to order it off when, taking a better look at the visage, she recognized it. "All drawn was the face, and horrid," said Mrs. Roundy, "pale like the belly of a toad, with large glaring eyes. 'What?' said I. 'Has the widow Waite raised thee up again?' Whereupon the thing shook its finger and made a wrathful countenance."

"And when did this apparition appear to you?" asked the magistrate.

"Why, it was the night of the great uproar, the night the wicked barn of Mother Waite was burned to the ground."

"And you are certain this spirit was Ursula Tusser?"

"Oh, sir," said the baker's wife, her eyes round with fright and her hands gesturing as though she were conjuring up the vision herself. "It was the girl I saw, and no stranger. She stood in the shadows, next to the lime tree, yet could I make out the features of the face. I asked her if she were Ursula, and made the sign of the cross to protect my soul. She nodded, by which I took her to mean it was even as I had said, and then cast at me such a dire grimace that I said, 'Get thee behind me, Satan.' As I did so, the spirit vanished."

The crowd murmured at this testimony and Priscilla Roundy began to shudder and shake, contort her face, and babble incoherently. Someone shouted that Margaret Waite had bewitched the woman, and there were hysterical wails from two young girls; however, order was quickly restored when the magistrate brought his gavel down sharply and threatened to have the court cleared if there were further outbursts.

The trial continued with the prosecutor asking for the report of the jury of women. This was read to the court by the clerk, and concluded with the information that the Devil's mark had been found on Margaret Waite's left buttock and that the smoothness of Jane Crispin's skin was equally valid evidence of her conjuring. This evidence was greeted by expressions of horror and amazement in the audience, and the people cast fearful, accusatory glances at the two women, who were much mortified at having their bodies discussed in public.

By now it was nearly dinnertime and the judges declared a recess until later in the afternoon. Matthew took his prisoners into the clerk's tiny office, which was adjacent to the courtroom, where he saw that food was provided for them. Neither woman was hungry. They sat as though stunned, Jane Crispin holding a prayer book with its pages open but not reading it, Margaret weeping quietly. Finally, Jane said, "We have put our trust in God. He will not fail us." She closed the prayer book. Matthew watched her with cold sadness. Jane Crispin's slightly faded beauty shone through her grief. She said she was reconciled to whatever God should decree as her personal fate. It no longer mattered to her whether she was vindicated in the eyes of the town or not. She had her faith, her husband's love, her dear daughters. She said she wanted nothing more.

"The worst is past for us, Mr. Stock," Margaret said, drying her eyes. "All that can be done now is for our bodies and spirits to be separated. But since that must befall us all sooner or later, how blessed are we to know of the sure hour when we will face God."

Matthew took these pieties in without comment, sitting upon a stool while the two women occupied a short, straight-backed bench against the wall. He wondered if Thomas Crispin was taking his wife's imminent conviction as calmly. Things looked very bad for the women. The afternoon promised worse. The jury had been affected by the fit into which the baker's wife had fallen at the termination of her account. Matthew had seen it in their horrified faces. The physical evidence—the witch's teat on Margaret Waite's left buttock (or had it been the right? And did it make a difference which side it was?) and the supernatural smoothness of Jane

Crispin's flesh—had also been telling. That Satan was at work in Chelmsford seemed no longer in question—at least to the townspeople.

A knock came at the door and one of the deputies looked in to say that Mr. Crispin was outside and wanted to know if he could speak with his wife. "Let him come in," Matthew said.

The tanner entered and his wife rushed to embrace him; then he turned on Matthew angrily. "I will be revenged on every one of them," he stormed, speaking, Matthew supposed, of the witnesses against his wife. "Shameless lying hypocrites the lot of them!"

"Peace, husband, do not speak so," said Jane Crispin in her soft, cultured voice. She put her hand on his mouth to still his ranting. He grasped the hand with his own and kissed it, tears running down his cheeks into the neatly trimmed beard.

"Preach me no sermons of forgiveness," Crispin said to his wife. "I have a bitterness within me that must vent itself or I'll explode. Let me have my words, then, I beg of you."

"Vent your wrath, husband," she said, "and then forgive your enemies as our Lord counsels."

Matthew left the room and waited outside the door while husband, wife, and sister conversed further. Presently, Crispin left and the parson came. He had taken his midday meal with certain London gentlemen of his acquaintance, and now said he felt obliged to give spiritual solace to the accused women. Matthew went into the office with him and listened while he spent the better part of an hour speaking of heavenly matters designed to lift the women's spirits. The parson seemed puzzled by the fact that their spirits were already lifted, although they explained to him how they had prayed and fasted too. "Satan has power to give us a false sense of security," the parson said. "We must remember our salvation does not proceed from *our* strength but from God's grace."

Jane Crispin assured him her faith was from God. "Before, in my pride, my faith was lukewarm," she admitted. "In my ordeal I have found Him without whom all human endeavor is vanity."

She said this with such fervor that even the parson looked schooled by her. He presently took his leave of them and returned to the courtroom, where the trial was ready to resume and the benches were quickly being filled.

Matthew took his prisoners to their places, and soon afterward the judges returned.

Matthew had earlier been given to understand that the afternoon would be devoted to an examination of the accused women and that it was in this examination the prosecutor was to show his skills. To this end, Margaret Waite was first called to the witness stand. She was sworn upon the Bible, but, unlike the witnesses who had testified against her, she was first asked if she professed the book to be the Word of God. She said she knew it to be the Word of God and was allowed, because of her frail condition, a stool to sit on. Malvern then asked her if she could recite the Lord's Prayer and the Ten Commandments. She rendered the prayer word-perfect but confused the sixth commandment with the eighth, whereupon a murmur of dismay ran through the court. Malvern cast a significant look at the jury as if to say, "Goodmen, did you notice *that?*"

They had noticed it; Matthew saw them nodding and whispering to each other.

Then Malvern asked her about her church attendance, and she said she had rarely missed a Sunday. Malvern laughed and said so did many a whore and linen snatcher, and put a good face on it too. "What do you say to these worthy women who searched your body for the Devil's mark—yea, and found it on your nether parts? Are they liars or are they good Christian women?"

Margaret was flustered by the question, caught as she was in the dilemma of having to choose between defending herself and condemning her neighbors. For a moment she gave no answer, and the prosecutor had to repeat his question, a grim smile of triumph forming at his mouth.

"It was a birthmark . . . a mere imperfection, which I had

since childhood," Margaret said tearfully. "It was in a privy place, but my husband knew of it and thought nothing amiss."

"Vile creature!" stormed Malvern in such a voice that more than one spectator in the court jumped in his seat. "Your husband is the Devil! That is the *husband* you speak of. Tell us, did he come to you at night, whispering in your ear. What did he whisper?"

"Nothing, sir . . . nothing . . . I—"

"Nothing? Then you do admit he came to you but said nothing?"

"He never came. I have no husband."

"You had a husband of whom you wearied! You conjured a spirit to frighten him and deprive him of his life. Admit that this is true!"

"It is not true!" Margaret shrieked, rising. "My husband died a natural death. His heart failed him. He had been long sick."

"Long wasted, you mean," returned Malvern with heavy sarcasm. "Long wasted with a mysterious ailment. This once hale and hearty man. I know. I have talked with his physician. The man was at a loss to explain the disease. A natural death, you say? Very natural. Yes, very natural indeed, when a man looks out his window and sees a girl six weeks dead glaring in at him. That's most natural, most wondrous natural."

"I did not cause my husband's sickness. I did not conjure Ursula's spirit," Margaret said quietly.

"And yet the spirit came. And how could it come, save it were called forth? Answer me that, woman."

"I cannot answer," Margaret said.

"Indeed, you cannot answer, Mrs. Waite," said the prosecutor. Malvern turned and gave a long look at the jurymen, who leaned forward intently. "Goodmen of the jury, you have heard this woman's words. I had to wrench the facts from her. Wherefore her reluctance, I ask you, but a vicious desire to conceal the truth? She would have had us believe her husband died betwixt sleep and awake, as they say righteous men do. But I can summon witnesses who viewed Malcolm Waite's corpse and it was no pleasant sight, I can tell you that." Malvern paused, then turned to Margaret again. "Are you not ashamed to have conjured such an apparition?"

"Why, no, sir, I am not ashamed," Margaret said indignantly.

"Oh, then you are not ashamed you say?" Malvern swung around to face the jury again. "What an infamous witch is this not even to show shame when she sups with the Devil and compacts with the Evil One to kill her husband."

The magistrate intervened, perhaps out of compassion for the stricken woman on the witness stand or perhaps simply because he was weary of the prosecutor's ranting and posturing. "Mrs. Waite, when you said no to Mr. Malvern's question, did you mean to deny you were ashamed or to deny you conjured?"

Margaret looked up gratefully at the magistrate and said, "The latter, sir. I never conjured, never in my life. I wouldn't know how to do it. I would not want to do it, even if I could."

The magistrate sat back satisfied and motioned to the prosecutor to proceed. Malvern went over to the little table behind which he had been sitting and shuffled through some papers. Matthew waited, as he had waited ever since the interrogation of Margaret had begun, for Malvern to bring up the matter of Philip Goodin, Margaret's brother. But when Malvern resumed his questions they dealt with Margaret's relationship with her husband. Matthew wondered if Malvern knew about Philip Goodin at all.

"Now, Mrs. Waite, it is well known in the town that you were a shrewish wife, a domineering woman who kept her husband in his place," said Malvern.

"I confess that was my wicked humor," Margaret replied after a few moments of hesitation. "I much regret it now that he is dead."

"I am sure you do," replied Malvern caustically. "Did you not wish your husband to die?"

"I did not."

"Speak the truth!"

"I speak it, if you will hear it."

Malvern tried another tack: "It was your barn in which Ursula Tusser practiced her witchcraft."

"Such witchcraft as she was said to practice occurred in my barn," Margaret replied.

"I'm surprised more was not made of that at *her* trial, for how could she do such wickedness under the nose of the barn's owner save that person knew of it? You did know of it, didn't you?"

"I knew of her meetings, but thought it not all of the Devil," Margaret answered weakly.

"Not all?"

Margaret repeated what she had said. She spoke very softly now. The courtroom was dead quiet, listening.

"Either Ursula practiced the black art or she did not. If some were evil, then all were. It follows, doesn't it?"

Margaret, obviously wearied now with the prosecutor's questions, looked confused. Thus far she had held up well under the grilling, but her pallor indicated how much the interrogation had taken from her.

The prosecutor went on, his voice growing louder and more insistent: "The fact is, Mrs. Waite, that you are as guilty now, and were then, as Ursula Tusser. As much in communion with the Devil as was she. It was only your so-called respectability as a merchant's wife that saved you from the gallows. Had you been poor, deformed, ignorant, a person without name or property—"

"I think you've made your point, Mr. Malvern," interrupted the magistrate, who undoubtedly felt that the implication of these remarks touched upon his own execution of justice as much as it did on the alleged guilt of Mrs. Waite.

"I only wished to demonstrate, sir," said Malvern in a conciliatory voice, "that this woman's practice was of very long standing. In admitting her involvement with Ursula Tusser she *ipso facto*—that is to say, admits to being a witch herself."

"I'll hold my judgment on your logic, sir, and the jury

will in due time render its verdict. Please proceed, but calmly."

Malvern made a stiff little bow of respect to the magistrate and glanced through his notes, which he now held in his hand. During his exchange of words with the magistrate, Margaret had sat down on the stool. Malvern was about to address another question to her when she slumped forward and would have fallen to the floor had not Malvern caught her in his arms. This sudden collapse aroused some consternation in the court, for it was immediately assumed a supernatural agency had been the cause of it. However, when a damp cloth was provided by the clerk and administered by Jane Crispin, Margaret revived. Malvern said he would put no more questions at present to Margaret, and she was helped by the clerk and her sister to the prisoners' bench.

Throughout Margaret Waite's questioning, Jane Crispin's expressions had been the mirror of her sister's suffering. She had wept when Margaret wept, cringed before Malvern's accusations, and cried out for mercy's sake when Margaret had fainted. Now Jane was called to the stand. She rose, her face suffused with revitalized conviction. She walked directly to the witness stand. Refusing the offer of the stool, she stood looking at the prosecutor with an expression of curious interest. She had dressed neatly and well for her trial and looked calm and dignified. She seemed conscious of a social advantage—and certainly a moral superiority—over her accusers. Malvern asked her first to recite the Paternoster. She recited it perfectly, rendering it with such passion that one would have thought her the author of it and that He to whom the words were addressed was seated in the court. The spectators, hanging on every word, were obviously impressed; when Jane said "amen," more than one voice echoed it. She also recited the Ten Commandments—in their proper order and without failing to include the negatives, the omission of which had sealed the doom of more than one poor woman accused of witchcraft.

When these tests were completed, Malvern stood regarding Jane Crispin for some time, as though she were some kind of freak that he might not have the opportunity of seeing again. She stared back at him. Without speaking, the two of them seemed engaged in a contest of wills. This went on until Matthew began to feel hot and nervous from sheer anticipation. A restlessness in the court indicated he was not the only one feeling this way.

"You have heard, Mrs. Crispin, the evidence against you?" Malvern asked.

Jane said she had heard it and thought very little of it too.

"You deny having conjured, then?"

"I do deny it most forcefully," she said. She turned her gaze on the judges, then on the jurymen, and finally on the spectators. Her gaze was bold and steady and caused unfavorable comment in the court. But Matthew admired her pluck. She reminded him of his wife—steady, no puling wench with only tears for her defense. He leaned forward, not wanting to miss a word of the exchange between them.

"Inasmuch as their testimonies," Jane continued, "given here or elsewhere label me as anything but a woman of unblemished reputation and a Christian, I do deny their charges most vehemently. My conscience is settled."

"Your neighbors are liars, then," said Malvern in a loud voice. "Isn't that the inescapable conclusion your words force upon us?"

"If they say I am a witch, they are mistaken and misled. The same is true of their testimony against my sister. I know nothing of witchcraft. I care to know nothing. I know only the Scriptures, the prayer book, and the verities I learned upon my good mother's knee. All these I have practiced since my youth. My heart is free from offense to God and my neighbor. Only God can know the human heart, and therefore if in *their* hearts my neighbors think ill of me, then my neighbors must answer to God for it."

"The name of Deity comes readily to your lips, Mrs. Crispin, by which stratagem you hope to convince us that you are not of Satan's party. But such words are cheap, are hawked at every street corner. They are easily had by rote memory, lisped on the tongue when the occasion requires—

to create a semblance of virtue when indeed there is no virtue at all."

"That's true, sir," answered Jane. "Words are cheap. But if my words are cheap, then so are yours. If words can gloss a lie and make it shine like a verity, then a slander may daub a truth and make it appear a falsehood. But there are facts too, sir, and they are at times more substantial than words. I was dipped in the baptismal font of our church when eight days old, and have lived a Christian all my life. Who judges me may well remember the words of our Saviour: 'Let him without sin cast the first stone.'"

These remarks of Jane's caused a murmur in the court and the clerk had to call for silence. In his heavy lawyer's gown Malvern was sweating profusely, and it was obvious he was growing vexed at Jane Crispin's responses.

"Very well spoken, Mrs. Crispin," he said. "I'm sure the court appreciates being preached to by a woman. But let that pass. Tell us now, your sister has made her accompliceship plain by confessing that she knew of Ursula's meetings, of her craft. In so doing, she has practically confessed to being a witch—"

Jane started to protest, but Malvern hushed her with a wave of his hand and continued forcefully: "It comes to that by order of logic, Mrs. Crispin. *Your sister is a confessed witch!* Now you, Mistress Eloquence, were that famous witch's employer. I mean Ursula's, of most detested memory in this town. Even she whose spirit has come to be called the Chelmsford Horror, to the dismay of honest Christians. What can be said of the mistress who allows her servant such liberties to the detriment of her soul and those of others?"

"I know not your logic, sir, having not been in school," Jane replied, "but the Scriptures I know, for I have studied them from my youth. Did Jesus not have one follower who betrayed him? If, then, the master is answerable for all that the disciple does, how is it our Lord escapes the blame for Judas's treachery?"

"What!" exclaimed Malvern, throwing back his hands in mock amazement and laughing hoarsely. "First you preach at us. Now you would liken yourself to the Son of God! Has the court ever heard such blasphemy as this? This is mere chop logic. Yet the woman claims no learning."

"Mrs. Crispin," interrupted the magistrate. "We will have no blasphemous similitudes in this court. Please answer Mr. Malvern's questions simply and without further resort to sacred writ."

"Your honor, may a woman not defend herself, then?" Jane asked calmly, turning in the direction of the three judges.

"She may defend herself," said the magistrate, "but as a woman, not as a man."

"As a woman," she said. "I understand, or at least I think I do. Very well, sirs." She turned to the jury. "Goodmen and neighbors, you have every one known me for a long time as a decent honest woman—as no shrew or backbiter, gossip or railing wife. My tongue I have kept disciplined and, I pray, clean of filth. How can you believe these lies and calumnies inspired by ignorance and malice of my husband's enemies? Curses against cattle and sheep! Strange characters scrawled upon paper! The Holy Sacrament administered to dogs! Why these are foolish fictions, every one, the fruits of idle—no, addled—brains!"

Several of those who had witnessed against the sisters rose up to protest these characterizations, and for a moment there was a great deal of shouting and name-calling, mostly from the baker's wife, whose enmity toward the Waites and Crispins was now painfully obvious. "Liar and whore! Devil's slut!" Mrs. Roundy raged. Over this din, the clerk shouted for order and the magistrate banged his gavel until the handle broke and he was forced to use his fist. Finally, Mrs. Roundy's husband silenced her and the other irate witnesses resumed their seats. Jane Crispin stared at the hostile faces in the court as though their rage and vile expletives meant nothing at all to her.

"Another such outburst and I will have the court cleared of spectators," growled the magistrate. "Mrs. Crispin, you will answer the questions put to you and say no more to the jurymen. Let your answers be 'yea' or 'nay.' Nothing more. Do you understand?"

Jane said she understood. She said she was weary of standing and asked if she might sit upon the stool her sister had used. The stool was brought forward and Jane sat down.

"Tell us plainly, Mrs. Crispin," Malvern said. "Were you aware of what transpired in your sister's barn?"

"By hearsay, sir, not by direct knowledge."

"Yes or no, Mrs. Crispin?"

"If I must answer categorically as you require, then I am forced to say no."

"No? Forced? Why? Because you don't want to incriminate yourself?"

"I *know* that which I have seen, smelled, tasted, touched, heard. Someone told me my servant was practicing witchcraft in my sister's barn. That's not *knowledge,* sir."

"Oh, very well, Mrs. Crispin," Malvern said with exasperation. "Tell us what you *heard,* then."

"I heard many things, but I hear many things about this person and that in our town. Not all are true, and certain it is that none ought to be believed without certain proof. It *is* certain proof you are interested in, isn't it?"

The magistrate reminded Jane that she was present to answer questions, not to put them to the prosecutor. Malvern was now dripping with sweat. The courtroom was stuffy and stale. The jury looked tired, and Malvern was in a rage.

"Were you aware," continued Malvern, "that your sister sought a familiar spirit of this Ursula Tusser, *your servant?*"

"I know not if there be such things as familiars," Jane replied calmly. "It is true that the Bible speaks of them, yet I have been forbidden to speak of that book and therefore will leave the text to the learned. Perhaps familiars are beings that belong to the old dispensation of Moses and the Prophets and are done away in Christ, such as they say miracles and the speaking in tongues are. In any event, they are not within the scope of my knowledge or experience."

"Well, then, Mistress Theologian," returned Malvern, "are familiars within the scope of your *sister's* knowledge?"

"For that, sir," Jane answered, "you are well advised to ask my sister, for the question pertains to her and not to me."

Someone laughed in the back of the room and Malvern swiveled around to see who it was. Red-faced with fury, he turned back to his witness. "Enough of this foolish talk, woman. Will you confess? Will you confess before God and man that you are a witch? Confess and save your soul from damnation! No one here is deceived by your clever tongue, for with such a tongue Adam was tempted to sin and thus the whole race of mankind fell."

"I am responsible for my sins, sir," said Jane. "Mother Eve must look to her own."

There was another ripple of laughter at this witty reply. Malvern mopped his brow and then looked at the magistrate, opening the palms of his hands to suggest that with a witch of this obduracy there was little more to be done.

"The hour is late," said the magistrate, who also seemed angered by Jane Crispin's answers. "The court will adjourn until tomorrow morning, at which time I trust this business will be brought to a conclusion. Mr. Malvern, will you have any more witnesses?"

"Just one, your honor. One I have saved for last. It will be a most important and conclusive one, I promise you." He leveled a look of hatred at Jane Crispin, who sat very still on her stool, contemplating the faces in the courtroom with a mild air of one far removed from the conflict her responses had generated.

SEVENTEEN

"I THOUGHT Jane Crispin gave as good as she got from that slippery pettifogger," Joan remarked the next morning at breakfast as she watched her husband attack his food as though he were on the rump end of a long fast. She was speaking of Malvern, to whom she had taken an instant and intense dislike. Great bag of guts, she had called him, mocking his red swollen face and mimicking his growl.

"The tanner's wife has a head on her shoulders," Matthew responded between mouthfuls. "Like *you*, Joan."

Joan acknowledged the compliment with a smile. Matthew turned his attention to the porridge. It was excellent—a concoction of turnips, coleworts, and barley made in a thick soup of wheat flour and eggs. Joan's recipes were famous in the neighborhood.

"I wonder what trick the prosecutor intends for today," she said. "How ominous his words were. Who could this witness be?"

"I don't know. But his methods will be subtle, true to his nature. Pray God that Jane Crispin proves his match for the second round. She's quite come out of her shyness in these circumstances. She's a fighter now."

"Yes," Joan agreed. "Strange, isn't it? Margaret was always the dominant one. She always insisted on having the last word on everything. Then these wicked charges. I fear for her life, even if she is found innocent."

"Mrs. Crispin doesn't seem afraid," Matthew said, signaling to his wife that he had had enough of the porridge and that she could return the ladle to the pot.

"She should be," said Joan darkly.

Joan was right, Matthew decided. The trial was not going well, despite Jane Crispin's clever retorts. Not going well *because* of her cleverness. Her witty tongue was working to her disadvantage as far as the judges and the jury were concerned. It didn't matter about the prosecutor. Matthew knew his fellow townsmen. Malvern was a type they didn't like. But it was a dangerous thing to make a fool of a prosecutor, especially if the one making the fool was a woman. If Matthew read the jurymen's faces right, their verdict was certain: Jane Crispin was either a witch or a shameless virago who had set a bad example for the wives of the town and needed hanging to learn to be civil to men in authority.

He and Joan talked some more about the trial, working themselves into a fit of melancholy. "Ah, if there were only some new evidence," he murmured.

"Another apparition?"

But he wasn't thinking of spectral evidence. God knew there had been a superfluity of that. He wanted something palpable. Like a bloody knife. Or a smoking pistol. Or an eyewitness, or even an intelligible motive to connect the case of the Chelmsford witches with the world of his own understanding—a world in which constables could do their job without mixing up with theology and the supernatural.

"It's passing strange that Ursula's spirit has made no further appearances. For a while, it was a busy spirit indeed."

Joan said this airily, as though she had not been scared out of her wits by the face in her window. Matthew remembered well how he had had to comfort her. For several nights afterward, she had made him get out of bed to see to every bump and squeak in the dark house. He had become the chief investigator of groaning timbers, rattling windows, and mice scampering in the pantry. But the ghost of Ursula had not appeared again. Not to Joan. And not, evidently, to anyone else in town. That *was* passing strange. "Well, let God be thanked for the dead that keep to their graves," he said, aspiring to her lightheartedness. "What, would you want another visit to our window?"

"Hardly," she replied soberly. "Unless someone has seen her since and has kept quiet about it, Ursula's visit to us was the last of her visits. It was the night the sisters were arrested and the barn burned."

Matthew agreed that if anyone else had seen the ghost he would have surely made a noise about it. No one in town seemed reticent on that score. "Every witness in the trial has become a local celebrity. Simon Roundy has done a booming business in his bakery since his wife confronted the ghost and proclaimed the fact from the housetops. Customers come in not for cakes and marchpane but to gawk at the woman and to hear the latest version of her ordeal. Before they leave, they buy some biscuit or cake for a memento. Roundy's well paid for his wife's fright."

"And so is her vanity. She's grown very tedious," Joan said cattily. She didn't like Mrs. Roundy either. "It is almost as if with the arrest of the sisters the spirit was satisfied," she conjectured.

"Or left town for fear of the riot," he said, trying to be funny but failing. Joan smiled charitably. He could tell she was still wrestling with the question.

"Brigit hasn't been seen again either," she said.

"No. She's vanished."

"I wonder if there's a connection."

"Well, the spirit has probably scared her off. That dark, gloomy house. Rank with death and failure. I'll wager she's gone home to her mother."

"But suppose," Joan went on, as though she hadn't been paying attention at all, "that the spirit—Ursula—had done whatever it was that she was intended to do?"

"Frighten Malcolm Waite? Terrify the town? You?" He looked hard at her, trying to figure out what it was she was saying. Her expression was one he recognized. It was the look she had when she had reached a conclusion for which he would have no satisfactory rebuttal.

She developed her argument with easy assurance. "The arrest of the sisters. The disgrace of both houses. Look, Matthew, doesn't it all make a terrible sense?"

"Vengeance?" he answered. "But why stop with the Crispins and Waites? There's the jury that convicted her, the hangman that hanged her. Mrs. Byrd who complained to the authorities in the first place. And the spirit's visit to you. What in God's name had you to do with *her* that she should visit this house? Were I a ghost, able to materialize where I wished and to whomever I wished, I would dog my enemies until they ran mad in the streets. As for the rest—they that had done me no ill—let them sleep of nights."

"Oh, but there's something—something in this all. If we could only fathom it," she said. "But one thing seems simple to me. The sisters have suffered too greatly from these horrors to be their authors."

"A reasonable inference," Matthew said, "and yet when I look at Margaret and Jane now, I see sometimes the women I know, and at other times the creatures I fear. Expressions I would have deemed sad suddenly seem sinister and conniving. Their very movements and whispers fill me with a kind of dread."

"Much of that is your own fear, Matthew. It distills from your brain. As for my vision—well, it was a true one. I swear it, but as I have said, I don't conclude from it that either Margaret or Jane was its cause."

At that moment Peter Bench looked in the door to say that John Waite was in the shop and wanted to speak to Matthew.

"What does he want?" Matthew asked, annoyed at this interruption of his breakfast.

"He wouldn't say, sir. He said only that he must speak to you at once concerning a matter of some urgency."

"Some urgency, is it?" Matthew got up from the table. He gave his wife a skeptical look, wiping his mouth with the napkin. He went to see what John Waite wanted, promising Joan to return presently. John Waite was browsing among the cloth-laden tables. When he saw Matthew, he immediately explained why he had come. "It's happened again," he said.

"What has happened?" Matthew hoped the young man did not mean the ghost had put in another appearance.

"It's the prowler again," said John Waite with a nettled expression. "Susan Goodyear woke me at midnight pounding upon my door without mercy. 'God help us!' she screamed, all in a crazy flutter and half-dressed. 'There's a spirit walking among the ruins of the barn with a lantern in his hand.' I leaped from my bed and flew to the window to see this marvel, only then remembering my window did not look upon the backsides and I must go to the chamber where my cousins lay. I did. Woke them at once and told them both what Susan had said. She had followed me into the room, terrified of being left to herself, and moaning and groaning as she was, she gave Dick and Edward a fright, I can tell you. She looked a very spirit herself, but a truly ugly one, with her hair flying every whichway and that sullen face of hers with her lower lip a-trembling. In a twinkling they were on their feet, half naked and shivering, neither caring that Susan stood there gaping at their bare legs.

"We all looked from the window and saw the flicker of light Susan spoke of. It was but a little light, as though the lantern had been hooded for secrecy's sake. I could see him that carried it, though. He was no more than a moving shadow, stalking around in the rubble as though he had lost something there and wanted desperately to find it. He would bend down, pry loose a board or two, then stand erect again."

"You're sure it was a man you saw and not a woman?" Matthew asked, thinking perhaps what the nephew had seen was a spirit, after all, and doubtless Ursula's.

"Well," John Waite said, pausing thoughtfully. "It was of mankind, not animal. Of that I'm sure enough. It might have been a woman. Of course, whoever it was wore a cloak and hat, so how was I or my cousins to tell? Susan Goodyear declared it was Ursula's ghost, as sure as she lived. But I told her spirits have no need of lanterns to see by."

"And did that persuade her it was no ghost you saw?"

John Waite laughed mirthlessly and stroked the hairs on his upper lip. "You must be joking, or you don't know Susan. The whey-face is addled beyond redemption. She's a giddy goose if there ever was one. My good aunt could not seem to employ better."

"What was she doing up and about at that hour anyway?" Matthew asked.

"A nightmare had awakened her and she had risen to use the chamber pot. Having graced it with her bum, she was on her way back to bed again when a dreadful fear came upon her. She looked from her window toward the backsides and saw the light."

"I see. Go on."

"At once I knew it was the prowler of whom I had complained to you earlier. I told Susan to go back to bed and cease her blubbering, and then I and my cousins armed ourselves and in our nightclothes stole downstairs and out the postern door, careful not to make a noise. We hoped to fall upon the wretch before he was aware."

"You feared no spirit, then, or armed man either?"

"Who, I?" said the young man, making a cynical face. "I thought at the worst him a flesh-and-blood thief or perhaps one of our fine upstanding loyal neighbors out to do us more mischief. Besides, there was but one of him and three of us and we had the advantage of surprise, or thought so."

"Well, what happened? Have you caught him?"

"Sadly no," answered John Waite. "We could see the light again when we were in the yard. He was digging. We could hear his spade at work. We were within a dozen feet of the fellow when my Cousin Dick stumbled over a piece of the wreckage and went sprawling, crying out as he flew. The cry alarmed the trespasser. We could hear him running off in the darkness, leaving the lantern and spade behind him."

"Did you give chase?"

"Did we not?" John Waite laughed. "We were unshod, you understand, and him whom we would have pursued was lost to us in a moment. Look, I have brought you both the lantern and the spade."

John Waite opened his cloak to show Matthew the lantern and spade. Clumps of mud mixed with ash clung to the blade's edge.

"Now why should anyone be digging around in the ruins of your aunt's barn? Had your uncle some treasure concealed there?"

"To my knowledge," answered the nephew dryly, "the only thing of value Malcolm Waite had in that pestilent ruin was the mare, now a rotting corpse. I doubt if the mysterious digger was some lover of horseflesh bent on giving the beast a decent burial."

"Well," said Matthew, conscious of the time and his need to bring his prisoners to the court, "he'll probably not return now that you've discovered him."

"Probably not," said John Waite ruefully. "But we intend to keep a guard just in case he does."

Matthew examined the lantern and the spade. Neither bore its owner's mark and both were of a common variety easily had in the town. "You have a good lantern and spade for your pains," he said.

"Yes," said John Waite. "I suppose I do." He sighed heavily. "Well, I thought you should know of this. I'm off now to the trial, where I expect to hear the worst regarding my poor aunts." The young man's face showed what seemed genuine sadness.

Matthew shook his hand and said he was sorry for his family's troubles. His words sounded flat and insincere even to himself, and he wondered what the nephew made of them. He watched the young man leave, then returned to the kitchen to tell Joan what John Waite had said.

"A prowler digging in the barn ruins. How strange," she said.

"Despite what the nephew says, someone might have thought there was silver or gold buried there," Matthew said.

"At least it was no ghost."

Matthew was about to leave to fetch his prisoners when Joan stopped him.

"You know, there's something very strange about the barn," she said mysteriously.

"What do you mean?"

"The barn. Ursula's loft. It was there I felt the intruder's presence and didn't know what to make of it. Now this strange and secret excavation. Oh, Matthew, I have the strongest feeling that the barn loft is the key."

"The key? Key to what?"

"Why, to the mystery. Why Ursula's spirit cannot rest."

"But the barn is a heap of ash now," he protested.

"The rubble must be cleared and searched," she said firmly.

"Impossible," he answered impatiently. "The Waites and Crispins are not about to do the work themselves, not with their women on trial. And they were unable to find anyone in town willing to help them for love or money. It would take all day, clearing that mess."

"We must do it, then."

"*We?*"

"The apprentices can be spared this morning. There won't be a half-dozen customers in the shop with the trial in progress and the verdict in the offing."

He stood stupefied. When his wife got a notion in her head, it was set in mortar and hardened a week. As for himself, he had not an idea in the world what the barn, ruin that it now was, would or could demonstrate about any aspect of the present business.

But she insisted, and would not let him out the door until he had relented to her request.

"Oh, very well. You're right about business anyway. The boys will only sit on their hands all morning, or sneak down to the Sessions House to hear fresh news of the trial."

He called to Peter, and when his assistant stuck his head in the doorway, he gave him his orders. "Go fetch Arthur Wilts. Tell him to come straightway."

Matthew lingered until Arthur arrived, which was not more than a few minutes. During the interval, Matthew tried to pry from Joan just what it was she thought would be found in the ruins besides ashes, but she wouldn't say. It wasn't clear that she knew herself. However, her uncertainty made her no less positive about what should be done. Matthew's apprentices were to do the dirty work. Arthur, who wanted to go to hear the verdict, was disappointed when Matthew told him he was to supervise the digging.

"You wish the horse buried, Mr. Stock," asked Arthur, curious, of course, why this project should be undertaken at all.

"Yes, yes, bury the beast. I'll come to you at dinnertime and inspect the work. If you find anything unusual"—he paused to glance at Joan—"anything . . . strange, bring me word at once."

Joan looked pleased. She was off to the Sessions House herself, and she planted a warm kiss on his cheek as he went out the door to fetch the women.

The horse and cart were ready, brought up before by Peter. By the time he was halfway to the Blue Boar, Matthew had forgotten completely about the Waite barn.

EIGHTEEN

THE journey from the Blue Boar to the Sessions House, a distance of not more than a quarter mile, was more tumultuous than it had been the day before, and therefore seemed the longer. Faces surged toward Matthew as they might have done in the worst of nightmares, in which the threat of physical danger joins forces with verbal abuse and calumny of the vilest sort. Hands clawed at his prisoners huddled in the back of the cart, grasped at the moving wheels and tried to restrain them. The cart was rocked and jostled, pelted and spat upon, yet Matthew drove it forward, thanks to the aid of three of the magistrate's men who rode alongside. The epithets hurled at him slashed like razors.

By some miracle, Matthew got the women into the court without injury to them or himself. The trial, scheduled to resume at eight o'clock, did not get under way until nearly nine, an unfortunate delay. By that time claps of unseasonable thunder could be heard in the distance, and these gave the onlookers and the jurymen even more cause for concern. When the great Bible, used for the swearing in of witnesses, was inadvertently knocked onto the floor by a flustered clerk, nearly everyone concluded that this second and final day of the trial had begun on an ominous note indeed.

The prosecutor Malvern rose first to make a short summary of the previous day's evidence against the accused women, as though it were not already etched permanently in the minds of all those who had attended the proceedings. He made much of the testimony of Mrs. Roundy, the baker's wife, He emphasized her special status as an eyewitness to the reality of the apparition, and interpreted her fainting fit as a clear sign of the Satanic influence that continued to emanate from the accused women. He summarized rapidly and with an air of confidence, as though to say, "This all is behind us, like the foundation of a great edifice upon the which I will now erect an even more spectacular superstructure." He gestured dramatically like a player on the stage, his bulging eyes fixing by turn on the judges, the jurymen, and the onlookers.

Finally it was time for the last witness. Seated rigidly next to Malvern was the boy with whom the prosecutor had arrived in town. Upon entering and taking his place behind Margaret and her sister, the constable had not noticed him. Now, in response to the clerk's summons, Michael Fletcher—or so he was called—stood up. He did not step forward to the witness stand, however, nor was his oath taken. It was quickly apparent that the young man was to be a witness of a different sort.

"Michael Fletcher, whom you see before you, was himself possessed of an evil spirit," Malvern explained when the magistrate asked to know who the boy was and what use the prosecutor hoped to make of him. "*Was* possessed, I hasten to add. For nearly a year he was afflicted. During that time, he languished, convulsed, spewed pins and needles from his mouth, vomited rocks and stones, to the wonderment of his friends and parents. At length he was freed from the possession through much earnest prayer, both of learned clergy and of his family. Since then, he has on many occasions done valuable service to towns such as yours cursed with this terrible malignancy of witchcraft."

A clap of thunder was heard; there was a visible shudder among the onlookers. Malvern paused, noting the sign's effect, and made a shrewd face. Young Michael Fletcher himself stood very still and stony-faced, as though Malvern were speaking of someone else. Matthew wondered what it was the boy would do. Give an account of his possession? Preach a sermon against witches?

But as Malvern continued, describing his protégé's powers without specifically saying how they were used, it became apparent that the boy was no accuser of witches, but a detector of them. He was a wonder, a prodigy—endowed with a marvelous gift, made more wonderful by its serviceableness to a righteous cause: the identification of others possessed by Satan.

"If a woman or man or child be *contaminated*," Malvern went on, shuddering at the word, "if that contaminated person has made room in his heart for the Devil, then Michael Fletcher will know of it. Since his own deliverance, he has become abnormally sensitive. He can no more endure Satan's presence in another than a rose the first grip of frost."

Matthew studied the face and form of this marvelous personage, who indeed looked like any other boy his age except for the good value of his clothing. The eyes were bright blue and intense, the skin of his face waxy pale, and at his chin was a crop of pimples. Beyond the white lace cuffs of Michael Fletcher's jerkin, his small delicate hands hung limply like little dead fish. There was something cold and watery about Michael Fletcher—certainly something intimidating about his reputed powers. Matthew began to feel uneasy.

Malvern said a trial would be made of the women, one that would lead to an inescapable conclusion. It would be a kind of demonstration, he said, that would make their possession all very plain, even to the most skeptical. He conferred with the clerk briefly and gave some instructions that resulted in a hiatus in the proceedings while the spectators in the first row were asked to move to the side of the room so that their bench could be shoved back to allow more space before the judges' table.

When this was done, Malvern handed the clerk a paper on which had been written the names of six women present in the chamber, women who were all reputable wives of the town and who had not previously served as witnesses. The names were called and the women were asked to come forward and stand before the judges. Among them was Joan.

Matthew had been first surprised to hear his wife's name

called, then anxious. It was evident the women called were also confused and embarrassed by this curious and seemingly spontaneous summons. Some smiled or giggled nervously, others looked on solemnly, waiting for further instructions or at least an explanation from Malvern. When they were all at the front, Malvern had them form a line and turn to face the spectators. Then he asked Matthew to bring his prisoners forward and place them within the line. This even more strange and unexpected development caused some consternation, both among the women standing and among the audience, for many were not happy to find themselves—or to see their wives—lumped with the accused witches, and those so distressed made audible comments to that effect.

When this was accomplished—Matthew now beginning to suspect what Malvern intended—the prosecutor pulled a handkerchief from his pocket and made it into a blindfold for Michael Fletcher, explaining as he did so that the blindfold would guarantee the validity of the demonstration. Malvern stepped forward and, planting his hands on the shoulders of several of the women, repositioned them so that the order of the line was different from that which his protégé had last viewed. By now every woman in the line, including Margaret and Jane, had grasped the prosecutor's intent, and the few among them who had giggled nervously when brought forward were as solemn and anxious as the rest. The whole courtroom was tense with anticipation, and those whose eyes were not fixed on the faces of the eight women were giving equal attention to the blindfolded figure of Michael Fletcher, who to many in the room must have appeared as the male counterpart of the allegorical justice, wanting only the scales and sword.

Now Malvern announced in sonorous tones that he was prepared to begin, and asked, unnecessarily, that all give heed to what was about to happen. Taking Michael Fletcher's hand, he led the boy toward the women and asked them to extend their hands before them, extending his own to demonstrate what he wanted them to do.

The women extended their hands. There was a little buzz

of talk in the court but it soon fell silent. Malvern led the boy to the first of the women, guiding his hand so that his fingertips merely glanced hers. The poor woman, who had obviously been holding her breath for fear, now let it all out in a loud "Whew!" that would have provoked laughter in other circumstances. She smiled broadly and Malvern moved on. The next woman, as it turned out, was Joan, and Matthew was seized by a sudden dread. It was clear to him that as theatrical as this so-called demonstration was and as spurious as Michael Fletcher's powers might be, his friends and neighbors in the room were convinced of the validity of the demonstration; it might have been Saint Paul himself performing the wonder. There was therefore real danger in the boy's touch. The cold white fingertips made contact with Joan's fleshy brown hand, and Matthew flinched and then, when nothing happened, sighed for relief, expressing in the sigh as fervent a prayer of gratitude as he had ever uttered in his life.

Inevitably, Michael Fletcher came to Margaret Waite, who was standing in the fifth position from where the demonstration had begun. By now, four of the women having been touched with no more response from Michael Fletcher than a twitch of his youthful nose, the spectators had been lulled into a false sense of security. But when the boy's hand touched Margaret's, the touch turned instantly to a vice-like grip, Michael Fletcher's face contorted violently, and he shrieked as if Margaret's hand were a searing brand.

"Satan! Satan! Satan!" Michael Fletcher screamed, as though each mention of the name were wrenched from his soul.

Everyone, including Malvern, appeared shocked at the violence of this outburst, and immediately the prosecutor began to struggle to break the contact his protégé's abnormal sensitivity had forged. It was as if the boy were unable to let go Margaret's hand, and this nearly proved to be so, for despite his greater physical strength and his intense determination, it was all Malvern could do to break the grip. It seemed an eternity until he did so. Poor Margaret shrieked and quaked, and with her free hand clutched at her heart in obvious terror.

Then it was over. The contact was broken, and the shrieking stopped. Malvern and the boy breathed heavily with exertion; Margaret fainted dead away and had to be carried back to her bench. For a few minutes the court was in an uproar; however, since everyone wanted to see if the boy would respond similarly to Jane Crispin, the spectators quieted down.

Malvern moved the boy down the line, touching two more women without noticeable response. Jane was at the very end. When he came to her, just as the audience expected, Michael Fletcher's performance was repeated.

But it was more dreadful than before, more ear-piercing, the jerks and wriggles more violent. Michael Fletcher ripped the blindfold from his eyes and, with his free hand, flailed about in the air as though fending off a host of winged and invisible devils fluttering about him and Jane Crispin. He whined and howled like an animal.

While Jane Crispin endured this with the utmost disdain for her accuser, some in the audience, terrified by this show of Satanic power, were making for the doors in an effort to escape. Others left their benches to get a closer view, while some fainted or began to imitate the boy's seizure, writhing in agony or snarling and howling like dogs. One would no sooner give over his fit than a new victim would appear whose contortions and shrieks were more dramatic and otherworldly than his predecessor's. For a half hour at least, the chamber was a perfect bedlam. The judges shouted themselves hoarse in their effort to restore order. A physician was summoned. The parson made the sign of the cross repeatedly, in a vain attempt to exorcise the disruptive spirit. The magistrate, bewildered by the reaction and appalled by the breakdown in decorum, ordered his men to clear the chamber at once, but they too seemed affected by the general hysteria and were more concerned to use their halberds to ward off any supernatural threat to themselves than to defend the civil order. Even after Malvern succeeded in his superhuman struggle to free Michael Fletcher's hand from Jane Crispin's, the uproar continued. Indeed, it did not begin to abate until the most vociferous of the possessed were prostrate on the benches or so raw of voice that they had to keep silent.

Young Fletcher too had been exhausted by his fit. When his grip was broken, he collapsed in a heap on the floor.

The howling and shouting finally stopped, and everyone gave their attention to the fallen boy, whose marvelous touch had proved the prosecutor's case, or so it had seemed. Malvern was down on his knees beside the prostrate form of Michael Fletcher, trying to revive him. The crowd was on their feet, pressing around for a better view. "Give him air! He's only fainted!" shouted Malvern. He called for water and water was brought. He dipped his handkerchief in the cup and wiped the boy's brow and cheeks. Some color could be seen in the smooth young face and within minutes the closed eyelids fluttered and opened.

Despite these signs of returning life, Mrs. Roundy cried, "*She's* killed him!" The baker's wife pointed an accusing finger at Jane Crispin, who all this while had stood taut-faced and apparently indifferent to the chaos around her. Now it was evident her apparent lack of compassion was construed as responsibility for the seizure, and from everywhere in the room the charge of the baker's wife was echoed: "Away with them! Away with them both!"

In time the prosecutor was able to get Michael Fletcher up, brush off his clothes, and help him to a seat. The court quieted, much sympathy was expressed, and the boy's revival was looked on as a miracle. A recess was called to allow sufficient time for the boy to recover from his harrowing experience.

Matthew led his prisoners to the clerk's office.

"Did you ever see the like?" stormed the previously unperturbed Jane Crispin when the door was shut behind them. "The boy is nothing more than a monkey on a string. What if he does wear a blindfold? He responds when cued and will denounce whom he likes. No woman, nor man either, is free from his accusations. Have my neighbors lost their minds?"

Margaret, more undone than her sister by what had gone on in court, wailed piteously, "Oh, God, help us now!"

Matthew was equally alarmed and disgusted. But what was he to do? It was all up to the jury, who were obviously taking in the whole spectacle with the greatest amazement and credulity; intoxicated as they were by their powers of life and death over the women, what justice could one expect from their hands?

He waited in the office commiserating with the women until they were recalled, then led them to their place. He watched while Malvern rose and, screwing up his eyes at the judges, announced triumphantly that the prosecution had made its case.

Then the magistrate asked if the women had any answer to make to the charges against them other than what had already been said, and Jane Crispin said she had. She stood and faced the jury.

"Goodmen of the jury, I rise to speak for myself and for my poor sister, who is too abjectly melancholy over these proceedings to speak another word for herself. You have heard what passes for evidence against us—idle gossip, speculation, the malice of enemies, and ignorance of the uneducated. It is a sorry bit of evidence, but this previous demonstration by the callow youth yonder surpasses it all for treacherous undermining of reason and justice. The Bible says, 'Answer a fool according to his folly.' But I confess, sirs, that I cannot conceive of such folly as would be fit to answer this foolishness with."

At this point, Jane was silenced by the magistrate, who said he had heard enough. He commanded Jane to say no more.

"The court has already been abused grossly, sir," Jane continued, ignoring the order to be silent. "If you have no charity for me or my sister, consider what peril your own wives, daughters, mothers, and grandmothers stand in when such as Malvern and this wretched boy are allowed to traipse about the country accusing whom they will. And what defense—"

"No more, woman!" cried the louring magistrate, rising to his feet and shaking a warning finger at Jane. He ordered Matthew to restrain her.

Reluctantly, Matthew moved forward to execute the magistrate's command. Momentarily, she resisted the pressure of his hand on her arm, and then allowed herself to be seated. Her eyes smoldered. "Don't say any more," Matthew whispered, leaning over her. "It will do you no good at all."

"I will be silent," she said, in a voice loud enough for the judges to hear. "I will say no more, no, not to any man. If I were a witch, I would empty my store of curses upon them all, but since I am a Christian I can only pray forgiveness for them who despitefully use me."

The magistrate sat down and said, "The jury is instructed to consider what it has heard from the witnesses against these women, from Mr. Michael Fletcher, and from the very lips of the accused. Let the jury now retire to consider its verdict."

At this, everyone began talking and there was a general movement toward the door. Matthew led Jane and Margaret to the clerk's office to wait the jury's decision, while the jurymen were led to the small adjoining courtroom to consider what they had heard. Matthew saw the women inside the clerk's office and made certain that guards were placed at the door. As he was preparing to leave, the relatives of the women descended on him with their complaints.

"A vile trick!" cried Thomas Crispin, who had been in the courtroom and watched Michael Fletcher's demonstration.

"Oh, Mr. Stock, can nothing be done?" asked Dick Waite.

Crispin asked to see his wife.

"The magistrate has given orders," Matthew said. "No one must see the prisoners until the jury has reached its verdict."

"What, does he fear escape, or a new round of bedevilment visited upon the town by these hapless women?" John Waite demanded in his cynical vein. "If my aunts be witches, how then can these walls and your guards prevent their curses?"

It was a good question, for which Matthew had no answer, but he did have his orders and they had been clear. He stood his ground despite Tom Crispin's pleadings and threats. The tanner's face swelled with rage. Alert for trouble, the two guards effectively barricaded the door to the clerk's office with their crossed halberds and regarded the tanner's pugnacity with concern.

Matthew caught the eye of the clerk, who, having remained in the courtroom talking to one of the judges, had become aware of the trouble. The clerk left the room and returned within minutes with three more of the magistrate's men.

Outnumbered and outweaponed too, Tom Crispin and the Waites now gave up their efforts and went off with some contemptuous words for the court, the guards, and Matthew.

Matthew pursued them to the chamber door, trying to reason with them. He did have his orders, but he assured them they would have a chance to see the women later.

"When?" stormed Crispin as they stood at the courtroom door. "When they are on the gibbet? What of my poor children? Will they be allowed to see their mother?"

The relatives of the accused women glared at Matthew resentfully and clattered down the stairs, calling him a base traitor and a scoundrel.

Matthew watched them go, their rebuke still ringing in his ears. He saw Arthur Wilts advancing toward him. The deputy was filthy with dirt and ash, and Matthew remembered what he had had him doing all morning. Arthur's flushed, excited face and breathlessness bore the marks of imminent revelation.

"We've found something, sir, me and the lads," he said in an excited whisper. "It is most strange and wonderful."

"What is it?" asked Matthew, sensing that this strange and wonderful discovery was more than buried treasure.

"You must come to see for yourself, Mr. Stock. None of us dared to touch it, nor understand what it is our eyes see."

The stench of decay was more noticeable than ever. About twenty feet from where the barn had stood, Matthew's youngest apprentice was bent over double, gagging helplessly and drooling into a pool of vomit at his feet. Beside him, his older companion, equally ashen, was seated cross-legged on the ground with the handle of the spade resting against his forehead. Beyond them, Matthew could see that the foundation of the barn had now been exposed, and to the right between the house and the garden were a pile of charred planks and beams and the blackened carcass of Malcolm Waite's mare.

Matthew and Arthur had come at a run from the Sessions House and both were out of breath.

"The barn had a kind of cellar, you see," Arthur explained as they advanced toward the ruin. "For the storing of roots, probably. The fire burned the floor above quite away."

Matthew pulled his handkerchief from his pocket in an effort to control his rising nausea.

At the west end of the foundation was a hole of about ten feet square and half that in depth. On closer inspection, Matthew could see that Arthur was right; it was a cellar with an earthen floor and walls, and with an access that had been somewhere inside the barn. Still holding the handkerchief, he got down on his haunches and peered into the recess, which was strewn with rubble.

The mare had not been the only victim of the fire. The collapsing floor had covered the bodies with debris and ash, but the human forms were unmistakable. They lay side by side, two of them. One was the missing Brigit Able. Death had not graced her homeliness. The glistening pupils of her eyes could be seen, despite the thin covering of ash that had given her a blackamoor's visage. The small mouth yawned grotesquely, preserving the shape of her scream when she had realized there was no escape.

By her side another human form lay face down. The legs were crossed awkwardly beneath the long russet gown, and one blackened arm, the sleeve burned away, draped protectively across Brigit's chest while the other was twisted painfully beneath the body. The hair, which was all of the head Matthew could discern from above, was long and fine and clearly a woman's.

He climbed down into the pit to complete the identification. Its rigor passed, the body yielded itself to his touch, and as it turned, the fine long hair splayed around the small heart-shaped face of Ursula Tusser's ghost.

N I N E T E E N

"NEW evidence? What new evidence?" asked the magistrate dubiously.

The magistrate sat at table where he was enjoying the company of several of his London friends who had come up to Chelmsford for the trial. He was not pleased by this interruption but Matthew was insistent. For the magistrate, the trial was virtually concluded; all that remained was the sentencing and on that point the law left little to his discretion.

While the conversation buzzed and tableware clanked, Matthew gave a hurried and confused account of the discovery of the bodies, of the excavation of a grave now in progress, and of the suspicions he proposed to make certain if he could only be allowed a few additional witnesses.

"More witnesses? My God, man. Have we not had a devil's plenty of witnesses? Would a cloud of witnesses make the guilt of these two viragoes more sure?"

One of the magistrate's companions at table had overheard Matthew's plea. A distinguished jurist himself, he reached over and placed a cautionary hand on the magistrate's arm. "It might be worth letting the constable question his witnesses, my friend," the jurist advised. "The trial has been more diverting than a bearbaiting thus far. I should not mind passing another hour if the constable will promise us good value for our money."

Matthew, hearing this, said that he would promise good value, but the magistrate continued to look doubtful. He reminded them both that the case had already been submitted to the jury, and that even now the jury may well have reached its decision.

"Come, sir, don't be an old grumble guts with more concern for procedure than for justice," said the London jurist, with a wink and a hearty slap on the magistrate's shoulder. "There's precedent for delay if that's your concern. It's not every year your town gets so much attention. Why, the Queen herself is aware of these proceedings and would gladly learn of your willingness to give these *women* every opportunity to defend themselves."

"Well," began the magistrate, ready, it seemed, to shift around in the wind but still hesitant at the tiller.

"Oh, sir, don't say 'well,'" chided the jurist, laughing. "Say 'very well' and 'so be it' and 'let it be done forthwith.'"

The magistrate laughed good-naturedly. "I am prevailed upon on all sides, I see. I cannot deny the Queen's wishes, can I? Mr. Stock, I shall convey your request to my fellow judges. Let's see how your credit stands with them. If they agree, the jury shall be recalled and their verdict delayed until we hear this new evidence, which I confess I cannot make head nor tail of in your narrative. But I warn you, sir," continued the magistrate, addressing his friend the London jurist, "if I am called to account for this irregularity, your own admonishments shall be my excuse."

"If you are called to account, I will join you in the prisoners' box and use simple charity and a love of justice as my sole defense," said the jurist pleasantly. "Now make arrangements to reconvene the court and let us return to our dinner while we can."

The magistrate beckoned to one of his servants, and the message was conveyed to the court clerk. Matthew thanked the magistrate and his London friend and went at once in the direction of the Sessions House.

But he did not stop there. He passed through the milling crowd and went to the churchyard, where in a remote corner a grave was being exhumed under Arthur Wilt's supervision.

"He'll come to the coffin anon, sir," Arthur said as Matthew came up. "They don't bury them as deep as they were wont."

Matthew looked down into the shallow hole. The grave-digger was working vigorously in the damp, clayey earth. His spade struck something hard, and within a few minutes the top of the plain oblong box could be seen.

The gravedigger put down his spade and wiped his sweating brow with a dirty rag he had pulled from the pocket of his leather breeches. He looked up with dull lusterless eyes at the two men watching him.

"Go ahead, man. Open it," Matthew said.

The gravedigger shrugged, and then, using the tip of the spade as a pry, he began working at the coffin's lid. Secured by a few pegs, the lid gave easily and the coffin was opened.

Of the three witnesses standing in the forlorn churchyard only one was surprised at what was now seen. That was the gravedigger, who swore by the patron saint of his trade that he had never seen such a sight. No, not in the twenty-five years he had digged.

The coffin was empty except for two canvas bags, securely tied, which upon inspection proved to contain a mixture of small rocks and sand.

At two o'clock the court reconvened. The magistrate had been true to his word. He had secured the agreement of the other judges, and they had determined to hear further evidence on behalf of the women. Informed of this, Malvern was furious. He objected strenuously, arguing that the jury ought to be allowed to render its verdict. Such was the law, he said, and he hoped the judges would abide by it.

But the magistrate was firm, nor did the spectators seem disappointed. They had enjoyed the trial to this point and had high expectations for what remained, even those who had called a great deal of attention to themselves during the morning by having been possessed, as they chose to call it. Matthew's only restriction was that his new evidence was to be relevant and briefly presented.

Matthew was no lawyer, and he lacked the lawyer's eloquence and subtlety, but he had attended enough assizes and quarter sessions to understand the procedure of the court. Moreover, he was undaunted by the opposition of the prosecutor, whom he thought, for all his learned terms and quiddities, a pompous self-serving ass, interested in little more than advancing his reputation as a witch-hunter.

His objections overruled, Malvern sank down in his place, folded his arms, and looked at the jury for sympathy.

Matthew gave the clerk the names of the additional witnesses and these names were read aloud to no little surprise and wonderment of those called. The first was to be Mrs. Roundy, the baker's wife. Flushed with pleasure at once again being the center of attention, she made a great to-do of coming to the witness stand, being as she was a woman of considerable awkwardness. In a loud voice, she begged pardon of those whose feet she stepped on in her eagerness to retell her experience, and when she arrived at her place Matthew had to wait until she had caught her breath, so excited was she at the prospect of once more speaking in public.

Since she had already taken her oath, Matthew proceeded immediately to his questions, asking her to tell her story again—the one of her vision of Ursula's spirit. Without asking why she should, Mrs. Roundy began to relate her dreadful encounter with the apparition, sparing no detail from the original version and adding a few new embellishments that made the story all the finer.

"Would you describe exactly the person you saw?" Matthew asked when she had finished her account.

"It was Ursula Tusser to the life," said Mrs. Roundy. "I have said *that*."

"Yes, you did," said Matthew, "but pray oblige us with the details of dress, of figure, the color of the hair."

"Ursula was well known on the street," answered Mrs. Roundy. "I can see no purpose—"

"Answer the constable's questions, please," said the magistrate, scowling.

The baker's wife cocked her head, and her brow furrowed thoughtfully. "Well," she said, "it was very dark and most of what I saw was the face, but I think she wore a plain gown with slit sleeves and a low bodice. The color of her hair . . . was . . . I cannot recall what it was. It was dark, you see. The figure was just standing beneath the lime tree."

"Did she wear a cap?"

"No, I think not."

"Then you did see the hair?"

"Well, yes, I did. It was like Ursula's. The way it was worn, I mean."

"Long to the shoulders?"

"Yes, sir, Mr. Stock. So it was."

"But that is not how I remember Ursula's hair," said the constable. "At least not when I saw her *last*. Her hair had been shorn in gaol. There wasn't an inch of it covering her skull. She looked more male than female."

Mrs. Roundy said that that was true. She had been at the hanging herself, had seen Ursula.

During Matthew's questions, Arthur had brought Susan Goodyear into the room. Now he led her forward to where Matthew stood. Matthew picked up a leather pouch and took from it what first appeared to be a small furry animal but, upon being shown to the court, proved instead to be a wig, a long wig of straight light brown hair. He asked Susan to remove her cap and fit the wig upon her head. This Susan did, smoothing the hair with her hands.

"I ask you, Mrs. Roundy. Is this the girl you saw in your garden, beneath the lime tree?"

Mrs. Roundy squinted and looked at Susan. She shook her head. No, Susan was not the one she had seen. She was very positive about that.

"But what of the hair, this wig. Was not the hair of the apparition of the same length and straightness as you see before you?"

"Why, yes, I believe it may have been. But the face I saw was definitely Ursula's."

"Or that of someone with like countenance," suggested Matthew.

"Well, it wasn't this girl," Mrs. Roundy said positively, frowning at Susan. "She doesn't resemble Ursula at all."

"No, she does not," conceded the constable.

Matthew said the baker's wife could return to her seat, and she did, a smug look of vindication on her face.

The magistrate now asked somewhat impatiently where Matthew had come by the wig he held and what it had to do with the accused women. Matthew said his question would be answered shortly, and the clerk called Arthur Wilts to the stand.

"Explain, Arthur, how you spent your morning while the rest of us were here in the Sessions House."

Arthur turned to the jury and told how he and the clothier's apprentices had cleared the rubble of the Waite barn, and of the finding of the two bodies in the cellar.

"And who were these bodies, Arthur?"

"One was the Waites' servant that ran off, Brigit Able."

As he said this, a moan of grief could be heard from Margaret Waite and there was a flurry of whispers in the court. But the clerk had no need to call for silence. The spectators quieted of their own accord. They were eager to hear the identity of the second corpse.

"And the other body?" Matthew asked.

"We thought it was a woman," said Arthur, "for so he was dressed, but when we lifted him up we discovered that he had male parts."

"He was a man?"

"Yes, sir, he was indeed."

"But at first you thought it was a woman—because of its dress?"

"We did. He was wearing this woman's garb, you see, and also the hair—or the wig, as I should say, for a wig it proved to be. The man was wearing a wig, and he was wearing a gown, sir, such as Ursula Tusser used to wear."

"In fact the garment was Ursula's, wasn't it? And the wig the body wore, that was Ursula's wig, wasn't it—made of her own hair?"

"I wouldn't know about that, sir," said Arthur.

"No, you wouldn't. But here is Susan Goodyear, who, as all the world knows, was a good friend once to Ursula. She can testify it is true."

Susan nodded. In a thin nervous voice she declared the wig was Ursual's, made of her own hair. "Ursula when she cut her hair would save it, and in time made a wig of it."

Matthew turned his attention to Arthur again. "Now, Arthur, tell us whose body it was that you found in the cellar beside that of Brigit Able?"

"It was her brother's, sir. Ursula's brother, Andrew Tusser."

The chamber resounded with loud murmurs of amazement. The clerk called for silence.

"Another ghost, Mr. Stock?" asked the magistrate when the audience had grown silent again.

"No, sir," answered Matthew. "Andrew Tusser died in the fire, just as Brigit Able did. Those who think what we found was a spirit may trouble themselves to go to the churchyard, as Arthur and I did shortly before coming hither, and look in his coffin. You'll find there no body but two bags of rocks and sand drawn from our own Chelmer. What's left of Andrew Tusser is laid out in the Waites' back yard."

"You mean, then," said the magistrate, "that the person the baker's wife saw was no ghost, but the dead girl's brother, who we all thought was dead himself?"

"Yes, sir. That is what I mean. Wearing his sister's gown and wig, he much resembled her, especially to those not close enough to detect the down on his chin, and full of the expectation of seeing Ursula and not him."

The prosecutor, who had been sitting impatiently during these revelations, rose to protest. "Come now, Mr. Stock. This is all very interesting, and were this lout you speak of— Andrew Tusser—alive, we could have him up on some charge or another, if only for parading in female attire. But he is dead. And whether by fire or otherwise, I see no way this bears upon the case against the witches."

"I beg to differ, Mr. Malvern," Matthew said. "The principal charge against these women is necromancy and murder. If there were no ghost, as it now appears is the case, there is no necromancy."

"There may yet be murder, however, Mr. Stock," interjected the magistrate. "Malcolm Waite was deprived of his life by a fearful shock of seeing what he thought to be Ursula Tusser at his window. The brother was dressed as his sister. Such imposture was as deliberate as it was deadly."

"I think, sir," said Malvern in his ponderous tone, "that it is a plain fact that the women made use of this wretched boy, who, by what I have heard tell, was too simpleminded to have plotted this himself. Whether they paid him money or granted some favor is immaterial. They had the motive and the opportunity. See now, the boy was found with the serving girl of Margaret Waite. And in her barn! Doesn't that argue complicity? What more proof is required?"

The magistrate stroked his chin thoughtfully and regarded the prosecutor first, then Matthew, as though he were trying to decide which counsel to follow. Then he said, "I think, Mr. Malvern, that our good constable has thrown enough light on this darkness that we should allow him to hold his lamp a little higher. Proceed, Mr. Stock. What other revelations do you have for this court?"

Matthew asked the clerk to call the next witness. Thomas Crispin rose in response to his name and made his way forward to the witness stand. His rage at the mistreatment of his wife, so evident in the strong set of his jaw and his blazing dark eyes, had now been replaced by a more complex set of emotions. He walked with a kind of reckless swagger, as though he were prepared to tell the whole court—and, indeed, the whole world—to go to hell.

"Andrew Tusser was your servant?" asked Matthew when the tanner had taken his oath.

"He was. All the town knows it," Crispin answered brusquely.

"You were present when he died, weren't you?"

Crispin hesitated at the question, then said, "He was dead when I got to the field where he'd been playing football. I was in your custody as a prisoner when the fire broke out that killed him, if you're implying I had anything to do with his death."

"I mean the day he collapsed and we *thought* he had died," replied Matthew calmly. "You remember, Mr. Crispin. You carried the body off."

"I did."

"You confirmed he was dead."

"Well, I thought he was. I'm no physician. He *looked* dead."

"But how could you have made such a mistake?" asked Matthew.

"You made it yourself, Constable Stock," Crispin responded curtly. "You told me he was dead, in fact. There was not a wisp of breath, no pulse. The flesh was growing cold. We thought the great exertion—or perhaps the blow—had killed him. It had happened before, even to young men of strong constitutions."

"I don't blame you for mistaking his death," said Matthew. "As you point out, I made the same error. I accuse you of concealing the fact that he later revived."

"That's not true!" shouted the tanner, his voice reverberating in the court and his great chest heaving. "I thought he *was* dead."

"And you saw to his burial?"

"I did. Ask the church warden. Ask the parson, who blessed the grave and said words over the body. I paid a shilling for the stone."

"The parson said words over two bags of Chelmer sand and rock," said Matthew, "sufficient in weight to give the impression there really was a body inside the coffin. There was no body because Andrew Tusser was alive. The bags were canvas. They bore *your* mark!"

"They did not!" Crispin said resolutely. "They bore no mark at all. They—"

Crispin stopped in mid-sentence, realizing his fatal error.

Matthew turned to the judges and spoke quietly: "Either Mr. Crispin has eyes that can travel far beyond the walls of this room, or he knows exactly what bags I speak of. He has said truly. The bags bear no mark—no mark at all. But how could he know *that*, save they were his and he filled them and put them in the empty coffin himself?"

TWENTY

A murmur of confused speculation swept over the room, engulfing the jury and judges as well, and it was some time before order was restored and the trial could continue. But the focus of attention had clearly shifted. Both Margaret and Jane, still under guard on the prisoners' bench, had become anxious spectators to the case building against Jane's husband.

"You revived Andrew Tusser," Matthew said.

Crispin made no answer. Beads of sweat could be seen on his brow.

"Speak, Mr. Crispin," the magistrate said. "The constable has put a question to you."

"I did *not* revive him," said Crispin through clenched teeth. "Like everyone who saw the body, I thought he was surely dead. I carried him back to the house and laid the body out. He was an orphan, but he was my servant. No one else in the town would have paid for his burial. I was putting him in his coffin when I heard him moan and then gasp for breath. He had been in a sleep. A very deep sleep. But he awoke."

"But you concealed the fact of his being alive and perpetrated the fraud of his burial?"

"Yes, I did that."

"Why?"

Crispin shook his head. "I'll say no more than what I have said."

The magistrate said, "I warn you, Mr. Crispin. You are in considerable peril in the law's eyes. You had better answer the constable's questions or be prepared to endure the penalty."

"I know the penalty," replied Crispin obstinately. "And I will suffer it, but I will say no more about Andrew Tusser. No, nor about his sister either."

Matthew walked up to where the tanner stood and looked at him keenly. "Your wife, sir," Matthew said slowly, "is on trial here for her life. Your silence will do her very little good. What, would you compound her suffering when there is a possibility that through your confession her reputation may be cleared, her life saved? Think of your wife, sir! And of your children! These must endure the obliquity of having a convicted witch for a mother unless you speak and cause these mists of confusion and error to disperse."

Crispin winced at Matthew's words. A little pulse twitched in his broad, sweating forehead, and his jaw locked firmly. Matthew realized that what was now in Crispin's eyes was not wrath but suffering. The man was in agony, his dark eyes bright with anguish. It was not death he feared—Matthew knew that now—but something worse. What was it? Whatever it was, Matthew realized that he had found the one argument that would break the strong man's resolve: his love for his wife. Now Matthew was sure Crispin would speak.

Since beginning his testimony, Crispin had not looked at his wife. After the constable's words, he did. Matthew watched as the hardness in the man's face began to dissolve. His broad shoulders slumped and he let out a heavy sigh.

Crispin said, "Whichever course I take, I lose. I will speak, and may God forgive my ill intents, even as he rewards the good."

Everyone strained to hear the tanner's words, which were softly spoken now, heavy with defeat. Tears glistened in his eyes. "I must go back . . . tell my story from the beginning," said Crispin, drawing his hand across his brow as if to clear his thoughts. "Else the story will make no sense at all." The tanner paused, struggling to control his emotions. "My wife once had a brother, whom she loved greatly. Some of you here today will remember him. His name was Philip Goodin. He was a hot-tempered youth, much opposed to my marriage with his sister. He died—was killed—some dozen years or more not three miles from this place. The Elephant. The tavern still stands.

"The night before my marriage was to be solemnized, I and a few of my friends went to this same tavern. I was the only single man among them, and it was their intent to celebrate the last night of my bachelorhood with good fellowship and drink.

"It was late unto the night when my wife's brother appeared among us. At first I thought that there would surely be trouble, but it was otherwise. He was in a companionable mood. He said he wished to make amends for our previous disagreements, join hands in friendship, and drink to my marriage to his sister. Because I never bore him the ill will he bore me, I did not hesitate to take his hand. Whether he was sincere in his profession or not, I do not know—neither then or now. But while he sat with us he drank long and deep. In his drunkenness our old quarrel flared. He called me names, defamed my trade, and said his sister might find a better man to father her children. He challenged me to step outside and prove myself other than a craven coward. I refused. I told him to go home and sleep away his drunkenness. I reminded him that his father had given consent for his sister's marriage. Within twenty-four hours we would be kinsmen. Brothers. This only made him the more belligerent.

"Finally my friends and I prevailed upon him to leave. He did. After that a sullen melancholy settled upon us all. We stayed awhile, conversing among ourselves, until the host came to tell us it was his closing hour and we must say good night. We did, and I and one other who lived in the same neighborhood commenced our journey homeward. The moon, which was full, would have guided our steps had it not been for clouds which passed before it in fits. We had gone no more than fifty paces along the road when suddenly, the great moon being obscured, from without a thicket came this raving figure, cursing and roaring like a bedlamite.

"I confess I thought it more devil than man, and in my surprise and natural desire to defend myself being thus attacked, I threw a mighty blow at it. My fist caught the attacker full upon the face. I heard the crush of bone. He fell down and just then the moon showed her face bright and clear, casting on all the scene a lurid light, by which I saw the battered bloody countenance of my wife's brother, flat upon his back upon the ground.

"Too stunned to speak to my friend, I knelt beside the body to see how Philip was. Would to God he had been as Andrew Tusser years afterward—asleep only, although he seemed dead."

Crispin's voice broke; he stifled an anguished sob and hid his face in his hands. After a few moments, during which not a word was spoken and hardly a breath heard in the room, the tanner continued. "He was stone-cold dead. My ill-considered blow had killed him."

"Why did you not make these facts known then?" Matthew asked, much moved himself by the tanner's narrative.

"My first thought was to do so. The blow was self-defense. I meant no harm. I had given him my hand in friendship and was prepared to offer him a brother's love. His intemperate nature was his fault, no worse than that. Yet it brought about his death. A sad tragedy. But then I thought of how my wife-to-be might think of me. The slayer of her own dear brother. Even though she were to understand the cause, would she ever forget that I was the *means*, that Philip Goodin's blood was on my hands? No, it was awful to think of. Awful for both of us. We were to be married the next day, you understand. Was ever a bridegroom so cursed as this?"

"Cursed indeed," murmured the magistrate. "But what has this sad tale to do with Andrew Tusser and the present case?"

"The companion and witness of my self-defense was Malcolm Waite," said Crispin after a moment's pause. "Standing over the body of Philip Goodin, we laid a plan whereby we would conceal the nature of his death. He understood my fears, you see, Malcolm Waite. We wanted to make it seem Philip was robbed and beaten by highwaymen. We stripped him naked and took his purse, the coins in which we later put in the church poor box for conscience' sake. Malcolm Waite gave me his word then that he would never tell a living soul what had transpired. We went home. The next day, my wife and I were married. Philip Goodin's body was not discovered until later."

"Was he not missed at the wedding?" asked the magistrate.

"He was, sir, but it was only thought he stayed away because of his objections to our marriage. It caused my wife and her father some sadness, but no considerable grief."

"And did Malcolm Waite keep his promise?" Matthew asked.

"For years he did so," said Crispin, "and I suppose it may be said he kept the promise until the end of his life. Yet I feared it might be otherwise. It fell out this way. When his fortune changed, as everyone knows it did, his health failed him. His business went from bad to worse. In his desperation he came to me for assistance, which I gladly gave according to my means, for I was in a prosperous way and my generous nature is well allowed. But his requests, first uttered with modesty, became as insistent as they were frequent. They grew into demands. I shoveled money after money into the great hole of his misfortune.

"Soon it became evident that I was now to pay the price for his long discretion. My wife's grief had been deep when Philip's body had been discovered, and was made worse by the fact that his murderers were never known or punished. I feared the truth now would be more bitter than before and my wife's love would turn to deadly hate should she discover it was I who killed her brother. I had no choice but to give Malcolm whatever he wished. But he was a poor husbandman of my goods. They did him little good."

"You could have explained the circumstances," Matthew interjected. "It was not your fault."

"Yes," continued Crispin. "I could have explained. But would she have believed it? She would have said, surely, 'Self-defense *you* call it. Wherefore did you conceal this so-called truth from me all these years if it be truth indeed and not some lately concocted lie? You lied for years, by your own admission. Why should I believe you now?' Such a response I expected from her. Feared it worse than death. But then a new danger appeared to make matters worse."

"Which was?"

"Ursula. That wretched girl. She was no witch, you know, only a silly child with a handful of conjurer's tricks to catch attention and make herself more than she was. But that was just my opinion. Others regarded her talents more highly. My sister and brother-in-law, for instance. They were of a credulous disposition, and when I discovered it was Margaret's desire to communicate with Philip's spirit, I knew there was a single motive to her wish: to know the perpetrators of his death. I feared no busy spirit coming at Ursula's command, but I knew that Malcolm *knew* the truth. Every day his confused mind, the victim of his wasting body, gave him less control over his actions and thoughts. My fate was in his hands, and trembling uncertain hands they were. I feared that somehow the truth of Philip Goodin's death would be disclosed."

"There were also his increasing demands upon your purse," Matthew said. "Which brings us to Andrew Tusser."

Crispin nodded affirmatively and cast down his head. "Andrew much resembled his sister in face, and once in their childish play I saw him don that wig that she had made of her own hair. They pretended each to be the other. He was a simple lad indeed, whose constant mischief proceeded more from his lack of wit than from guile. The deception was my idea. When he awoke from his trance, I told him what had happened, gave him something to eat, and told him the whole town thought he was dead. He laughed. He thought it was a good jest. He wanted to walk down High Street at noon and give the burghers a fright. I told him I had a better plan. I knew his bitterness at his sister's death. They were very close, you know. I agreed that she had been grossly wronged and said I shared his desire for revenge. I reminded him of how Malcolm and Margaret Waite had testified against Ursula at her trial, concealing their own participation in her mysteries. 'What should I do, then?' he asked, hearing this. I told him to conceal himself in the Waites' barn. He knew of the old cellar long unused. So did I. My father had helped Malcolm's father to dig it. I told him what a pleasant revenge it would be to give Malcolm a good fright if he would put on his sister's wig and gown he had of hers and haunt the house for a week or more."

"And he agreed to this scheme?" asked Matthew.

"Readily," said Crispin. "He had no love for Malcolm. Malcolm had once threatened to whip him for some abusive language he had used, and that, compounded by Malcolm's testimony against Ursula, made Andrew's loathing all the more intense. His simplicity, you see, had not lessened his capacity for vengeance."

"So he disguised himself as his sister, as you instructed," said Matthew.

"He did. I knew Malcolm's condition. I knew his health was failing more each day and that he would never stand the strain. The wish was father to the event itself. What more is there to tell? The foolish boy enjoyed the little trick he played, unmindful of my plan to make him the instrument of murder. He kept it up, appearing first to one and then the other. He came and went as he pleased, hiding out in the barn. I suppose he told someone—probably the girl who died with him."

"You suspected he had died in the fire," said Matthew. "It was you who was prowling around the ruins of nights."

"I believed that during the riot he would find refuge in the hiding place and therefore must have been trapped there when the barn was set afire. I needed to be certain. I was afraid if someone else found the body first, he would conclude as you did, Mr. Stock, that I had concealed the boy's revival for my own ends."

"And what of your wife and her sister—these poor women who stand in jeopardy because of your stratagems?"

"That was never in the reckoning. God knows I love my wife," said Crispin, with moist eyes. "I had no way of knowing that first her sister and then she would be accused of witchcraft. After the charges were made, I could see how my own device for sealing Malcolm's lips had made my burden worse. But what could I do? I couldn't reveal the identity of the ghost for fear of revealing my own murderous intent and what I most dreaded, that my wife should discover it was my hand that killed her brother."

Crispin turned to look where his wife was sitting. She was returning his gaze, her eyes also filled with tears. But whether in her gaze there were compassion and forgiveness as well as grief and shock would remain to be seen.

Then the magistrate ordered Matthew to take custody of his new prisoner and said the charge against him was to be murder—murder of such a strange and perverse sort as never to have been heard of before in England and certainly to rival the devilish practice of the Italians and the French, who were the most famous murderers in Europe. The magistrate had to speak loudly to make himself heard over the excited talk that now reigned in the courtroom and had broken forth at the end of the tanner's confession.

The clerk called out for order, and cried out again and again. The uproar continued. It was not clear whether the spectators were more amazed by the tanner's confession or disappointed that there might not be witches to hang, after all. Although the truth of Malcolm Waite's death now seemed determined beyond reasonable doubt, still the debate continued throughout the room, especially among the citizens of the town who knew all the parties in the case. Mrs. Roundy could be heard above the din screaming that it was Ursula Tusser she had seen despite what Crispin had said, and Alderman Trent had come forward from his place to argue with Roger Malvern about his conduct of the prosecution. Finally the uproar subsided and the magistrate was able to address the jury, who had all this while been in a great state of consternation about what they were to do now.

"I have conferred with my fellow judges," said the magistrate in his deep authoritative voice, "and we are of one mind. The jury, if it wishes, may have opportunity to reconsider its verdict, now that new evidence has been heard. If that is your wish, you may retire now. Otherwise, deliver your verdict."

At this the poor foreman, whose bladder had been swollen and aching for the past hour and was beside himself with agony over it, cast a hurried eye over the faces of his fellows. Then he said the jury would like to reconsider. He thought, however, with a sheepish grin, that the verdict might be quickly arrived at, and that this could be done well enough where they sat.

"So be it," said the magistrate, pleased himself at the prospect of a quick finish to the proceedings, which had now gone on well beyond the usual hour of his supper.

There was an air of excitement in the chamber while the jury deliberated. They did so within a few minutes of whispers and nods, gestures and signs. Then the foreman rose and announced, "Sir, we find the accused women, Margaret Waite and Jane Crispin, not guilty of the charges made against them."

The magistrate thanked the jury for their pains, but no one could hear beyond the uproar that now resumed and that no clerk's commands would quell. Since the magistrate and his colleagues departed hastily through the side door, the turmoil of recrimination and congratulation that followed, the cheers and cries of shame mixed oddly together, went unchecked.

Matthew led Thomas Crispin away. Jane hung upon her husband's neck, weeping copiously. It had been forgiveness Matthew had read in her face, after all, and the thought of it gave him the only joy he had had that long miserable day.

TWENTY-ONE

EARLY next morning, Matthew and Arthur took Thomas Crispin up the road to Colchester. Colchester had a gaol, which Chelmsford did not, and the tanner was to be tried at the next assizes, in April.

The journey turned out to be a memorable one.

All the way it drizzled; in places the road became a virtual quagmire. In time Matthew and his prisoner were forced to forsake the cart for Arthur's spare horse, and the constable and his prisoner ended up riding double into Colchester, with anyone's guess which of the two men was the more drenched and begrimed. But strangest had been Tom Crispin's cheerfulness along the way. Despite his heavy manacles and the prospect of months of imprisonment and heaven knew what beyond, he acted more like a man just born to a new life than one on the verge of losing the old. He spoke generously of his wife, whom he praised for her gentle, loving, forgiving nature, and quoted many pleasing proverbs the gist of which was that the man who had not lost God had lost little besides. "It's a wonderful woman I married, Mr. Stock," Crispin said more than once as they rode, the rain streaming down their faces, the horse clomping down in the ooze, the fields bleak and soggy.

When Matthew returned to Chelmsford the day after, he found much changed in the town. Although Tom Crispin was a confessed murderer—the law making little distinction between the doer of an act and the procurer thereof—he was also the object of much sympathy, now that his story had been told, and it was thought that his long record of honest dealings and his well-allowed charities would hold him in good stead when his case was finally heard by a jury. As for the animosities inspired by the trial of the sisters, these were mostly forgotten, at least by those who were not among the principals in the case. The prosecutor Malvern left town at once, it was said, to go to York where there was another outbreak of cursed necromancy and witchcraft. He took young Michael Fletcher with him. Those who witnessed the departure of the two said that Malvern was much dejected by the outcome of the Chelmsford trial, but that the boy was apparently indifferent to the fact that the accused women had been exonerated. Malvern was asked to explain how the young prodigy could have so erred, but declined to answer. It wasn't clear if Michael Fletcher remembered anything that happened to him when he was seized with one of his fits, but the outcome did not seem to have shaken his confidence in his own powers.

Alderman Trent said he questioned the wisdom of the magistrate's allowing the late evidence but had no quarrel with the verdict. While he may have been disappointed in seeing Jane Crispin go free, the arrest and ruin of her husband, his old enemy's brother-in-law, more than made up for it. He discussed the case with anyone who inquired his opinion.

As for the others involved, what passions had not been cooled by sheer exhaustion were now quenched by the continuing bad weather, which some said signaled God's displeasure at the entire episode. A grim succession of cold, gray days in which it was always raining or threatening to rain fell upon the town like a pall, and the subtly undulating countryside took on a drab, melancholy hue that depressed the spirit and provoked Chelmsfordians to keep indoors. There they talked gloomily of an early winter and of the witches' trial as though it had been another town's nightmare.

Of course, life for the families of the accused women changed dramatically. Margaret Waite's health worsened.

The sadness that had fallen upon her at the death of her husband, and that indeed had tempered her willfulness and stridency, now deepened as a result of her experiences. She looked twenty years older than she was and would hardly speak to anyone, especially to those former friends who she felt had betrayed her. Something in her had been destroyed. She had an empty, hollow look, a cadaverous look that made strangers shun her. She put her house up for sale. She told Joan, who was practically her only remaining friend, that if there were no ghost haunting her house before, then surely there would be one now, and she could no longer abide its dusty drafty rooms, the awful emptiness of her husband's side of the bed, and her bitter memories of the living and the dead.

Bitterest of these memories was her feeling against Thomas Crispin, who had deprived her of a beloved brother and husband and by consequence built a wall between her and the society of her sister. For if Jane Crispin could forgive Thomas Crispin, Margaret could not. The breach was recognized by both women and lamented, but it did seem irreparable. Margaret went to Lincoln to live with her son Dick, and John Waite went back to London, which he declared he was a fool to have left in the first place, despite the threatening of his creditors and several cuckolded husbands bent on revenge. He said that the entire episode of the Chelmsford witches convinced him of the small-mindedness of towns and that he hoped never to leave the more enlightened society of London again.

The house was sold to the baker, Mr. Roundy, whose wife often afterward gave tours to neighbors and strangers, and recounted her terrifying confrontation with Ursula Tusser's ghost. Susan Goodyear was kept on and promoted to housekeeper.

For the Stocks, life resumed its normal course. Joan managed the house and Matthew his shop, and during the winter that followed—and it was a bitter one—his constableship became a secondary concern.

But they often talked of the Chelmsford Horror.

"Ah, what a pity it was for them all," Joan remarked one particularly dismal Sabbath eve, about a fortnight after the trial. She and Matthew were seated before the great kitchen fire nursing their hot caudles and what Matthew feared was for him the beginning of a bad cold. He knew what she spoke of at once.

"It was a pity," he agreed, sipping the hot sweet liquid. The spicy aroma of the drink cleared his head, which was covered in a shepherd's cap that he had pulled down over his ears. He wore a woolen muffler around his neck, and over him Joan had thrown a heavy quilt. He sweat for the warmth of his body. All that could be seen of his face was an inch of forehead, the deep-set eyes, and the nose, reddish from the sniffles. He sneezed and wheezed as the fire snapped and popped and Joan talked.

"It was never clear to me why poor Brigit Able was in the company of Andrew Tusser," she said, puzzled. "What was she doing in the barn? Was she a conspirator herself, or a victim?"

"Both, probably," Matthew replied nasally. "After the trial, Susan Goodyear told me the truth of it. Brigit had told her how the spirit of Ursula had come to her in the night. The girl was beside herself with terror, but Andrew had something more in mind than scaring her to death. I imagine he revealed himself as flesh and blood, and got her to go to the barn where they took cover during the riot, thinking they'd be safe. It seems Brigit and Andrew were a little more than friends while he lived, and she may have not been too disappointed to find that he was alive, after all. With the town up in arms over the ghost, it was likely he was planning on leaving soon. Things were getting hot for him. Perhaps he told Brigit he would take her with him."

"So it must have been *them* whispering in the barn the day I was so afraid."

"No doubt. Andrew probably thought he'd pay off old scores around town, but he didn't plan on the riot or the fire."

• 224 •

"Any more than Tom Crispin expected his wife and sister-in-law to be accused of witchcraft."

"It was risky business for them all," he said.

"Poor Jane Crispin," she said. "What will happen to her now?"

"She'll be fine. She's a strong woman, as these events have shown. The arrest and imprisonment of her husband have proved her mettle, if any ever doubted it. She's turned over the management of the tannery to Will Simple, provided he engages in no more tavern brawls, for which he has given her a solemn oath. I myself witnessed it. The children miss their father, but Jane has promised he will return to them in the spring."

"Was that wise?" Joan asked, concerned. "*Promising,* I mean."

"I pray God it prove to be," he said. "Tom Crispin murdered his brother-in-law. There's no denying it. Whether the jury will find extenuating circumstances in his story, I cannot say. Of all my duties as constable, conveying that man to gaol was the saddest. I told you how merry he was, didn't I? Along the way he never complained of his lot or cast one of us a threatening look, even though he was in manacles and we his appointed guardians."

He had told the story to her several times, but she didn't remind him of that. Matthew went on: "Save for Tom Crispin's desire to rid himself of a false friend and blackmailer, he was virtually without guile in this business. His mistake was in not being honest with his bride. He should have told her how it was that Philip Goodin had died. He should have used Malcolm Waite as a witness. We would have a different story then."

"Oh, but he feared to lose her," she answered.

"There was small chance of that," he said. "She's a very reasonable woman. She may have loved her brother but she knew what a hothead he was and how he detested the thought of her marriage to the tanner."

"I don't think it was that easy," she said.

He looked at her with surprise. "Why wasn't it that easy? It seems to me the obvious course. Telling the truth."

Joan smiled tolerantly. "But there was love, you see. Don't speak of reason in these matters. It had nothing to do with that, neither on his part or hers. She loved her brother well—despite his quarrelsome nature and hostility to her betrothed. And Tom Crispin loved her beyond measure. He couldn't bear the thought of losing her, even though there was but a small chance of it. The very thought of that small chance terrified him."

"Well," said Matthew disapprovingly, but in a tone suggesting that he was prepared to allow his wife her way, "he was not the first man bewitched by love, then. Hell is full of good meanings and wishings—"

"And so is heaven," she answered, "or who of us would have hope of it?"

Their dispute, such as it was, was at a stalemate. They fell into a companionable silence, watching the dancing fire. Matthew felt a tickle in his left nostril. He struggled against the urge to sneeze and then yielded. The sneeze was violent and competed with the raging of the storm outside.

Joan sat up, startled.

"It's only me," Matthew grumbled apologetically, wiping his nose with his handkerchief. "It's this pestilent cold."

"Jesus bless us both," she said, looking at him wide-eyed. "I must have dozed off. And what a dream came upon me of a sudden! I was sitting as I now am and heard a noise at the window. A tapping. Then a lightning flash illuminated a glaring visage. It was the same as before."

"Andrew Tusser dressed as his sister."

"Yes. Then you sneezed and I—"

"Awoke to find no spirit present but your husband. Thank God for sneezes, then."

"Yes, thank God for them." She rubbed her brow, as though to wipe away the dream.

"The house is full of noises caused by the tempest. It's only winter in advance of itself, beating upon the door."

She looked relieved and reached out to stroke his hand. "It

is bedtime, isn't it?" she asked. "Go early to bed and late to your grave, or so the proverb goes."

"And a true proverb it is," Matthew said, rising with difficulty, swaddled as he was in so many wraps. His joints were stiff, his head throbbed. "Although grim and untimely, given my condition, this talk of graves," he went on, thinking still of the proverb. "I feel a hundred years of age or more—and an unhealthy hundred at that. Which reminds me of a song on that very theme. I'd give you a verse or two along the way, but this cursed cold has put me quite out of voice. No more sweetness than a bullfrog."

On the way to bed he hummed the first few notes anyway, just to spite the rude elements without and disarm whatever restless spirit of the dead might be lurking at the top of the stairs.

EPILOGUE

MARGARET Waite blew out the candle at her bedside and watched until she could gauge the strength of the pale and sickly moon against the darkness of the room she had been given in her son's house. Absolute darkness always aggravated her tormented memories and made the cold nights colder still; were it not for the cost of candles, she would have had hers burning all the night. Below in the house, the voices of her son Richard's family had long ceased, and her wonted loneliness descended upon her, making her subject to gruesome thoughts and unspeakable fears. Of these, the worst was the sensation of someone or something lying beside her in the bed. When her mood was most dreadfully upon her, she thought she could hear breathing, and once, upon the midnight hour, she was awakened by what she thought was a sudden snort of the kind with which her husband used to punctuate a long stretch of snoring. She had called out his name and listened for the familiar voice at her ear, then thanked heaven that no answer came.

Yet she knew it was Malcolm, and after a while it made no difference. She would creep into bed, extinguish the light, and wait. He would join her in the bed, never showing himself, but she could feel the weight of his body on the mattress. She took it all philosophically. In life they had been one flesh; it no longer seemed possible to her that death should divide them in any meaningful way, and soon—this she could feel in her marrow—she would go the same path into the absolute darkness.

But this December night, the tapping at her window insinuated itself into her consciousness like a twitch of the nerve. The taps were too regular and insistent to have been the wind, although God knew the house was full of groans and rattles enough. No, it was a summons. The summons for which she had been waiting since the night of Malcolm's death.

When she realized what it was and what it portended, her heart seemed momentarily to stop. She gasped for breath, but got up out of bed straightway and walked toward the window under the eaves.

There was no curtain to pull aside, and no reflection of herself to distort what she beheld beyond the little panes of glass where there was no ledge to stand upon and no ground nearer than the cobblestone street a dozen or more feet below. The long, straight hair framed the pale, distraught face like a cowl. The eyes of the apparition were without expression, but the lips, swollen and dry, curled slowly into a smile of grim triumph.

"Ursula? Ah, Ursula," she heard herself moan.

Her legs gave out and she sank onto the rushes. She looked not at the window again but at the rough-hewn beams of the ceiling that seemed to descend upon her. In the few seconds before she lost consciousness, she imagined the discovery of her own body the next morning. There would be no witnesses to the cause of her death, which would seem the natural consequence of age and prolonged grief. But she would not regret that. She had been enough of a burden on her son Richard, on his unfriendly wife, on the rout of ill-mannered grandchildren, the names of whom were always slipping in and out of her memory like those of ill-mannered guests. Thinking of these things, she could almost bless the visage staring in upon her.

She heard the tapping again, the summons; she smiled into the gathering gloom, at the beams that kept descending upon her like the boards in her coffin. She thought: Have done, Ursula. Have done. The reckoning has long since been settled.

The tapping continued, more insistent than before, and Margaret felt herself slipping away now, slipping out of the old sick body the way a clever apprentice, weary of his work, escapes his master's vigilance by a sudden deft movement. One moment he's there, the next he's gone like a whisper on the wind.

Quartet  Qrime

MEL ARRIGHI
Alter Ego

MEG ELIZABETH ATKINS
Palimpsest

DAVID CARKEET
Double Negative

ANTHEA COHEN
Angel Without Mercy
Angel of Vengeance
Angel of Death
Fallen Angel
Guardian Angel

RUTH DUDLEY EDWARDS
Corridors of Death
The St Valentine's Day Murders

SHIRLEY ESKAPA
Blood Fugue

DAVID E. FISHER
The Man You Sleep With
Variation on a Theme

ALAN FURST
The Paris Drop
The Caribbean Account
Shadow Trade

JOHN GREENWOOD
Murder, Mr Mosley
Mosley by Moonlight
Mosley Went to Mow

ELLA GRIFFITHS
Murder on Page Three

RAY HARRISON
French Ordinary Murder
Death of an Honourable Member
Deathwatch
Death of a Dancing Lady